Food Court, ⌣ , ...

would see it as a sick joke. Various food stalls and mini restaurants and chrome tables had been set up on the second floor of a giant, glass-roofed atrium, three stories high. I crouched under a table, and peered over the railing, down to the floor I'd just been on. It was like peering into the depths of hell.

Early dawn light revealed the space below me, perhaps a half acre, of total carnage. Dead bodies- human, horse, deer, and animals unidentifiable- lay in all stages of decay. Legs, hoofs, and massive cattle rib cages rose from the mess like dead tree limbs rising from a swamp.

And it was a swamp. The oldest bodies were liquefied, a thick goo that shimmered faintly in the dawn. From the fresher, more bloated corpses, gas escaped in obscene burps and wet hisses and farts.

I crouched behind the glass balcony and quietly puked up my Powerbar.

My shocked mind had barely even registered the aliens growing down below. A forest of new aliens, hundreds of them, growing at regular intervals in the body soup, still and tall on their hind legs, metallic lion's manes reaching as cheerily as sunflowers for the rising sun,

For Margaret, of course.

Freerunners

By Curtis Symons

Prologue

Where were you the night of the invasion?
This is the question people ask now. Every generation has a question like this. For our parents and grandparents, it was where were you on 9-11? Or when John Lennon/Kennedy/Regan (or whoever was shot) was shot? But now, it's *where were you the night the aliens invaded?*

Well, on the night the aliens invaded, I was far from the action. I'll get to that later. But the story I like to tell is where Claude was, so I'll start there. He doesn't like to tell it, but I pulled it from him in bits and pieces, and I've made up the rest. My dad always says you should never let the truth get in the way of a good story.

Claude and his buddy Ollie were at a party, the grand opening of a big sporting goods store on the outskirts of Toronto. It was a hot night, and the power had gone out all over the area.

"Hey man, come out with me for a smoke," Ollie called to Claude. The power had been out for half an hour, but the party was still rockin'. A hundred people had shown up for the grand opening of *Adventurer's Haven* - timed to coincide with the summer solstice- and between the band, the dancing and the dead air conditioner, the place was getting pretty ripe.

"Fucking–A," Claude replied, and they worked their way through the press of bodies, and out through the main doors. Ollie knew his younger friend didn't smoke, but Claude kept him company. Ollie was sixteen, a tall lanky kid with messy blonde hair. He was a year older than his friend, who was visiting from Quebec. Ollie was trying out smoking that summer, in the same way Claude was trying out English swear words. They grabbed their skateboards from the entry way.

1

"Check out *des aurores boréales*, man!" Claude said, looking up at the northern lights. They waved and skipped across the Canadian sky like something alive, some beautiful creature that was distant, and not quite tame.

The boys pushed off down the quiet street, the trucks of their skateboards rumbling into the night. It was hard not to keep looking up; the northern lights were a dangerous distraction. But the two teens road with the fearlessness of youth.

Claude would rather have been on foot, freerunning the city's bones- cars, benches, lamp posts, roofs- but Ollie wanted to make some distance, so they rode fast, with purpose. The party at *Adventurer's Haven* was cool, but all the girls were a lot older, and out of their range. Ollie's parents would have no idea the two boys were gone.

It's amazing how far a couple of kids can get on skateboards through deserted streets. Most adults have no clue. They see kids practicing tricks in the driveway or a skate park, and forget that those little boards on those little wheels are an effective means of transportation.

That night, the boys didn't get all the way to downtown Toronto. But they got near.

Suddenly, there was a strange pressure on them, like a wind pushing straight down. Yet there was no wind. Their skateboards faltered, as if the little wheels were stumbling. All around them, cars groaned as a magnetic force from above pushed them down on their shocks. Claude felt the pressure on the chain on his wallet, on his pants zipper, and even on his wrist, where the old Omega Seamaster wristwatch his *grandpere* had left him was repelled from the force from above.

They looked up.

A vast object above. It was sleek, shaped vaguely like an elongated egg or seed pod. It gave off no light of its own, but thousands of tiny metallic facets reflected the rainbow of colours from the northern lights.

2

It passed overhead, getting gradually lower as it headed south.

The strange pressure stopped abruptly as the giant object moved on, and the boys stepped off their boards, stunned. They tracked the descent of the impossible ship - for there was no doubt it was a ship - as it fell like a judgement on the downtown core of Toronto.

Claude and Ollie looked at each other, mouths and eyes open wide.

It's a strange thing I've noticed about teenaged boys- a testament to our bravery or our stupidity - that if we see trouble, we tend to run toward it. (Unless the trouble is of our own making; then we get out of there before someone assigns blame.)

The fires started soon after the alien ship disappeared behind the wall of dark high rises. Accompanying the fires, there was a soundtrack of explosions and screams; but no sirens. Every car battery remained dead, so even if the authorities were notified of the invasion, how would they get there?

Claude and Ollie got there. They rushed on their skateboards. And as a tide of (sensible) adults and small children washed toward them, Claude didn't even pause to wonder what they were rushing *to*, what everyone else was running *from*.

They crested a low hill in a residential area. The scene before them was like something from one of those Michael Bay movies, or the Bible. Destruction, flames, chaos. People running and screaming.

And marching slowly and inevitably toward them, bizarre alien shapes. Huge metallic wings stretched out from tall bodies; but the wings didn't flap, and the creatures stayed on the ground. A quiet part of Claude's mind recognized that the wings were more like a shield, spread wide; and from the calm spot on the hill he saw that the purpose of the shield was to create the illusion of size, like a

3

frightened cat that turns itself sideways and puffs up its fur. The scores of people who fled away from the creatures, toward Claude and Ollie, fled like cattle before a farmer waving his arms. Which that small, quiet part of Claude's mind considered, and asked, *'What were the people being herded to?'*

And old man shuffled out of a run-down townhouse, and stood beside the two shocked teens. He was in a housecoat, and pulled a little oxygen tank behind him on a dolly. Even above the screaming and explosions, Claude heard him breathe in deeply through the tube in his nose.

"Well, hell then," the old man muttered. He pulled a pipe from his housecoat pocket and fingered it absently. "Never thought I'd see the day," he said to no one.

Claude managed to recapture his earlier thought. The aliens were definitely herding people. Wild tentacles waved, but only made contact if a human was foolish enough to try to run south, through the advancing line. Then, a ropy arm would shoot out, grab the unfortunate person, and slam them against the pavement. Slowly, slowly, the teen from Quebec turned around.

"*Tabernac*," he muttered, forgetting his resolve to only swear in English. Ollie and the old guy turned too.

"Well, hell then," the old man repeated, at the same time Ollie said "Fuck *me*."

Behind them, a forest of spikey spheres, six or eight feet tall, rolled awkwardly toward them. Claude could think of nothing but sea urchins, those mindless ocean creatures he had seen at the Ripley's Aquarium. Sea urchins taller than a person.

The first wave of people who had passed the boys had come up against the spike pods. A few tried to rush through the tiny gaps between. Their screams of pain drowned out the general screams of panic and fear. And as the pods rolled forward, the poor souls were impaled further.

4

The old man studied the gruesome scene quietly, then spoke above the din. "You boys gotta smoke?" Ollie looked at him as if he were mad. Claude's mind was starting to work though. He reached into his friend's breast pocket, and fished out the crumpled pack of Luck Strikes.

"Thanks, friend," the old guy said with a grin. "It's not pipe tobacco, but it'll do. Lighter?" Ollie handed him a lighter dumbly.

"You sure, *grandpere*?" Claude asked.

"Sure as sure," the old timer replied. He handed Claude a key ring from his housecoat pocket. He nodded to a shiny old car parked pointing north. "Use the Chevy to break a hole in that line of spike things. I reckon that's the way to run." As he spoke, he was breaking up a cigarette and filling his pipe with tobacco. "I'll see if I can slow down these bastards so you and some other folks can get away."

The man trundled off down the hill. He walked slowly, tamping his pipe. He waited until he was five meters from the advancing aliens, then flicked the lighter to life. Claude imagines he saw a grey plume of pipe smoke for a moment before the oxygen tank ignited, and then the night turned to day. The boys were flattened. The aliens were turned into giant torches.

Claude and Ollie picked themselves up off the pavement, and Claude found the Chevy's keys where they'd fallen. "Let's go, Ollie," Claude said, unlocking the ancient car. "We'll have to really get this old boat rolling. And we've got to warn the party, *non*?"

And so they began their first Freerun.

Now, like I said, I was far away, so I like to tell Claude's story of the invasion night. But my night wasn't without its drama. I was fifty kilometers north, in the little farming community where I grew up.

5

"Hey Will, grab me a beer while you're in there!" Dad yelled from the back deck.

"Jeremy, we've talked about this;" Mom didn't quite use The Voice, but was dangerously close. She moved through the open sliding door out to where dad leaned back in his plastic Muskoka chair, but I could hear the exchange clearly. "He's eleven years old, and he's your son, not a bartender. Kids imitate what their parents teach them."

I brought two cold Coronas out, a neat wedge of lime stuffed down in the long neck of each. I handed one to dad, and managed to keep a straight face while I presented the other to mom. "Your beverage, ma'am."

Mom rolled her eyes, but took the beer.

"See hon? I'm not teaching him to drink, just to serve." Dad took a swallow, holding the bottle by thumb and two fingers up near the mouth. "He's going to need a job one day, when he's in university."

I scooched into another deck chair and leaned back, looking up at the darkening sky, enjoying the family banter. Mom settled in on my other side and took a pull on her own beer. I was safe in the middle, the frosting stuff wedged neatly between two wafers in a family Oreo.

"Well, you'd better teach him properly then," she said to my dad; and then to me, "See, the bartender only places the lime wedge in the top. It's all about presentation. The customer gets to stuff it down in there."

We were all three quiet for a time, looking up through the warm night, waiting to see some northern lights. It was supposed to be a really cool show tonight.

We didn't even notice when the power went out, because we'd turned out all the house lights to see the aurora borealis better. Dad went in for another beer- no more for mom; she was training- and only realized when the fridge light didn't come on.

"Laurel, did we pay the hydro bill?" he called through the screen door. I didn't pay attention to the grown up talk, I was totally drawn into a shimmering world of reds, pinks and greens. Mom called it "the most psychedelic laser lights show ever"; dad had tried to make me understand excited electrons; I just got lost in it.

Soon dad was standing beside my chair, sipping thoughtfully. "Northern lights are caused by solar flares; back in the 1800s, electronic communications were disrupted by solar flares, and in 1989 Quebec lost its power for a few days from the same thing. I wonder if the power disruption is just local?"

"If it doesn't come back on soon, I'll scoot over to Mark's, see if it's the whole area," mom said. Mark was Mr. Nelson, the old timer down the road.

An hour later, no power, and the atmospheric light show was getting even more spectacular.

Mom grabbed the car keys and gave us each a kiss.

"Will, limit your dad to just one more beer; if he keeps opening the fridge, the food will spoil."

"Maybe he'd better just grab two or three each time, save energy," I replied cheekily.

She ruffled my hair. "Just like your dad, always thinking, and always speaking. Well, while you boys are pondering the secrets of the universe, and how to justify getting tipsy on a Wednesday night, I'm going to go out and actually *do* something."

A few minutes later, mom was back. "Jeremy, the car won't start, won't even turn over. Could the solar flares do that?"

"I think so, but I don't really know much more than what I told you," Dad admitted.

"I'll take my bike; I only had a light workout today anyway." Mom looked up at the light show. "There's more than enough light to see the road by."

We weren't sure exactly how long mom had been gone, since none of the clocks worked. But it had been hours, and dad and I went to Mark Nelson's, and woke him up. He hadn't seen her.

Of all the horrible things an eleven year old can think up to explain why his mom has gone missing in the middle of the night, I never guessed the truth. I mean, sure, I was a kid, but 'alien invasion' just never crossed my mind.

1
Five Years Later: *Race Day*

One klick, three distinct terrains.

The opening leg, 400 meters of County forest, known as The Gauntlet. Straight rows of towering pines planted, according to faded signs, some 40 years before the Blackouts.

Second leg, the Hill. The specific hill changed every year, but it was always steep and painful; that one was my real weakness.

And finally, the Field. This was where I excelled: clear trails, few obstacles, just 400 meters of hell-bent, legs-burning, puke-yer-guts-out sprinting. Yee-haw.

I wrapped another layer of duct tape around my ancient hand-me-down Adidas and tried to calm my breathing.

Next to me on my fallen log were the Cox twins, Frankie and Theresa. The twins looked calm. Both had long blond curls tied in ponytails, both were barefoot. Only a year younger than me, but like many of the youngins they seemed to have more thoroughly embraced the post-Blackouts world. They only wore footwear when it was time for winter boots; and when a group of us older kids retold old episodes of Scooby Doo or the plots of Disney movies, Frankie and Theresa listened, but didn't participate. It was as though they had never lived in a digital world.

The competition was rounded out by five others, all warming up and psyching up nearby: Sitting on a fallen log at the edge of the clearing was Mike, a lanky 16 year old who lived a few farms north of us, big of shoulders and long of legs. He was a good guy, a tireless worker on his parents' farm, and a solid athlete, but not a real threat.

Over there was Andrew "Ace" Mathews, on his feet

and never still, the favourite to win this year's Run; he was neither tall nor short for a teen, maybe a few centimeters below my 185, but he already had the sculpted leg and arm muscles of an adult. He oozed kinetic energy, always stalking or twitching.

We'd been in the same Grade 2 class together, before the Blackouts. Ace was a year older than me, but had been held back a year. Probably because he spent more time in the principal's office than in the classroom.

Mom said he probably had ADHD; dad said the Blackouts were probably the best thing that had ever happened to him. At 17, Ace Mathews, who'd been a failed student back in the civilized world, was now an apprenticed mechanic and accomplished carpenter, whose skills were respected and much sought after in the community.

I'd been scared of him in Grade 2; he had been bigger and older than the rest of us, and his natural energy and frustration with school had made him a mean kid. Now all that was channelled into fixing farm machinery and fixing his neighbours' homes. Now I was in awe of him.

Stretching her long legs just a few meters to my left was Magda, my friend, one day maybe more than my friend. Long, tanned legs, long honey-coloured braid. In motion, she had the kind of unhurried and graceful gait of a loping wolf. She was a great runner, but built more for distance than speed.

Sitting nearby in the long grass was a strong, compact kid from way out east (funny to think that 10 km away was now 'way out'); he had mocha skin and black, shaggy hair. His name was John. I thought my mom had said their family was Indian, but whether she meant Native Indian or India-Indian, I wasn't sure. I knew him vaguely, enough to nod a greeting if I saw him go by on his bike, but maybe not enough to actually say hi.

The final entry was a complete unknown. More like Ace than the rest of us. It wasn't a matter of age, but of confidence. He wore cut-off army cargoes, baggy with the pockets still above the cut; a dirt-coloured tee with a faded logo: Dead Milkmen? Weird. And peeking out from the tee, some kind of tight black shiny undershirt, similar to my mom's running tights. He was calmly stretching, and ignoring the rest of us.

I felt a soft touch on my knee, just the tips of three slender fingers. "Good luck, Will. Go hard," Magda said quietly at my side.

"You too," I replied, "But you've been training for this. You don't really need luck." I'd seen her out almost every morning, jogging the trails between our farms. Once I figured her schedule, I timed odd jobs near the barn so I could catch sight of her as she passed out of the northern tangle of deciduous trees, through a brief clearing, before loping off through the rigid rows of Ministry forest.

Now she gave a smile, just a tiny widening of her already wide mouth. "Tell you a secret?" She asked and I nodded. "I haven't really been training."

"Bullshit," I softened the swear word with my own smile. "You run almost every day!"

Magda arched a coy eyebrow at me. "Oh, really? Have you been spying on me, Will Dunmore?"

"No, I just…I mean…" God, how did girls do that? Didn't I just catch her out in a lie? So why did I feel like I was the one who was tripped up?

She saved me by explaining, "I don't really want to race today, never did. I just like to run, to be by myself, sweat out some bad energy." She was picking at the seeds on a piece of long grass as she talked, so didn't notice me studying her face. "My mom says it's a 'waste of time and energy, and exercise for the sake of exercise is a vanity of the before-times,'" she finished in a poor imitation of her mother's nasal tone. "So I tell her I'm training for the Race, to make the family proud." Now she looked at me with the smile back in place. "So either I run with you maniacs, and actually try, or I lose my alone time."

"My mom's the opposite. She's been working me hard." Mom had been about to take one last shot at the Pan Am games when the blackouts happened. She'd been a really good hurdler and sprinter before I was born, but was training for the heptathlon when the world went to hell.

She never got her shot at the big leagues, but when the invasion started to push north, and there were no telecommunications to warn people, she was one of a handful from our area who spread the alarm. Through the Bruce Trail, she ran all night to reach the soldiers at Base Borden. They sent two squads on forced march to meet and stall the aliens on Airport Road, just south of our farm.

"I think she's pushing me partly to pass on her dream, and partly to make sure I'm prepared, in case they come this far north again," I said. Magda nodded, and we didn't speak any more. We'd be racing soon.

When the younger kids had run their sack races and fun relays, one of them was sent to the clearing to summon us teens. Ace was already near the path, so was first to go. The rest of us followed more or less single file.

Each one of us was locked in the mental solitary confinement that had probably always preceded intense competition, from the Olympics and high school sports that both ceased to exist more than five years ago, to the battle of Thermopile that had ended more than 3000 years ago.

I rolled my shoulders and shook my hands as I walked, expelling nervous energy. Ahead of me the twins bounced on their toes as they walked, a little hop-hop-HOP rhythm not quite in time with each other. Only Magda seemed truly calm, walking as though on the way to see a friend.

"These young men and women are about to embark on more than a race, more than an obstacle course," the Widow Cox began. "Five years ago, our world changed."

12

She searched out each set of eyes in the crowd, pulling us together through her retelling of our story. "It changed, and we faced our doom. The lights went out, and the enemy took full advantage. The lights went out, and the alien enemy marched up our own roads, intent on our annihilation.

"We had become reliant on electricity, reliant on gasoline and coal; and when the lights went out, we thought we were without power.

"A handful of our own stood up and showed us otherwise. Seven individuals recognized the threat, and proved that while we had lost electricity, we had not lost our power. They set out on foot, on horseback, and on bicycle and spread the warning. Through forest, field and through enemy lines, they raced. They rallied a militia such as has not been seen in Canada for 200 years. And while farmers, teachers, plumbers and even children held off the invaders, one woman, one of the five, made it the twenty-six kilometers to Base Borden, and the enemy was stalled at last."

Even the grasshoppers seemed to fall silent as the Widow Cox turned her steel gaze upon us. Despite myself, I stood taller as she addressed us directly.

"As you run, you symbolize the strength and endurance that saved us; you honour the past. But you also represent our future. The adults of this community will one day soon pass the baton of responsibility on to your generation; you will not be found lacking. Each of you has made three bracelets for this race, your entry fee as it were," A few chuckles at the old joke. "*Courage, Strength* and *Will*, you have written on each Token. As you run today, you will gather these Tokens that represent the courage, strength and will of our community, these qualities that have kept us alive, and will ensure that we thrive for generations to come!" The small crowd cheered, and the eight of us lined up at the edge of the orderly rows of pine forest. It suddenly

13

occurred to me that there were only supposed to be seven of us.

The sound is deadened by 50 years of decomposed pine needles. Short and quick strides, so I can turn without losing much speed. The trees, planted as evenly as soldiers on parade, whip by on either side, like I'm standing still and they are on hyper-speed treadmills.

Quick feet quick feet quick feet! Don't slip into my normal long stride till I'm out of the forest. A hint of yellow off to the left- there! The marker. I'll need to cut left, damn, Ace is in that lane already, he doesn't need to change direction. Make the cut left between the pines, crap, close call, dead branch scraped my arm. Gotta keep the strides even shorter, quicker.

Acutely aware of Ace ahead of me, maybe 10 meters, but if there are no more cuts, I can lengthen my stride, reel him in...Shit! He cuts right again, he must have seen the next marker- god! He's smooth, doesn't need to slow down, just changes direction like a cue ball off the break. I don't see the marker yet, but a wider gap appears, I cut right to follow Ace, lose time lose footing....where the hell is he? Why did the markers bring me back to my original lane? Bastard tricked me! He's already back in the left lane, he knew the turns would slow me down more than him. I scoot back again... Now the gap is twelve meters.

A new presence, off to the left...the new guy? About even with me, man, he's cookin' too. The three of us have got to be the forerunners. Sloping downhill now, easy to lose control. The youngins who were in the kids' races are just up ahead, high in the branches, cheering and hooting, a strange, spread out murder of crows. Spectators mean we must be near the first Token now- that means few cuts, so I pour it on. I've got the advantage now over Ace with my leg length and lighter frame, but he's still got a serious lead

The grade gets sharper suddenly; do I keep the same pace, risk a spill, or gear down? Risk the speed, gotta make up ground. I see sunlight up ahead to the left- a clearing at the bottom of this hill. Ace is out of sight through the trees, but the new guy is behind me, he must have slowed up for control on the hill.

Breaking into full sun is like surfacing from the bottom of a cool lake: warm, stunning, explosive. I skid at the edge of the forest, must let my eyes adjust. Twenty meters away and down, in the centre of the clearing is the yellow marker. It's tacked to an old white birch in the middle of the clearing; three birches really, growing out from a central point. There's a 6 foot piece of rebar about four meters up, set horizontally across two of the birches. The Tokens will be up there for sure. A knotted rope hangs from the rebar; Ace is already grabbing the rope. Damn! Another setback- he's way stronger, faster up the rope than I'll be, and I can't start up till he's down.

I'm jogging down to the last few meters to the trees as Ace drops to the soft grass. I'm thinking *At least I'm in second, I'll get him on the last leg,* when "Aiee! Clear out, farm boy!" and a grey blur nearly knocks me over. The new guy hits the three birches top speed, and somehow converts his momentum *up.* Three clear steps, inside the triangle of trees: one trunk, change direction but still moving up, 2nd trunk and up, third and he's above my head, spinning gracefully toward the rebar, grabs the bracelet Token from its hook, and has the presence of mind to slip it on his wrist, all before he hits the ground.

He smiles at me, gives a mocking bow. "And you?" he asks with a slight French Canadian accent.

What the hell? I shrug, back up and go for it. I can see the mark his first step made on the papery bark, I hit it dead on. I push off, too much! Hit the second trunk hard, knee bends too much in order to absorb the impact, and I lose momentum. I'm in the hang-time spot between impact

15

and falling; desperately I push off, lunge for the rebar. I grasp it with my left hand as my legs swing wildly in front of me. I know I'm going down, hard; somehow I hook a finger on one of the leather bracelets before gravity starts to win.

Sometimes time is fluid. I was horizontal, arms and legs akimbo, about four meters above the ground, but I somehow had time to think, to notice things. The vibrant green-on-white of the tree; the bracelet in my hand, *Courage* burnt into the leather, and the little flower design that told me Magda made this one. And I remember thinking of the French guy, his moves, and I thought *I want to be able to do that.*

Then, boy meets ground, air leaves boy, and I was left with the sound of the French guy laughing as he ran off after Ace.

2
A Racer's Lullaby

"You okay, Will?" Magda called from the edge of the forest.

"Unghh," I replied, the wind not yet returned to my lungs.

"Well, get your ass up then!" Nice caring girl, huh? She was starting up the ropes as I struggled to my feet.

I slipped the *Courage* Token on my wrist, heaved for air. I started out after Ace and the French guy, still stunned and stumbling, but my limbs were starting to respond.

The next yellow flag led out of the little clearing, up a game train through weeds and twisted crab apple trees. By the time I hit a decent stride, Magda was on my heels.

"The twins and Mike cleared the pines," she panted. "They won't be long."

Damn! Gotta make some ground; I picked up the pace, scanning for a hint of yellow.

We pushed it on the trail, the pace made faster by some weird combination of companionship and competition. The next flag appeared over a rise, and we could see the front runners. The little hills were behind us; a solid chunk of the Niagara Escarpment was in front. The yellow flag was planted firmly at the top.

We slowed to a jog as we considered our options. The ridge we faced was perhaps 100 feet of porous rock, dotted by occasional hearty little shrubs that clung to the rock face. A crude road ran parallel to the cliffs, upwards at a steep 45 or 50 degree angle. I'd been back here before, the previous spring, on horseback, hunting wild turkey. I knew the road was steeper than it looked, and surfaced with deep sugar sand, lousy for running or even walking.

Ace, with a solid lead, had chosen the safe bet, the road. He was halfway up, but moving slowly in the deep sand. Mr. French was at the base of the ridge, mapping his route before starting to climb. If he could do it without falling, he'd steal Ace's lead.

"Easy choice for me, Will," Magda said, and took off for the start of the road.

Decision: Follow Ace and Magda, and hope I could make up the difference in the Field? Or follow the Mad Frenchman, make some ground right now, maybe even hit the Field even with Ace?

I made my favourite kind of decision: no decision. I took off at a sprint for the road. Why couldn't I hedge my bets, have it both ways? I set my eyes on a spot roughly half way up the road; I'd start rock climbing there. I zoomed past Magda with a quick "Hi there!" and hit the base of the hill. Mr. French was perhaps three meters above me to the right. I tried to keep the sprint going, but after ten strides, the sugar sand and the slope reined me in. I leaned forward to keep momentum, but soon I was trudging, not running. I could see Ace near the summit, moving even slower than I was; I had no idea how high up the French guy was behind me.

Really labouring now, my knees and thighs started to feel like jelly. I was panting, sweating, grunting. The July sun beat on my left, my mouth felt like ashes. Would I have any strength at all to tackle the cliff towering at my right side? I was only a third up, made a snap decision to start climbing.

Bad decision. The old, weather-beaten rock was slick as glass. The bits where moss grew actually had more traction for my fingertips. The glaciers that created these formations probably moved faster than I climbed them. I finally pulled myself up onto the lichen-laced cliff's edge, paused to catch my breath. Three figures were on the road below me: I recognized the matching blonde ponytails of the twins in the lead, and the lumbering frame of Mike a fair way behind them. The trees started back from the edge, obscuring my view of Ace, French guy and

Magda. I had no idea where John was. Overall, I was now running blind. Panic dragged me to my feet, and I started off along the ridge to where I knew the next Tokens must be. My hands and forearms were aching, unused to the kind of abuse the climbing inflicted.

I spotted the yellow flag through the bush, and bulled my way ungracefully through the dense foliage rather than finding a trail. No time for subtlety now. I snatched a leather bracelet from the small cluster of them on the stump by the flag and took off, scanning for the next marker. *Strength,* I knew this one said, but I didn't pause to read it. Go go go!

I knew where the finish line was, and I had a rough idea where I was now. I sprinted away from the Hill, trying to make up ground. Where the hell were the other racers? In front or behind me?

I found the marked trail, and the underbrush thinned out. Tried to control my breathing, get some oxygen to my lungs and limbs. Grasshoppers ricocheted around me as the trail began to cut through field more than forest. Soon I was running parallel to a split-rail fence, with fallow field on the far side. I found a rhythm again, let my stride open up. Here we go, I thought.

There! Ahead and to the left, through the tall weeds: movement. But who? I poured on the speed, focused on catching him. And it *was* a him: the mad Frenchman! He was a lot shorter than I, and I was reeling him in with my big stride.

I followed the fence around a corner, leaned into the turn to avoid losing any speed. I was vaguely aware of spectators again, kids and adults, cheering and shouting, a smear of faces in my peripheral vision as I focused on the Frenchman. I was on him now! I worked my arms, but kept loose, relaxed.

The fence right-turned, but the trail went over. There was a stile, a little up-down ladder for hikers. He was headed

19

for it: I had other plans. The stile was a full step higher than the fence itself. I scanned left and right, found a low spot where the old cedar rails sagged between posts.

Mom had been a hurdler, and she was my trainer for the Run, so I knew hurdling theory, had even practiced a bit. You don't jump a hurdle, you *stride* it. A good hurdler's head doesn't move up as he or she goes over. You stretch your lead leg out straight, lean down over your knee, and drag your trail leg over bent and to the side. Any motion up is a loss of momentum forward. The other guy was headed up, over the stile; he'd lose speed, and travel a longer distance.

A very rational, but quiet part of my mind recognized that I, myself, was not a hurdler. And this fence was not a hurdle. For one thing, hurdles were lower. For another, they were designed to topple forward when hit. This was an old fence, but if I hit it, it wasn't going anywhere. And if I hit it wrong, I could forget about ever having kids of my own.

The low rail of the fence was dead ahead. My strides beat a steady tattoo on the grass. I was almost parallel with the Frenchman. If I timed my strides right… We hit the fence at the same time, and neither of us slowed down at all. I stretched out my left leg, bent low… three meters to my left, the Frenchman was at it again; he didn't climb the stile, he vaulted it. Time slowed again and I was suspended, stretched out over the rail as low as I could get, and the Frenchman spun, arms tucked at his sides, body out straight, even higher than the style, spinning on two axis.

How the…?

My crotch grazed the rail, and I refocused: time went normal, I hit the ground clean, and was accelerating again before he'd landed his crazy jump. Go go go! I can win this! I urged myself on, and the trail was lined with my friends and neighbours, and they were doing the cheering for me.

20

A hundred meters of homestretch. I could hear the footsteps behind me, and I pushed it hard. *Don't tighten up, don't let your head go back, stay loose and lean forward, breathe!* I could hear mom's voice in my head.

I kept the speed on full until I 'dipped' out across the finish line as my mom had taught me. The Frenchman crossed less than a half stride behind me. I collapsed on my back, the wave of cheers and faces a blur of sound and colour that somehow merged into one sensation, a musical mix of senses that danced to the beat of the blood in my ears. I was vaguely aware of the French Canadian guy plopping down beside me.

He patted me on the shoulder, and said *"Bon courier, mon chum."*

"You too, man," I panted back, and there was no breath left for either of us to speak further.

The Widow Cox came over, said "Well run, boys," and slipped the final Tokens on our wrists, the ones marked *Will.* She also had a water bottle for each of us. I drank greedily between breaths. "Great finish, Will!" Widow Cox said. "You sure made it an exciting contest. Third place is very respectable."

Third...? I tried to ask, but I was out of breath and she was gone to greet the next finishers.

The French guy saw my expression, and apparently found it hilarious.

"Mon chum, I like you, I really do!" He was panting and laughing at the same time. I wished he'd die from lack of oxygen. "Your girlfriend and the big one, they played it safe," he laughed, and clapped me on the shoulder again. "Sometimes that works. But they lack our style, *non?"*

I closed my eyes tight, and lay back in the grass. I think I passed out then, the sound of the French guy's laughter my only lullaby.

3
Barn Dance

Mr. Nelson's barn was one of the oldest in the area, and one of the strongest. His wife's grandfather had built over a hundred years ago, probably with the help of all of his neighbours. It soared five storeys high, constructed solidly with massive hemlock beams hewn from the virgin forest that his people cleared when they settled the area over 200 years ago. There was not a single nail used in the interior construction; instead, joints were held together with wooden pegs, spikes really, carefully fitted into hand-drilled holes.

Before the blackouts, the barn had been filled with hay. Mr. Nelson had been old even then, and hadn't had his own livestock for some years. He'd only hayed the farm for the little money it brought from neighbouring farms, and for something to do. The winter after the blackouts, he carefully distributed the hay to local farms in need, helping to load the old-fashioned square bales onto horse-drawn wagons, working faster than a man half his age.

The barn had been empty of hay for five years now, but tonight its windowless heights were full of light and life.

Mr.Nelson had been living with my family for a bit, but his old barn remained the social hub of our community. Lanterns hung from chains at different heights from the unseen rafters, giving the illusion of a starry night.

The crowd was like a living organism, a giant cheery amoeba, constantly moving, made up of dozens of small groups adjusting and growing. Distant neighbours arrived and were absorbed in hugs and handshakes; individuals and pairs slipped out in occasional acts of mitosis, to find fresh air or a corner of cool privacy away from the larger body. Out a small side door, a tin lean-to covered the fire pits where two pigs had been on the spit since early that morning; smoke and the insane smell of roast pork occasionally surfed in on waves of fresh night air.

In spite of my foul mood, I smiled as I took in the scene. The post-blackout world could be lonely. Mountain bike or horse were the most reliable forms of transportation, so you wouldn't really drop in on even a close neighbour without a pressing need. Besides, free time was at a premium; basic survival meant filling almost every second doing something productive.

So the festival, two days and nights of games, gossip and revelry in the height of summer, was the highlight of our community's long lonely year.

And the party in Mr. Nelson's barn was the shining jewel in the festival's crown.

Determined to hold my bad temper, I fixed a mild scowl on my face and made my way through the throngs toward the fire pit door. We salted and jerked most of our meat and stored it for the winter. The only fresh stuff I'd had in the last 6 months had been small game, like groundhog and porcupine. (If your Grandma made it through the blackouts and the badtimes, ask if she has her original copy of *The Joy of Cooking*. It has some surprisingly good recipes for porcupine, and even tells you how to skin it safely.) So anyway, I'd have to be seriously *seriously* depressed not to be drawn by the prospect of freshly cooked pork.

"Good run Will!" A hearty farmer's backslap nearly knocked me on my face. I turned but my wake was already filled by the crowd. Now I was suddenly being hugged; "Great job, sweetie!" Old Aunt Betty (not my real aunt, but everybody's aunt, you know?) was giving me a great matronly embrace. I gave her a quick kiss on the cheek, disengaged almost politely, tried to move on. "Better luck next year!" Backslap, handshake, hug…god! This was worse than the Gauntlet!

"Dunmore." Who was that? No one called me by my last name.

"Dunmore. Here." I looked up. Ace Mathews sat on a cross beam, one dangling foot at about my head height, the other tucked under him. His back was against a massive vertical support.

Normally the youngins owned the beams at these parties, climbing and scampering about above the crowds, playing tag or Freerunners and Aliens. There was nothing childish about Ace though. He seemed above it all, figuratively as well as literally. He was like a calm gargoyle, more part of the building than the party, watching over the people of his community, but not one of them. The barn party was chaos, lively, loud; Ace was so still. I'd never seen him so still, so…*not* in motion. He reached down suddenly with his right hand, as smoothly as anything he did in the race. Unsure, I reached up and grabbed it.

He pulled me up, almost a clean-and-jerk, while I scrambled with my feet and left hand to gain purchase up the vertical beam. Suddenly I was sitting beside him, closer to the hanging lanterns than to the people below. Ace reached around to the other side of the tall beam, came back around with a couple of Marissa Shockley's home brews. Handed one to me, opened the other for himself and took a long pull.

Despite my mother's fears on that long-ago night, I was not a beer drinker. An unwritten local code had developed in the absence of real laws: you were an adult when you did an adult's work. And when another adult recognized your maturity or your contribution, they treated you as such. Maybe they asked you to stop calling them 'sir', or asked you when you and your girlfriend were going to tie the knot. Well, Ace was less than two years older than I, but he had standing in the community. He had converted John Bascomb's hay bailer to operate as a horse-drawn machine. When my parents wanted built a bedroom for Mr. Nelson in the basement, they had Ace do the job. Ace was an adult.

I, on the other hand, milked the cows and cut hay. Important jobs, don't get me wrong, but kid jobs. Unskilled jobs. And if you need a hand mucking out the pig pen in the

24

spring? Call Jeremy and Laurel's kid, Will. My parents loaned me out all the time. I did what I was told, I was a reliable kid. But I still called Mr. Nelson Mr. Nelson, and no one asked me if Magda and I were getting married; they teased me because they knew I had a crush on her.

I accepted the beer from Ace, and suddenly I didn't give a crap that I'd come third. The fiasco with the first token seemed less vivid. I didn't care that I got beat by someone who only ran in order to maintain her 'alone time'. The conflict I'd been feeling, between pride in Magda that she'd run so well, and embarrassment that she'd beat me, faded to the background.

I smiled to myself, took a pull on the beer. Root-cellar cold, rather than fridge cold like those Coronas I'd served my parents five years ago. Made from local wheat, apricots from Marissa's Shockley's tree, and hops from my dad's little garden. It tasted fresh and earthy, amazing. I looked down on the happy crowd below me. My first beer offered, rather than snuck; it tasted like pride somehow. Pride in this community, that pulled together to help each other, when the rest of the country was in anarchy; pride in myself, that someone I respected, someone I don't think I even liked very much, offered me a token of his own respect

I was halfway done my beer and already feeling it before Ace spoke again.

"I was always scared, you know," he said quietly, barely audible above the noise of the party.

"During the race?" I asked, stupidly. Somehow I knew that's not what he meant.

"Naw. Back in school. When we were kids." It was the most I'd heard him speak at once."

What?" The idea was ridiculous; Ace had been the big kid, the mean kid. "We were terrified of you!"

He smiled, drained the rest of his beer. "I know. I was angry all the time. I guess anger was my..." he made

25

little circles in front of him with the empty bottle, trying to round up the right word.

"Defense mechanism?" I offered, "Like a shield?"

He shrugged, nodded.

"See? You can find words. I was no good in school. Couldn't sit still. Always being told to do things I couldn't do." I was thinking that Ace had made up for lost time: people asked him to do things now, things he was the best at.

He continued, "I had no control. You think it's scary being a bunch of small kids seeing one big kid walk into your class?" He reached around for another beer, offered it to me. I accepted it, but noticed he didn't get a second for himself. *Control.* "Try being the big kid sometime. Christ, I was big compared to kids my own age. When they dropped me back a grade, well, for such a big kid, I sure felt pretty little."

Huh. We both fell silent, thinking about this. If this wasn't the weirdest day...

"There." Suddenly Ace gestured to a corner where a small group sat on sawhorses around a lantern. Mr. Anderson, one of the local council men, had his arms crossed; Mrs. Smith, also on the council, leaned forward, talking animatedly to a strangely dressed man I'd never seen before; and in the corner, the new French guy from the race, the one with the crazy moves. He had a beer and watched the crowd, seemingly uninvolved in the tense exchange going on around him.

"Who is he?" I asked Ace. "I've never seen anybody move like that. At the trees, and the cliffs, he ran...*up.*"

"Exactly." Ace was back to single-word communiqué. "*Freerunner.*"

It took me a moment. "A Freerunner? Like, *coureur des bois*?" I leaned back in shock and sudden understanding, forgetting I was two and a half meters off the floor. Ace grabbed me by the shirt front and righted me.

"The older guy?" Ace indicated the other man I didn't know. "He's with the Freerunner. Up from the city." My companion turned to me, with a complicated smile that didn't reach his eyes. Ace's normally calm face expressed, what? Irony? Bitterness? Yes, and something I recognized from our shared childhood: anger.

I felt a hand on my foot; looked down at my dad's upturned face. Mr. Nelson and my mom were with him. "Ace, you might want to join us." Dad considered for a moment, "Will, you too." And the three of them walked toward a room at the side of the barn, the former tack room. The council members and the outsiders with them were headed in the same direction.

I followed my parents, Mr. Nelson and Ace, once again feeling like a puppy scampering behind the big dogs. My former delusions of manhood had vanished, as surely as one of my beer burps into the crowded barn.

The tack room was empty of saddles and bridles now, all transferred to our own barn. A loose circle of straw bale seats and sawhorses filled the hot, low-ceilinged space.

Little Frankie Cox, silent as ever, closed the door behind me and set up against it like a guard, shutting out the noise and delicious smells of the party. The air in the tack room was spiced with the healthy smell of hay dust, and human and horse sweat.

There were no spaces left to sit, so Ace and I stood against one wall, barely in the glow of the lanterns. Opposite, likewise on the fringe of the light, was the Mad Frenchman, the Freerunner. He met my eye, and gave a brief nod. The city guy was sitting in front of him, alone on a bale. He was dressed like the Freerunner, in a mishmash of grey fleece and loose cottons, but his manner belied his thrown-together look. The Freerunner wore his loose clothes naturally, like an animal wears its fur. The older man wore them like a wire hanger wears a tuxedo. This older man was not a Freerunner: he was military.

27

Sitting around him, but clearly not sitting with him, were my parents, Mr. Nelson, and four other council members: Mr. Anderson and Mrs. Smith had come in with the outsiders; already in the room were Mrs. Cox, mother of the twins, and her own mother-in-law, the Widow Cox. The Widow Cox and Mr. Nelson were the eldest of our community.

Where Mr. Nelson bore smile lines etched deeply from eight decades of amusement at the absurdity of the world, no one had ever accused the Widow Cox of being amused. Her steel-grey hair was always pulled back from her face in a severe braid that never seemed to change in length; she wore sensible men's clothes, jeans and flannel shirts that probably came from her deceased husband's closet; she raised the fastest and smartest and best-trained quarter horses around; and if she were ever to smile, I bet her face would shatter. I didn't know what was going down in the tack room that night, but I knew the city guy was in for it. I subtly shifted my position against the wall so I was behind the Widow Cox, out of her line of sight, out of her mind.

The military man from the city gave the opening salvo, but it felt like the battle had been waging for a while already. "The agreement is clear. The fact that it's been five years is irrelevant. Five years ago, you got your weapons; now we get our recruits."

Widow Cox's spine was an iron rod. "The agreement *is* clear: we got our guns, you got your *volunteers*. And we've been supplying your army with food ever since."

The military guy wasn't cowed. "Five 'volunteers', for only one year each, versus twenty-five semi-automatic weapons, and reams of ammunition? Ha! Listen, old woman, there was no expiration date on this contract, and you haven't supplied us with a new Freerunner in over two years." He leaned forward, "However, I do believe we

28

shipped a crate of ammo just last spring. Plus, you've had our protection."

I knew we sent food when we could, but I didn't know we had ever supplied the military with any Freerunners. Joyce McKee had left to join the military a few years back, to train at Base Borden, not to the city to be a *coureur des bois*, but to be a soldier.

It was my father's turn to speak. "You can have your ammo back, Jackson. We still have two thousand rounds from the initial shipment, which brings up another point: we don't need your protection."

We had fewer raiders every year, and only six or seven real threats last year. Most people who migrated by our community on the way north were stragglers, little desperate family groups. If they had no specific goal, like relatives farther north, they were adopted into our community.

The military guy, who my dad had called Jackson, turned to my dad. "Raiders are not your real problem, and you know it. Perhaps your lovely wife would like to entertain you with some stories of the real enemy."

All eyes turned to my mother, who'd been staring at the city guy with steel eyes, and one side of her lip slightly up, like a dog at the start of a growl.

I was confused. I knew my mother had volunteered in the city in that first year. How could I *not* remember the hardest year of my life, and my own mother absent for most of it? But she'd been helping the medics in the sick bay. She'd never even seen the aliens up close.

One year... volunteer Freerunners?

"Oh-" a single syllable signalled my sudden understanding.

"That's right, boy," his pale eyes searched me out in the gloom. "Your mummy was a Freerunner. *The* Freerunner, you might say, one of the illustrious individuals who started it all. If you've heard a story about wild, insane

29

Freerunners with a death wish, you've probably heard a story about your mother." His eyes narrowed, and shifted minutely to my left. I was dismissed, and his focus nailed Ace to the tack room wall. "And now we need more."

My dad motioned Frankie Cox over, whispered to him. I read the word *bridge* on his lips, and Frankie slipped out of the room. I knew what that meant.

Dad addressed the military man again. "You're not taking anyone against their will, Jackson. Canada hasn't had conscription in a long time."

"Canada ceased to exist five years ago." Jackson opened his vest as if suddenly aware of the close air. The butt of a handgun poked out from a holster under his left arm. "This is not conscription. This is *need.*" He looked around the room. "Humanity *needs* defence. It has the remnants of the Royal Canadian Armed Forces, a ragtag army with no chance for reinforcements, but an army just the same." His gaze settled on Ace. "But an army *needs* communication. And until the lights come back on, that means we *need* Freerunners."

The tack room was becoming a Dutch oven. The kerosene lanterns hissed into the silence. Eyes shifted from the city guy to Ace. I waited for one of my parents to speak, to defend, to deny; for Widow Cox to rip this stranger to pieces with her lash of a tongue. Why wasn't anyone speaking up?

I surprised myself by speaking first. "Dad?" He held my gaze, and his silence. "Mom?! Come on!"

My mom spoke, but not really to me: "It's Ace's decision. Not the Council's."

Ace looked miserable, angry, unable to vent. He was rigid with impotent fury. He was 8 year old Ace, all eyes on him, no skills to express himself. But the difference was, he was a man now, and people were going to treat him that way, even if it meant we lost the best mechanic and craftsman we had. And Ace would lose his place in the world.

"Pack your things son, we leave early for the city," Jackson looked around the room smugly. "I'll take you outta this cow patch and give you something to be proud of. You're a soldier for the human race, now."

Faces drooped around the room, but still no one spoke. The tension left Ace's shoulders. His already lowered head nodded slightly.

4
A Low-held Blade

"No."

All eyes turned to me. Ace wasn't good at speaking, but as my mother often said, *I* never seemed to stop. I put my hand on Ace's shoulder, gently pushed him back against the wall. I stepped into the lantern light.

"You can't have him." I moved toward this stranger in our midst. He was on his feet, meeting my challenge with a cold smile.

"You gonna stop me, boy?"

Mom was suddenly between us, shoving the guy hard. He laughed, didn't defend himself.

"You need mommy to protect you?"

"It's okay mom, let him through. I'm not gonna fight him." Damn straight I wasn't; he'd kick my skinny ass. "I'm gonna reason with him." I held up a fist as my mom stepped uncertainly to the side. I put up one finger. "Reason number one: Ace doesn't want to go." Jackson huffed, about to interrupt but I pushed on.

"Hey," I addressed the French Freerunner. "Didn't get properly introduced- I'm Will." His tight-lipped smile was back.

"Claude," he said politely. "Pleasure to meet you Will."

"Okay, Claude. Why do Freerunners run?" I was pretty sure I knew what his answer would be.

He shrugged. "Because they love it," he said in his light French Canadian accent.

I looked back at the man called Jackson. "A Freerunner who doesn't want to be there is no good. Ace goes with you, he's angry, he's bitter, he's thinking about home. What happens, Claude?"

Claude shrugged. "He dies quick." That ironic smile came back, "Okay, he dies even *quicker*."

I thought it best to ignore that last, and pushed on. "Reason two." I looked back to Jackson. Now that I knew Claude was my ally here, I could focus on this bastard in front of me. "Ace isn't your best choice."

Jackson laughed openly now. "Oh, kid, you've got a set. I know you're not selling out your little girlfriend out there; I can see where you're going." He turned toward my mom again. "Laurel, isn't this sweet? The pup wants to follow in the bitch's footsteps."

Dad did stand up at that insult, slowly, intently. Dad was not one to jump to his feet.

Surprisingly though, the young Quebecoise intervened. He was on his feet too, and laid a casual hand on Jackson's shoulder. "Sergeant? A quick word?" His tone was light. Jackson turned and leaned in close for a conference with his companion. He'd already dismissed my father as a non-threat. God! The arrogance of the man!

Out of all the others gathered in that sweatbox, only I was close enough to hear the exchange between the two outsiders. "Sarge", Claude said quietly, "You step outta line this time, *non*?" he tilted his head toward my mom. "Laurel has been gone some years, but she is still *coureur des bois*." He looked straight into Jackson's eyes, held them. He was a fair bit shorter than the military man, but they were clearly equals in Claude's eyes. "Maybe you should apologize, *non*?"

Jackson started to react angrily, stopped short, stiffened. My body blocked the view from the rest of the room, as I'm sure Claude intended. I followed Jackson's wide-eyed gaze downward. Claude held a short, wickedly curved blade against Jackson's pant zipper. He drew it up slowly, making a faint zit-zit sound, then tapped it twice against Jackson's crotch. Jackson graciously nodded, once.

The blade disappeared up Claude's sleeve as Jackson turned to my parents. Claude sat back down.

"Laurel," Jackson said with a nod to my mom, "Jeremy," to my dad. "My apologies. I spoke in the heat of the moment." Boy, was he pissed. He looked over his shoulder at Claude. There were some serious undercurrents in *that* relationship. He continued, much in his former commanding tone. "But the fact remains, we don't want a runner-up." He turned back to me. "We need a real *Freerunner*."

The interaction between Jackson and Claude had given me a bit of time to gather my arguments, but part of me wondered what the hell I was doing. Sure, I was a bit bored with farm life, but I loved it too. And my pride was pretty battered from the race. But I remembered Claude's crazy moves, and the thrill trying to keep with him. Man! I wanted that control! That freedom!

"Listen," I began again. I was still addressing Jackson, but I was beginning to think Claude was the one I needed to convince. "Listen, Ace can beat me right now, he's proven that. And I'll never be able to deke side to side like him.

"But I'm still growing, man. Dad says in six months, I'll probably add 15 pounds." I looked back at my dad, who was sitting again. I couldn't read his expression. Thoughtful? Proud?

I turned to Claude, took a chance. "Claude?"

He stayed where he was, but leaned into the light. "Ace is stronger, quicker in a sprint, and has good endurance." He gave a little one-shoulder shrug. "But this kid, he has real potential, Sarge. He's damn fast on a straightaway already, he thinks on the fly, and he wants to learn *parkour*." What the hell was *parkour*? I wondered. "Give me a few months with him, I think he might be able to beat me." And he directed that shrug and a challenging grin at me.

"I beat you today, *mon chum*," I shot back, and suddenly we both laughed. I was starting to wonder how hard he'd been trying.

Jackson muttered some obscenities under his breath, and pointed a finger at my mom. "It's not on my head if he doesn't come back, Laurel. And if your runt can't keep up, he's on his own." And he stalked out of the tack room, ramrod straight. When the door opened, fiddle music wafted in on a breeze of cooler air. They were starting the square dance out there, a hundred and fifty people oblivious to the tensions in this little room.

When the door closed again, the Council were all on their feet. Mom gave me a big hug, then dad came over.

"You sure, Will?" he asked.

I nodded, lying; then they moved back to let Ace through. He looked into my eyes intently. There was a question in his eyes; I nodded once. He seemed satisfied, and wrapped me up in a big man-hug.

A weird day, indeed, I thought.

5
Revelations on the Porch

A very similar night to that one long ago. A warm evening, crickets, no electric lights.

We were on the back deck once again, staring up at those glorious reds, greens and pinks as they danced and faded, rippled and shot across the black, so lively that you could almost hear the music they danced to.

Five years ago, I had been a kid, sitting with my mom and dad. Now, maybe I was man; I don't know. Can you point to one place in time, a moment in your life and say that's where I grew up? Like spotting Waldo in one of those kids' books, and knowing you could now turn the page, and look for the next milestone in your life?

Our family had grown since the blackout began. Mr. Nelson was one of us now; he lived in the basement, but I wondered how long he'd be able to manage the stairs. Maybe I should offer him my room. I'd mention it to dad.

Mr. Nelson had had a small glass of moonshine when we got back from the barn dance, and now snored away in the lounge chair. Magda had come back with us, too, a comforting presence in the dark beside me. Dad had invited her over for my last night. Her hand rested on her chair arm, centimeters from where mine rested on mine. I didn't bridge that small gap, didn't touch her hand, but I wanted to.

There was beer this night, too, but dad brought it to me this time. I sipped carefully. Sunrise would come early, and we had a lot of k's to cover.

Dad was talkative that night. "Will, I'm proud of you, son. I could list a hundred reasons for you not to go, but none of them outweigh the reasons you chose for going." It wasn't like dad to ramble like this. If he had a point to make, he'd usually think it through before he said it.

36

"I mean, I don't want you to go. You should really be here, with your family and your community. But it's time you made your own decisions." He paused for a moment, changed direction abruptly. "I hope you don't mind that I didn't stand up when Jackson challenged you. And Laurel, I hope you don't mind that I did stand up for you." To my right, Magda was stifling a giggle.

I think I knew what was making dad nervous. My parents had lied to me, or at least kept secrets from me. Why didn't they tell me mom had been *coureur des bois*? I would have been so proud of her, and it would maybe have given me something to grab on to for that hardest of hard years.

"No dad, I'm glad you didn't," I said reassuringly, honestly. "He would never have respected me if you had."

Mom leaned over and gave dad a kiss. "And I thought you were quite gallant, honey. You got him to apologise. Only *you* are allowed to call me rude names." Magda and I were both laughing now. I saw no reason to explain the real reason Jackson had apologized. Mr. Nelson snored on.

"Well, you always say I'm a thinker, not a doer. But sometimes-"

He paused, and I had the impression mom had laid her hand on his.

"Honey, could you walk Magda home? I told her mom she'd be back tonight." He got the hint.

"Of course! Come on, Mags. Do you want to borrow Laurel's bike? We could ride?"

Magda stood up, and I did too. Suddenly her arms were around me, my face in her hair. I breathed in deep.

"Be careful, you," she whispered, and then she hurried out.

Dad put his hand on my shoulder, patted once, and followed her through the house and out the front door.

I'd been trying to puzzle out how I felt about mom's newly revealed past. The silence wasn't uncomfortable as we

37

sat there, but there was an expectant feeling flowing between us. Mom broached the subject before I could ask.

"Will, I'm sorry we deceived you. We thought it best at the time."

I felt that I should be angry or hurt, but there was too much going on in my own life. Maybe this was a symptom of how I'd been feeling: I couldn't even decide how I felt. I simply asked "Why?"

She let out a big sigh. "Our community was instrumental in preparing the armed forces for the aliens. I'd personally both seen the aliens in action, and helped repel them."

I nodded; I knew this stuff. I was there too, running messages with the other kids.

"Actually, when the soldiers from Base Borden arrived," mom continued, "mostly what they did was clean up. The action was largely done. We were a rural area, and the aliens were after livestock more than humans, so they hadn't sent a large force this far from the city."

We both contemplated the vivid night sky. Mr. Nelson's sleep was quieter, more restful now.

"Jackson was a communications officer, on his way up," mom continued. "When the battle was done, he approached me, your dad, some others. Called for a pow-wow, to use his words." She smiled; I couldn't see it, but I could hear it. "Your dad and I really liked him at first. He was persuasive. Insightful. With no communications technology, he knew his job in the army had changed, and he was innovative. He recruited me to come south in an advisory role, and to help put together his team of message runners."

"But why not just tell me that? I know I was just a kid, but I could have handled that." It was really easy having this talk in the dark, looking up. Usually I didn't know where to look or put my hands during difficult discussions.

Another sigh. "We knew there was going to be

danger, Will. Your dad wanted to be open, honest. But there was some old fashioned part of me that felt guilty for putting my baby's mommy in danger." I heard her settle deeper into her Muskoka chair. "Then by the time I came back here for my first leave, there were all these crazy stories about Freerunners: the danger, the risk-taking, the recklessness. There was no way I wanted you to know I was one of them." "So, are the stories true?" I just had to ask.

"Ha! No," then she paused, "Well, yes, sort of." I turned to look at her now. What else didn't I know about my mom? "There is often a lot of risk, I'll give you that," she explained. "But it's calculated. They aren't just going to throw you out to the aliens, if that's what you're worried about." Shit. I wasn't worried about that *before*. "There's some serious training, and one of my jobs was to make sure it was adequate training." There was pride in her voice now, an echo of those long gone days when she'd been an elite athlete.

"What about the rest?" I asked. "The 'recklessness', as you call it; the death wish, the thrill-seeking. The partying?" How do you hope something isn't true because of how it reflects on your mom, but hope it is true because you're sixteen and about to leave home for the first time? A balled-up tea-towel hit me in the face as an answer.

"Well?" I pressed. "What exactly am I in for? What did you get into?" I chucked the towel back, missed; it landed in Mr. Nelson's lap.

"Okay, fine. Anytime you put a bunch of young people together, things are going to be pretty crazy. Emotions, hormones, territorial fights. Add in a real element of danger, and they find ways to let off steam. But you listen to me: I was about ten years older than the next youngest person, married with a kid: you. I was the universal mom down there; my job was to make sure things did not get out of hand. Most of those wild stories are propaganda spread around to get impressionable young boys like you to run away from home for an adventure."

"Did you do a lot of Freerunning?" I asked. I was reluctant to steer us back to serious stuff, but I wanted to know what the job was really like.

"Yeah, a fair bit," she answered quietly. "At first there were just a few of us, and we all Ran. And you can't train people for something like that if you've never experienced it."

"What is it like? I mean, really?"

"Ah, Will...it's life and death. For you and others. It's a rush, I don't deny it. The squadron you're assigned to is manoeuvring blind, except for its Freerunner. You run the gauntlet, you're their lifeline.

"Sometimes, you risk your life to get to the next squad with an important communiqué, but they're not where they're supposed to be. Sometimes they've moved, and you've got to find them.

"Sometimes they're just...gone. But you don't know that, so you're looking, running, chasing an entire squadron of people that no longer exist. So you need to decide: am I putting more lives in danger if I don't deliver the orders and return to my squad, or if I keep chasing ghosts, and my squad makes its move, expecting reinforcements that are never going to come?"

The crickets were quiet now, and the chill of late night dew was settling on us. The northern lights danced on, oblivious to the wrench they'd heaved into the human race's machine.

Neither of us wanted to end this last night on a dark note. But I didn't know where to steer the conversational ship. "So if it's a lot of propaganda, maybe I'd be better off in this wild farm community if I want to party."

It was lame, but mom laughed.

40

"Listen up, kid. You'd better be careful out there, and I don't just mean with the aliens. I'm too young to be a grandma."

"Mom!" I exclaimed, at the same time Mr. Nelson let out a bark of surprised laughter. I wonder how long he'd been awake!

His laugh turned in to a cough, and mom sent me into the house for a glass of water.

"Will- while you're in there, there's a canvas pack at the top of the stairs," Mr. Nelson called. "Grab it for me, will ya?"

"Sure thing," and I was back in a moment with water and pack. The pack was mostly empty, but held something of substantial weight.

Mr. Nelson took the water, drank, but waved the pack off.

"Something for you. Open it up."

Intrigued, I reached in, grasped hard leather. A sheath? I pulled out the object, and mom lit a lantern and brought it over.

In the white light of the kerosene flame, I examined a huge, strange knife, almost a machete, in a black leather scabbard. Mr. Nelson nodded me to draw it out. The noise was smooth, metal on leather, not that metal on metal 'shwing!' from the movies I remembered from my childhood.

The blade was heavy, and had a dramatic angle. The dull side was thick, extending straight for maybe 20 cm, then the heavy blade bent at an angle and widened out in a wicked curve, like a poplar leaf, but bigger than my hand. It wasn't pretty or adorned with anything fancy; but it was beautiful in its craftsmanship and its lines.

"Where did-? Is this really for me?" I asked lamely.

"For you, Will. I've been holding on to that thing for so long- got it in Nepal a million years ago, when I was a

41

Reserve. Missed WWII, but got to travel a bit just the same."

I was watching the light glint off of this impressive gift. I'm not violent by nature, but what guy isn't enthralled by a well-made weapon, be it knife or gun or nunchuck?

Mr. Nelson continued, "That there is called a kukri, don't know if I'm sayin' it right. It's the traditional weapon of some very tough fellas from Nepal called the Ghurkhas.

"Now, I've got my service revolver too if you want it, but the way I understand it, a blade is more the tool you'll be needin'."

"Thank-you, Mr. Nelson. I don't know what to say."

"Well, you can start by sayin' 'Mark' instead of Mr. Nelson. Mr. Nelson was my dad, and he's been dead nearly twenty-five years."

"Thank-you, Mark."

"Now, don't go doing something stupid like running your thumb along it. It's sharp enough. I had a go at it with a whet stone when your folks said that Jackson fella was comin' up for the races."

I shot a look at mom, who just shrugged sheepishly. I guess my parents knew me a lot better than I knew myself.

"You're gonna have to learn to care for it. That French boy has a few blades on him, he's a good one to ask."

I slipped the kukri back into its home, and ran my hand along the leather-wrapped handle. It felt solid and real, like the way any well-made tool feels.

"Well boys, I hate to break up this male-bonding session, but I'm sending you all off to bed." Mom kissed Mark on the cheek and shooed him into the house with the lantern. "Will, I'll put together some supplies, and you can pack them with your extra clothes and such at first light. Go get some rest; you had a tough run today, and you've got about six hours on the bike tomorrow. Go."

I was pretty wired up, but slept hard. My last night in my childhood bed.

42

6
What Mom Saw

The morning came in crisp and bright. Only dad biked out to the road with me; mom busied herself around the farmyard, doing my chores and trying not to let me see her crying.

We had a few minutes to wait for Jackson and Claude. We were quiet. When you've done a lot of farm work or any physical labour with a person, you don't feel the need to fill silences.

When we saw a small group of bikes approaching from the north, dad finally spoke. "Remember Will, you're going to be *coureur des bois*, not a soldier. You don't have to follow orders blindly, no matter what Jackson says. Use your head, and keep it attached to your body."

I nodded, and we hugged. "Remember your bandanna?" He asked, and I nodded. "Good luck, and be safe."

Three bikes arrived, not two. Jackson, Claude and-"Hey, John," I said, surprised to see the guy who'd finished seventh place at the races. "How'd you get sucked into this?"

"Hey, Will." White teeth shone out from his dark face when he smiled back at me. "I volunteered, same as you. I'm going for the bike division of the Freerunners." His jet black hair curled out from under his helmet. He had a nylon pack, with a small steel hatchet strapped to the side for easy access, similar to how I had my kukri strapped to mine. "And please, call me Bear. Only my mom calls me John."

He did resemble a bear, with strong legs and shoulders, and that shaggy black hair.

Dad gave Jackson the evil eye, hugged me, and we were gone.

43

We cruised toward the lip of the valley, and the last of the cultivated lands fell away. Old Mrs. Rainey's place sat near the valley's edge, a yellow stucco spinster of a house, alone, old and proud. Mrs. Rainey died before I was born, but in the way of small communities it was still her house. It was fairly well maintained, though no one lived in it full time; as the building on the southern-most edge of our communal grounds, it served as boundary marker and occasional guard house.

There hadn't been a raid of significant force in months, so Mrs. Rainey's was still. Our little convoy of mountain bikes was a smear of motion as we passed it, a swipe of dull paint blurring past the house's yellow canvas.

Jackson led, and didn't pause at the top of the hill. When the man walked, spoke or talked it was with a military arrogance, like he was trying to convince you he was the best. When he biked though...there was no arrogance, no swagger. He seemed to absorb the bike as a part of him, and he and the machine moved like a poem.

He dropped over the lip of the hill, then Bear, then it was my turn, with Claude bringing up the rear.

I leant in low over the bars to reduce wind resistance. The leafy top of the valley stretched out vastly east and west to my left and right. The paved road was steep and sunlit for the first hundred meters, then it was swallowed up by the valley forest. It was like dropping into a green, verdant tunnel.

The wind surrounded me like a warm bath, and I smiled into it. Birches, weedy Manitoba maples and evergreens whipped by. Another klick, and I would be out of the safety of the community's embrace.

The hill gave me enough momentum to coast a long way on the valley floor. Claude and I caught up to where the other two had stopped, still astride their bikes, a hundred meters from the bridge.

Jackson was staring thoughtfully at it.

I unwound the purple kerchief from my neck, slowly wiped the light sweat from my face. Shook the kerchief out, let it dangle from my hand. Waited.

Bear was getting restless beside me. Claude was casual, but his eyes were all over: on the trees, on the slow moving river, back to me, on to something else. Jackson watched the bridge, thoughtful.

Claude spoke to me while we waited. "You handle that bike okay. But not so good as Bear here."

"Huh," I replied, and wiped my face again. "Rather have a horse under me."

"A horse!" Bear exclaimed. I knew he was a bike freak. "Stupid animals! Big, loud, smelly stupid animals!"

"Come on, Bear. You ever fall asleep on your bike, and it brings you home on its own?" I argued back, good naturedly but half-heartedly. I was watching Jackson, and watching what he was watching. Past the bridge, high in a Manitoba maple, a flash of sunlight on metal. I wiped my face with the kerchief.

"Bloody amateurs," Jackson muttered to himself, and suddenly turned his bike off road. The three of us followed, slow peddling down into the ditch. A giant black walnut had created a clearing under itself with its toxic roots. A drunken split rail fence met at the tree, so there was shade and seats on the half-fallen rails. Jackson leaned his old Iron Horse up against the tree and rounded on me.

"Bloody amateurs!" he yelled it this time. I dismounted, kept the bike between me and Jackson's fury. "Your damn father and that old crone think they can play war games with me!"

I pushed my bike slowly toward the fence on the left side of the tree. Jackson kept pace, still yelling. "We had a deal! You volunteered! And I see a fucking sniper waiting to take me out! Bloody amateur hour! That bridge is the only ambush spot on the whole bloody road! Did they think I wouldn't smell a trap a mile away?"

My bike was at the fence now, Jackson was at the tree. I finally spoke.

"Why are you yelling at me? What makes you think I knew about this?" I was aware of Bear and Claude watching the spectacle, Bear looking scared, Claude slightly amused.

"You're the one who tipped me off!" He was right in my face now, and I could feel flecks of hot spit hit my forehead. "You're so bloody nervous, you started sweating and wiping your face with that fucking rag as soon as we got in sight of the bridge! God! What have you got waiting for me, a bloody farmer with a shotgun?"

"Nope, a little kid with piece of glass," I replied, having fun now. Suddenly Mr. Scributan stepped out from behind the tree, the bore of his long gun inches from Jackson's shocked face. "The farmer is right here, and he has a deer rifle, not a shotgun."

Jackson looked to Claude for support. The wiry Quebecer was openly laughing now. Mr. Scributan lowered his rifle, and promptly ignored Jackson.

"Good god, Will!" Mr. S. exclaimed. "Thought you'd blown it with all that face washing. I got the message! Purple flag for all's clear." He turned to Bear. "You're Millie and John's boy right? Run tell Frankie and Tee to come down here, and we'll get these men some breakfast."

With that, Mr. Scributan pulled a pack from the bushes and started to set up food, oblivious to the red-faced Jackson behind him.

I tucked the purple kerchief back into the side net pocket on my pack. Claude peeked over my shoulder, spotted the yellow kerchief. "What would have happened if you'd wiped with the yellow rag?"

I shrugged. "You'd be dead, I guess."

Surprisingly, he laughed again at that. "Well, *he'd* be dead," nodding his head at a suddenly sullen Jackson. "I'd be long gone, but pretty much alive." I shrugged again; he wasn't really boasting, he was just telling me.

Frankie and Teresa arrived, quiet as ever, and began setting out leftovers from the party. Jackson was stony-faced, but he didn't refuse the soft bread and cold pork. Times like these, it doesn't matter how angry or embarrassed you are: you eat when you can.

After breakfast, the four of us rode all morning. I hadn't been so far from home since before the invasion. The hilly country was hard on me, and for a while we had little energy for conversation. Jackson and Claude stopped occasionally, not to rest but to scout for danger. Bear and I were grateful for any breaks.

By mid-day, farm land was starting to give way to abandoned subdivisions, vacant cookie-cutter houses that weren't faring well against the elements, even though they weren't that old.

We were out of the hills, so riding was pretty steady; no painful climbs, no exhilarating downgrades, just flat and steady. Why would there be houses packed onto this beautifully flat farm land? I asked myself. Right next to a major city, it would have been convenient and efficient for farmers and city dwellers alike.

Jackson remained apart, in the lead and ever vigilant. With the hills behind us, the rest of us were starting to act like old buddies, and I wondered about Claude's age. He was so confident and cynical, and probably quite deadly; but when Bear let one rip and it vibrated on his bike seat, Claude laughed like me, like a kid.

We were coming up on a break in the houses, where a bunch of box stores clustered around acres of parking space. Burned out and tipped over cars littered the cracked pavement. I was in the back, trying to do my duty as rear guard. Claude and Bear rode side by side in front of me. Claude was trying to teach Bear an old Quebecois drinking song. They were laughing at how badly Bear was messing up the words.

The three bikes ahead of me gave wide berth to a small crater in the road. I stopped peddling, coasted to a stop at the lip of the hole. I was pretty sure I knew where we were.

I knew the story of my mom's Ride south by heart. She'd headed out on her mountain bike, to check on neighbours and find the extent of the blackout. Seeing the flicker of candlelight in old Mr. Nelson's house, she knew he was fine so impulsively turned south.

In large part, we'd been following her route from that long ago night. She'd paused at the top of the escarpment as I had, taken in a new perspective of the shimmering curtain of colours. They started in the north, but wrapped the entire sky, shooting south in an arch, like when someone throws a ball with a bunch of colourful streamers attached, and they billow out behind it. Even my ever-practical mom, a self-proclaimed "doer, not a thinker" was awed by that unearthly display.

How long did she sit there astride her bike in the almost-dark, before she realized what she couldn't see? The city. Toronto and the attached smaller cities, which wrapped around the end of Lake Ontario, collectively known as the Golden Horseshoe, were dark. Some eighty klicks away, it usually glowed orange on clear summer nights such as this one. On really clear evenings, you could even spot the CN Tower, for decades the tallest free standing building in the world.

But that night, all was black.

Mom headed south, doing, not thinking that we'd be waiting for her at home. When she got further south, she saw more and more cars stalled on the side of the road, bewildered occupants sitting on the roof, lost in the lights.

She saw no other bikes. She doesn't know what part of her brain or gut drove her ever south that night, but the warm night and her own breeze made the ride tireless, and urgent. She rode.

Till she reached the outskirts of the Golden Horseshoe, the place where farmland was being eaten by cookie cutter homes, and big box stores. Normally loud yelling would have been drowned out by the hum of air conditioners and the rumble of traffic, by the sounds of a vibrant community. But normally, she wouldn't have impulsively ridden 40 k on a Wednesday night, while her husband and son grew increasingly worried in their country home. So, she heard the screams long before she came upon the carnage.

Soon, there *were* people on bikes, coming toward her frantically. And then people on rollerblades, and lots of people on foot, carrying babies and children, swarming toward her on the road, screaming and crying. She pushed on, slowly south through the tide of north-fleeing humanity.

The aliens had landed a small ship in the communal parking lot of a Wal Mart, Home Depot and Longo's supermarket. Shock and awe, they call the tactic in the military. That first attack, coordinated with who-knows-how-many others throughout the world at the same moment, sure shocked and awed humanity.

Mom hid her bike and climbed on top of a cube van to watch the slaughter.

She says it was strange to see a cityscape (or a suburban-scape, I guess) lit by fire instead of electricity. Burning cars cast hellish shadows, and the aliens were like something from mythology: vague, massive, shadowy forms, sometimes glinting metallically in the flickering light. They moved nightmarishly slow, a stiff shuffling gait that should have been easy to dodge.

Mom saw some people try to sneak between the trunks of the aliens, ducking low under the metallic shields

49

they seemed to carry on their backs. But where their mobility was slow, long whip-like tentacles shot out like lightning, to grab a human by the leg, bash them bodily to the ground, and leave them lying there, crippled or unconscious on the tarmac. Then the line of aliens marched slowly on, herding the smaller, faster humans before them.

What mom thought were tentacles whipping about we now know are more like vines. And they don't hold shields: they *grow* them, a movable canopy of hard, overlapping metallic leaves that can shift to block a bullet or a firebomb. And we suspect they act like conventional leaves, too, and capture solar rays for energy.

Mom watched, sickeningly transfixed. Did she stay put out of fear or fascination? Or did she have some insight that what she watched and reported back to our community would save lives? I don't know, and she's never said.

The bloody spectacle was moving toward her position, and she decided it was time to get out. She prayed no one had found her bike.

As she was sliding down the back of the truck, she saw the first signs of resistance: not police or the military, but a bunch of kids. Teenagers with low-slung jeans and ball caps, acting somewhat in concert, popped out from between the houses with Molotov cocktails and barbeque propane tanks. They lit the hoses on the tanks, rolled them down the street toward the shuffling monstrosities. They hurled the bottles of gasoline; mom saw the silvery canopies of the aliens shift and ripple like the overlapping scales of giant snakes, to block firebombs before they reached their more vulnerable bodies.

When the first propane tank blew, mom was mostly protected by the truck. But it managed to take two of the monsters out. Mom said it also blew a crater in the middle of the street.

The aliens learned, and further tanks were hurled back at the teenagers by their ropey vines.

50

She'd seen enough, and could offer little help to the poor families being mown down in their own streets. She snuck to her bike, and began the long trek home.

I guess my companions noticed I'd stopped, and Jackson rode back to get me. I kicked a bit of loose asphalt with my toe, and it skittered into the scorched hole. The remnants of the two exploded aliens were long gone. Jackson coasted over to stand astride his bike beside me. He hadn't said much since the incident at the bridge, and nothing to me.

"Mom's first glimpse, huh?" he asked.

"Yeah."

"Keep it in the back of your mind, kid. The real enemy."

"Jackson?" I began. "Give me a chance, okay?"

He grunted, and slow peddled off toward where the other two were waiting. I hawked, spat into the hole, and followed.

7
Ambush

You Are Now Entering the Oak Ridges Moraine: a World Heritage Biosphere the blue provincial sign read.

The high edges of the moraine left a deep gash in the earth that cut across the flat land. The protected area was undeveloped for several k. on either side, running about 200 klicks in an irregular line roughly east-west through the province.

We paused at the top as was Jackson's practice, to scout for danger and likely ambush spots. Claude told us small groups of raiders had been active in the area. I was grateful for the rest. We'd had a short break at lunch, but otherwise we'd been riding steadily all day.

"Hey Jackson," Bear said, "Can I do this one?" Jackson had largely been ignoring us, except to give directions at camp. Claude, however, had quietly been giving us tips and hints about scouting and even biking. Jackson handed the small military field glasses to Bear, shrugged and said "Knock yourself out, kid."

Walking through the ditch weeds at the side of the road for a bit of cover as we'd seen Jackson and Claude do, Bear approached the lip of the hill. I followed. It was steeper and deeper than the escarpment hills from home. The road went halfway down, and where it levelled off it was sided by steep man-made embankments that dropped off into the forest below. The fissure itself was full of a tangle of pine and mixed deciduous trees, and looked pretty jungly for a northern forest.

Bear scanned the road ahead and below with the glasses. There were four cars littered across the road at its lowest point, so we wouldn't be able to use our downhill momentum to aid the steep climb up the far side. I quietly prayed I wouldn't embarrass myself by having to walk my bike up the other side.

"Will, do those cars look a little too random to you?"

"Huh? Whaddya mean?"

Jackson had ghosted up beside us. He held out his hand for the binocs.

"Well done, Bear," he said, still scanning below. Wow! Praise, and a real name? Jackson continued, "Those cars weren't there on our way north." He signalled to Claude, who joined us silently. He took a turn with the binocs, gave his assessment while still scanning.

"The cars are set up to slow down someone coming from the south, bottleneck them. There are probably men in the front and rear vehicles, and more in the weeds beyond the guard rail."

Jackson nodded once. "Options?"

It was a mark of real respect that Jackson consulted Claude on this. Jackson was military, and had training in tactics; mom told me he was also experienced in real combat, against humans and aliens alike.

Claude gave his characteristic shrug. "They're looking the other way; we could sneak up on them easy, get some weapons and supplies, make the roads safer for all mankind." Shrug. "Or go bush. There's a deer trail back a way, we could avoid the whole mess."

"I don't like messes. We've got to meet up with the other recruits at sundown in Caledon. Show me the trail." And Jackson started to return to the bikes in a crouch.

"Wait!" Bear hissed. We all turned. At the top of the hill opposite us, roughly even with our height above the valley, a small group on bikes was about to descend. They hadn't scouted, and were heading straight for the trap. From behind the binocs, Claude said, "Looks like a couple of, no-three adults, one kid. Maybe a family." I fingered the three leather bracelets I wore. *Courage. Strength. Will.*

My mom always says my dad is a thinker, and she's a do-er. My dad is my role model, but my mom is my hero. As I saw that little cluster of bikes heading for the ambush, I didn't think, I *did*. I ran back to my bike, hopped on and headed down the hill at break-neck speed. Jackson stagewhispered "Jesus Christ kid!" as I whipped past.

On the bike, I was *forced* to think: if I shout, will the other cyclists hear, or will I just warn the bad guys to look behind them? What was I going to do when I got down there? I didn't know how many raiders there were, and I didn't know if my group was following. At this speed I didn't dare look behind me. These thoughts passed through my mind just as the guard rails passed past my periphery, unbelievably fast, blurry, indistinct.

I crouched low over the handlebars and became part of the bike. Adrenaline was kicking in like an afterburner, and my tearing eyes scanned the front and rear cars for enemies as gravity pulled me toward the trap.

The other group of cyclists had a head start on me, but they were riding cautiously; it was going to be close. They were probably focused on the cluster of cars and didn't even see me barrelling down the other side of the valley. I wondered if I should draw the kukri, but some part of me resisted. I'd lived the last five years with human raiders being a constant threat, and violence was not unknown to me. I'd fired at a group of raiders, maybe even hit one. I'd had a few fist fights when I was younger, given as good as I'd got.

But some part of Jackson's propaganda speech rang true: other humans were not the real enemy, no matter how amoral and violent. And I just couldn't imagine actually slicing into another person with that deadly angled blade. I left it in its sheath on my back, beside my pack.

I thought again about yelling a warning as the road levelled out, but the decision was taken away from me. Ten meters from the cars, I was so focused on looking for raiders ahead of me, I ignored the sides of the road.

I hadn't yet hit brakes when I had the impression of movement to my right. I instinctively ducked and swerved as a man leaped the guard rail and swung an axe handle at my head. If I hadn't already been so low, the swipe would have clotheslined me, probably crushed my throat. Instead, it glanced off my helmet, and I lost all control of the bike. I tried to swerve as I saw the first ambush car dead ahead, didn't make it; the bike stopped, I didn't, and I flew over the hot metal of the hood.

Chaos in my brain. The helmet had protected me twice in five seconds, once from the axe handle and now from the pavement; it hung, split almost in two pieces, covering my left eye. I sat up and ripped it off. The newcomers from the south were surely alert to their danger now; I could hear a man's frightened orders "Get back! Get back!" and a woman's voice yelling "Watch out!"

I stumbled to my feet to find Axe Man ready for another swing. I opened the door of the car I'd catapulted over to slow him down. He kicked it closed. I was dizzy, could see two of him.

"Aiee!" A battle cry I'd heard once before, and suddenly Claude was vaulting the car, feet first. Axe Man turned, startled, in time to take Claude's hiking boots to the face. The little Quebecois changed directions off the enemy like I'd seen him do off of the trees, and landed in a smooth roll that absorbed the impact.

I was coming out of my shock, and lurched over to Axe Man and kicked him in the gut, hard. I grabbed his axe handle. I guess I was the Axe Man now.

Claude gave me that shit-eating grin of his, and gestured behind me with his chin. I turned as another thug was about to crush my skull with a cricket bat. He had it cocked back for a massive baseball swing, but it left him wide open; I used my new weapon like a spear and poked him hard in the face. There was a sick (but satisfying) crunch as his nose broke, and dark red blood started to run like someone had turned on a faucet. He went down, holding his face. I heard Claude laugh behind me.

"We should help the others, *non*?" I wasn't sure if he meant the family or Jackson and Bear. He cleared it up for me: "Will, get those people over the guard rail to the west. Tell them to follow the valley until they get to the next road; we'll rendezvous there when we can."

He looked behind him, where I could now see Jackson and Bear fighting off some more of the raiders. It was two against three right now, but more bad dudes were climbing over the eastern edge of the railing where they'd been hiding. I wondered briefly why Jackson hadn't drawn his gun. Thought maybe I knew. I ran off to the family.

It was two adults, a teen and a little kid. The woman had an old .22 rifle aimed at me, the man had a hatchet and his free hand out in front of him, and he was crouched.

The teen was a girl about my age, and she had a small hunting knife in one hand; the other kept the little boy behind her. I thought that very sensible; I've seen parents being protective of their kids by holding them in front, with their arms across the kid's chest; instinctive maybe, but it essentially made the kid the primary target.

Their bikes were a jumble beside them. They knew they couldn't get back up the hill; a man on foot could overtake even an adult trying to start biking that steep grade from a dead standstill; but they hadn't yet committed to the only option left: over the side.

"I'm a friend!" I yelled, hands wide. "Get over the edge! I don't know how long we can hold them off!"

The man looked untrusting still, and the woman raised the .22 to her eye. "Let's go!" I yelled.

At least the girl didn't hesitate to listen. She sheathed her knife at her belt, and lifted the kid over the metal guard rail. "Over you go, Orion." Her voice was surprisingly gentle and calm for the situation. She started to straddle the rail too, while the adults were still sussing me out. She turned to me, as though her companions didn't have deadly weapons trained on me. Big brown eyes searched into mine from beneath her bike helmet.

"What about the bikes?" she asked. Smart girl. Bikes were life out here on the road, but there was no way a kid, or even most experienced riders, could ride down that steep slope.

I made a decision. "Chuck them over! You can pick them up at the bottom. Ride west till you get to the next road! We'll find you there!"

The man and woman were finally on board. They stowed their own weapons, and set to work throwing the bikes over the steep edge. I could hear the twang as the light frames tumbled, wondered what kind of shape they'd be in when they reached the bottom.

I heard the scrape of a boot behind me and turned. The broken nose had slowed Cricket Man down, but he'd decided to get back into the fight. His face was a frightening display of blood splatter, like one of those abstract paintings in my dad's art books. I raised the axe handle in a twohanded grip, like a quarter staff, but I wouldn't catch him by surprise again. He was a full grown man, probably near twice my weight. I was gonna lose this round.

POP! Shwizzz. The little .22 hissed a round past my ear, and the bullet found its mark in Cricket Man's head. He crumped. It may not have been powerful enough to even penetrate his skull, but I sure wasn't worried about him anymore. I turned to the woman.

"Thanks," I said, and meant it on two levels. She'd saved my life, sure; but she may have killed for me, too. I was starting to realize just what that meant.

She just nodded, and hopped the guard rail. "See you at the next road," she said in a steady voice, and she started picking her way down the slope after her family.

I hefted my weapon and headed back into the fray to help my friends.

Ducking low to use the jumble of cars for cover, I snuck up to the melee. I was done with charging in blind. Jackson was central, swinging a policeman's baton like a tornado, whirring and swinging, blocking and cracking off of opponents' bats, machetes and skulls. Maybe this was why he didn't use his side arms: he didn't need to.

Claude was moving as much as Jackson's baton, rolling, diving leaping, never still. I don't know how many times he was actually landing blows, but he kept two or three men occupied with just trying to strike him.

Poor Bear was as out of his element as I. He was behind Jackson and to the side, guarding the flank. He had his hatchet up and ready, and I saw him swipe at raiders trying to circle behind the real threat, Jackson. I figured I'd add my new axe handle to this rear guard.

I peeked behind me to make sure Cricket Man wasn't making a miraculous recovery, and saw the cavalry arriving.

Unfortunately, it was the bad guys' cavalry. Four men on horseback were coming out of the brush hallway up the southern slope, and I could make out the distinct shape of rifles in their free hands.

"Jackson! Trouble behind us!" I yelled.

He glanced back, and decided to quit farting around. Sliding his baton into his belt, he simultaneously used his right hand to cross-draw the gun from under his left arm. Calm as can be, he shot a machete-wielding raider in the chest. A puff of blood spray misted the summer air.

"Grab your bikes," he ordered, "over the edge."

The threat of the gun held off six or seven raiders while Bear, Claude and I hurriedly found our bikes and lifted them over the rail. I could see the woman collecting hers at the bottom of the slope. It was a long way down, and steep. I mean *steep*. I found myself lamely wishing I hadn't already cracked my helmet.

For once, Claude was serious as he issued instructions. "Don' try to go straight down. Switchback, you know?" Bear and I nodded. Game trails back home always zigzagged down steep hills, never straight down.

I looked up the road. The horsemen were getting close, and gaining speed as the road levelled out.

"When the gunmen arrive, we'll have to really scramble, and change directions often." Claude held my gaze, then Bear's. We nodded again.

"What about Jackson?" I asked.

"Don' worry about him. Worry about Will." His accent got thicker under stress. "I lead." And he was off.

Over the edge, trying to follow the faint track made by Bear's tires, like a single-bladed furrow through the tall weeds. We took a sharp angle, half downhill, half side-hill. I could feel my back tire trying to skid down, had to adjust, point the front tire at a steeper pitch.

Bear was confident, actually pedaling, keeping pace with Claude. I was standing in a crouch on the pedals as I descended, trying to get a feel for this. I was having trouble controlling the bike. Steering was like dragging a spoon through oatmeal. I must have bent my tire up at the ambush.

I found myself strangely worried about Jackson; *I hope he's okay- he pulls some pretty heroic stuff for such a douche.* I actually laughed out loud at the thought, lost focus and my back end slid out again. *Stay sharp, Will!* I thought.

Bear tacked again: he turned the front wheel sharply and used the momentum and gravity to slide his back wheel around in an arc, and suddenly he's going in the opposite direction. I can do this, I thought.

Pivot, swing, *shit*. I didn't swing the back wheel around enough, and I was suddenly looking straight down the hill.

Immediately the speed picked up. Don't panic, use the back brakes gently, don't endo over the bars...despite the angle, I got more or less in line with Bear, but now I was below him, I couldn't follow his lead.

A few more tacks and I was getting the hang of it. We started to shorten the stretches between cuts, started to pick up speed and therefore distance.

We were almost halfway down the hill when Claude shouted a warning from below. "Go! Go! Go!" and a shot rang out. Not a pop like from that lady's .22, but a big boom, a hunting rifle.

I chanced a look up, saw man-shapes silhouetted against blue sky. I pointed my bike straight down and let gravity be on my side for a change. I forgot about being a hard target and just stared at the tangle of trees ahead, willing them to be closer. The weeds were so thick near the bottom that they actually siowed me down and I had to pedal.

Three more shots rang out, and I swear I felt the heat from one on my arm. Suddenly I was among the trees, gnarly thorny tangled branches grabbing at the pack on my back, ripping at my skin and clothes.

After breaking through the outer jungle, the forest floor was surprisingly open. The foliage reached upward for the sun, leaving the valley floor cave-like, cool, dark and damp. A flash of colour in the gloom indicated where Bear and Claude were waiting for me. The Quebecoise was peering through the outer leaves when I walked my bike to them.

"Jackson's led two of the horsemen off somewhere, but the others are picking their way down here. We better find that family quick, or Will's little display of heroics will be for nothing."

I refused to apologize, but I knew he was right. That little kid would be slowing them down, especially if he was scared. We had to help them away from these baddies. There may have been as many as two dead dudes up there, so the rest would be out for blood and mayhem. I didn't like the lady's or the girl's chances if they were caught.

"Let's go, boys," Claude said, and off we went. There was little underbrush, and the lower branches were about head height: a minor inconvenience for us on bikes, a major headache for men on horseback. On the downside, we were already tired from a long day of biking, and the slight incline through the forest soon had my legs aching.

Claude led once again, and Bear seemed to have no trouble keeping up. I found the trail challenging. I was in good shape, but this was more technical riding, and keeping constant vigilance a few meters ahead for rocks, logs and overhead branches was wearing on my mind, not my body.

My world became a tunnel, with Bear's back tire as the light at the end. I was always chasing, it was always receding, like some ancient Greek punishment. Gradually, the gap between us widened. I didn't dare look back for fear of getting beaned by a branch. There was probably nothing to see except trees after a few dozen meters anyway. We had to take it on faith that those bad guys were right behind us.

Claude took us across a little creek, riding a thin old cedar log across like it was a tightrope. I managed it okay, but my rear tire slipped off at the last moment, and I lost a bit of momentum in the mud. Bear was getting away on me. I stood up on the pedals to get my weight into it, and immediately found my face scratched up in a low dead branch. "Fuck fuck fuck!" I whispered harshly.

I remounted, spun my wheel a bit in the black thick soil, started to get some speed gain. I heard faint voices ahead, and suddenly Claude was coming back through the bush to me.

"Will? Can you keep up?" There was no judgement, he just wanted the truth. I wouldn't offer false bravado: I wasn't keeping up.

"I don't know, man."

He stopped in front of me, examined my front wheel.

"You're pretty bent up here. Probably from when you rammed that car, *non?*" He asked, smiling. How he could find humour at these times I didn't know. "You won't go far with a bent wheel. I sent Bear to find the family. We'll do something else."

The light was in his eyes when he said that last.

8
The Rabbit and the Monkey

Turns out the horsemen weren't behind us, they were parallel to us. Claude had heard harness jingle off to our left a while back. They knew the valley was funnelling us west, so they were keeping pace on the edge of the tree line where the low branches wouldn't hinder them. We ditched the bikes under some leaves, and crept to the south edge of the forest.

"Our first objective is to discourage them, keep them away from those kids," Claude whispered as we crept along. "But we drew serious blood back there, they won't turn back."

He sized me up, and asked, "You think you can use that chopper on a person?" I paused, thought about the kukri, and what it would feel like to slice through skin, muscle, hit bone. The slash of red, like early dawn, growing brighter and wider and redder...

I shook my head no.

"Okay. Grab a big branch then. I already know you got no problems smacking a man with a big stick." Well, I did have problems with that, but I had bigger problems with being smacked myself. I found a suitable fallen branch, about the same length as the axe handle, but heavier at the end. It would probably break apart after one good whack.

Claude snuck out into the sunlight, was back a moment later.

"They're ahead of us. Let's go."

We were off at a quick trot, an easy pace that felt good on my legs after so many hours on a bike. This was my element. The stick felt solid in my hand. The sun snuck through the canopy, dappling the forest floor as we jogged along.

We wanted to get near the horsemen, and draw them into the forest where their mounts would put them at a

63

disadvantage. Soon I heard a muffled curse, and the snort of a blowing horse. We got a bit ahead of them, and Claude signalled me to a crouch.

"You wanna be the rabbit, or the monkey?"

I smiled back at him. "The rabbit. I can't climb trees like you, yet."

"Okay. Keep a hold on the club. You might need it. Lead them under me. I'll let the first pass, take out number two." And he started to scamper up a thick spruce near the edge of the forest. The big old tree left enough room under it to make a man on horse think he might be in the clear.

When he was set up, squatting on a thick branch, he gave me a nod. Grasping my stick in both hands, I crept out toward the dying sunlight. The sea of dry weeds offered as much camouflage as the trees, and as soon as I cleared the forest I was wading more than walking.

My pack felt heavier because I was hunched over, and I briefly considered ditching it. Short term gain, long term loss: there was no guarantee I'd be able to come back for it, and it held my whole new life.

Our reckoning was good; I was maybe twenty meters in front of the horsemen, and they were working toward my position.

I needed to time it right. I had to 'accidentally' be seen close enough that they'd follow my path, rather than find their own opening into the forest to try to cut me off.

Closer...wait...sweat trickled into my eyes, the weeds tickled my calves.

I could make out the features of the men and horses. The lead man was heavyset, older, with hard lines on his face. He carried his rifle in his right hand, the butt resting on his thigh, the barrel pointing up. He neck reined the quarter horse casually and confidently with his left, Western style.

His companion was younger, and no horseman. He'd slung his rifle over his back, and sawed awkwardly at the reins with both hands. The poor horse was fighting him, not

64

misbehaving, but confused at the mixed messages its rider was sending. The lead man scanned the forest edge intently, steering his mount subconsciously, letting the horse avoid obstacles.

The rear man paid no attention to his surroundings; he was engrossed with just staying upright. If things went according to plan, Claude would take care of the skinny, inexperienced man, leaving the competent one to chase me. Figures.

Deep breath...now! Up I popped; the horse saw me first, shied. I froze, as if in surprise, gave the lead man enough time to shout and start to lower his rifle-time to go! I scooted into the woods; a shot rang out, nowhere near me I hoped, but loud enough to get me going.

Under the big cedar, I had to resist the urge to look up for Claude. I ran a good ten meters into the undergrowth and turned to make sure of pursuit. The leader came into the gloom more cautiously than I'd hoped; he paused right under Claude's hiding place...don't look up don't look up I prayed.

Rifle lowered, he waited while his eyes adjusted to the cool darkness; he spotted me and urged his horse forward with his knees as he took aim. I bolted to the side, putting tree trunks between me and his aim. He'd pursue, but would he dismount? Not this guy: he was probably more comfortable in the saddle than on foot, and wouldn't want to give up the advantage, even in the low forest.

I crouched behind a dense stand of whip-thin trunks, maples that had focused all their growth into piercing the canopy above. Through the trees, Lead Man was in slow pursuit.

The second man should be near the big cedar by now. I waited, as the lead man came close. He examined the ground, but I don't think he was a real tracker; I'd sprinted through soft earth to get to my spot, and left pretty obvious marks.

A distant yell, thump, and a horse's whinny told me Claude was in play. Lead man heard it too, and he looked over his shoulder to find out what was happening to his companion. I quickly crept up; his horse saw me coming, but still spooked when I suddenly yelled in its face. The rider's head was thrust into scratchy branches when the horse reared, but he managed to keep his seat. I darted away from sharp unshod hooves, and zigzagged away through the brush.

My man ignored his friend and came after me. I tried to channel Ace's moves from the race back home: sharp cuts left and right without losing speed, fast feet, fleet feet, go go go!

A quick cut around a big sugar maple and a peek back. He'd slung his rifle and was in full pursuit. His horse deked beautifully like a real cattle horse, and the rider was in total control.

Despite my tiredness and fear, I found the zone, and felt like I could lead this chase forever. Adrenaline and the strength of youth were high octane fuel; in the trees, I was actually pulling away from horse and rider, and it got me high. But I knew I'd tire long before the horse, and I couldn't handle a man with a gun. Slowly, I started a wide circle to bring us back toward Claude.

My legs were burning now, the euphoria wearing off. This guy and his horse were good herders. Every time I tried to circle back, they cut me off. He was no longer chasing, and I suspected he was biding his time, wearing me down. Where the hell was Claude?

I thought about finding a tree to climb. Could I get high enough before he got close? If I could find a big one, I'd be able to hide in the branches until Claude found us. I knew from raccoon hunting that it's really hard to shoot straight up.

But I didn't like the idea of being treed. I feinted back the way I'd come, backtracking to get behind the horseman. I glimpsed him through the trees. The rifle was at the ready, he was preparing to make a move.

Motion on the forest floor behind him...Claude! He had the other raider's rifle, but he held it in a two-handed grip by the barrel. The man might not see him, but horses have rear-view eyes: his mount would alert him. Gotta buy Claude some time.

I dropped my club and stepped out from behind a dead tree trunk. "I give up! I can't do this anymore!"

He raised the rifle to his shoulder, sighted on me from ten meters away.

"Please! Don't shoot!" I held my hands up. He kneed his horse forward.

"Where are your friends, asshole?" he demanded.

"I bent my wheel, couldn't keep up. They ditched me." Well, that was close to true. The horse kept advancing. They had halved the distance between us. The bore of the gun stayed locked on me.

The horse blew through her nostrils. She was a beauty. Nicely shaped head, a small white blaze between the eyes; well-muscled legs, long for a quarter horse.

"Hey," I said softly to her, and slowly lowered my right hand out to her. She snuffed at my sent. "I think I know you, girl."

"Hands up!" The rider barked. I ignored him. His mount stopped on his command, but she stretched her neck out, sniffing toward my hand.

I did know her! One of the Widow Cox's, stolen in a raid two years earlier. "Hey girl," I cooed, and stepped up for a nuzzle.

"Listen asshole, if-" Chunk! The sound of rifle-butt hitting the back of a head, and the rider pitched forward, landing head-first beside me. The mare started a bit, but I had her by the bridle by now, and was still scratching under her jaw.

"Thank you so much, Claude," I said mock-formally, still getting love from the mare. He stepped around toward me, shouldering the rifle.

"My pleasure, William. Now, would you care to get the hell out of here?"

We collected the other horse, and strapped my damaged bike awkwardly to the saddle. We left both of the raiders tied and gagged beneath the big cedar. Both were motionless, and I honestly wondered if the one who'd chased me was even alive. Claude had hit him pretty hard. I told myself it didn't bother me that much.

I mounted the mare, pulled the other along by the reins, and Claude got on his bike. We set off west to find Bear, Jackson and the little family.

It was full dark by the time we found Bear and the newcomers in a little hollow a few km on, right where Claude had instructed Bear to go. The woman was on sentry, and she called softly to us before we saw the camp.

"Gentlemen- here."

We followed her voice. I didn't see the fire until we were right upon it. Bear, the man, the teenage girl and the little boy sat around the fire, the whole camp screened by bushes. Either Bear had been taking Jackson's lessons to heart, or the newcomers were competent woodsmen.

Jackson! He wasn't back yet?

I dismounted, tied the horses to a tree and started taking the saddles off. Bear came over to help, handed me a water bottle, another to Claude as he leaned his bike against the same tree.

"Two down," Claude said to Bear by way of greeting.

"Make that five," Bear replied. "Jackson's been and gone, should be back soon." Bear pulled my bike down from the second horse and whistled. He quick-released the front tire, held it up to the firelight. It was so warped it resembled one of those infinity symbols more than a circle.

68

"Nice riding, Tex!"

I was exhausted, too wiped to defend myself. I pulled the second saddle to the ground, dragged it over to the fire and sat on it.

The man handed me a metal plate of canned beans and some hot bannock still on the stick, and introduced himself. "I'm Gabe, this is my wife Elizabeth, our son Orion." The boy gave me a tentative wave. "This young lady is Hannah Pike." So they weren't one family.

"I'm Will," I replied, around a mouth full of beans.

"We'd like to thank you boys for helping us out. Bear here and your friend Jackson filled us in." He tilted his head toward where Bear had sat near Hannah, still idly examining my tire in the firelight.

I nodded, started on the hot bannock.

"Where'd Jackson get off to?" Claude asked.

"Turns out Hannah here is one of the other recruits we set out to meet," Bear replied. Beside him, Hannah nodded, staring into the fire. Her eyes glinted gold in the flickering light. Her blond hair was cut in straight bangs above the eyes, the rest in twin braids hanging over either shoulder.

"But Caledon got hit by the aliens last night," Bear continued.

"Ah, man. Sorry," I said.

Gabe nodded, put his arm around his son. Orion leaned into his father. Elizabeth bustled around the fire. She was a lean woman, almost boyish, with hair in a neat brown ponytail.

"How bad?" I asked Hannah.

"Pretty bad," she said, still staring into the fire. "I was all packed up to meet you guys, just waiting till meeting time. They came at high noon, landed a small ship on the soccer field. Everyone scattered out of town."

I knew their tactics a bit; there was more coming.

69

"Turns out they'd dropped the spike pods out of town before, surrounding us. Everyone ran out; the pods rolled in." She shook her head.

"And you?" I asked.

"I remember the invasion; I hid. That's how I met up with the Jensons."

Elizabeth Jenson picked up the story. "We were only in town for market day. Gabe and I have been telling people for a year that the town was getting too big, it was ripe for those monsters to pick." She sighed, sat down, bookending her son between herself and her husband. "So when it started, we got under an old trailer. Hannah here crawled in after us. We watched the whole thing, till the herders passed us. Then we found our bikes, snuck out of town."

Claude addressed Hannah: "Any sign of the other two? Scott and Evelyn?"

She shook her head. "We were supposed to meet at the old high school in the early afternoon, then head out together to meet you at the water tower. That's where Jackson's gone. See if they made it."

I nodded, and started rummaging in my bag for an old shirt to rub the horses down with. I was exhausted, but that wasn't the horses' fault. They needed to be looked after. I was outside the circle of light, rubbing down the pack horse when I sensed another person.

"Got another rag?" Hannah asked in the dark. "I'll work on this one."

"Check the saddlebags. I don't know what's in 'em."

We set to work quietly, calmly. I loved working with animals. It was what I'd miss most about farm life.

When we were done, we led the horses down to the stream that trickled through the valley, and then picketed them in a little clearing that boasted a few clumps of tall grass.

I only got a few hours of rest before Gabe Jenson woke me for my turn at sentry. He stayed awake with me for a bit and we talked quietly as we circled the small camp. The fire was down to hot coals, and the comforting soft sounds of our sleeping companions played counterpoint to the symphony of the forest.

"Where're you headed to?" I asked quietly.

"Don't know, really. Our farm is too close to the town, don't expect any of our livestock will be left alive, or any buildings still standing." He paused. "And no town left nearby."

He was trying to be factual about it, but there was a catch in his voice. The idea of rebuilding again was daunting, demoralizing. The idea of another group of friends and neighbours dead, fodder for aliens...

"Bear tell you about our community?" I asked.

"A bit. Sounds like a good place."

"It is. We've got some good ground rules, too, about population density, size of large animal herds. Aliens shouldn't bother us if we stay loosely grouped." I shrugged in the dark. It was strange to be discussing adult business as an equal. I could practically hear my dad's voice coming out of my mouth as I said 'population density'. Good grief.

"That mare is the Widow Cox's, stolen a few years back." I continued. "Mrs. Cox is unofficial head of council."

"Mmh hmm." He was waiting to see where I was going.

"She'd be pretty grateful to have it returned to her, and I know her family's got more land than they can farm. And you could take the gelding as yours, the rifle if Claude doesn't want it." I knew he didn't; he'd only use it as a club anyway.

"You think we'd be welcome, times being what they are? Winter's coming, and we've got nothing set away." There was a hint of hope in his voice.

"They're good people, Gabe. I'll write a letter to my parents and to Council. Introduce you." He put a big hand on my shoulder. There were no words.

71

"And I'll get my folks to gather up my old stuff, toys, clothes, sling shot, the works. Orion can take it all, or what he wants."

I was suddenly engulfed in a great big man-hug.

Gabe went off to sleep, and I finished my rounds happier than when I'd started.

9
At Camp

Jackson cruised into camp while I was finishing my tour on watch. My eyes were grainy, my muscles limp and sore from the rigour of the past two days, all reserves depleted from the adrenaline rush of the day's chase and fight.

I was thinking of Magda, and my parents. I was looking forward to my sleeping bag, but it wasn't to be.

"Dunmore," Jackson spoke low in the dark. I hadn't heard him approach.

"Did you find them?" I asked, referring to the other two Freerunner recruits.

"Maybe one. Wake the boys. We'll need all of us."

"Hannah and the Jensons, too?" I asked.

He thought for a moment, then I saw his silhouette nod curtly, once. "Yes. The girl will want to come. I'll wake the Jensons to tell them where we're going."

I was thinking that I'd like to know where we were going too, but I just moved about camp, touching Bear and Hannah on the shoulder to rouse them. Claude woke before I got to him.

The teens started to ask questions; but Claude was silent, and immediately started getting his gear together. He was an old campaigner, and knew the information would come when Jackson was ready to tell us.

We gathered near the bikes for our debriefing, away from camp so as not to wake Orion. His parents joined us to listen in. Jackson kept it brief.

"I've found someone holed up near the enemy's aircraft, and I think it's Scott. No sign of Evelyn though." He searched out our eyes in the faint glow of the fire. "It's a tight spot. The aliens are bringing in their harvest, so there's a lot of traffic going in and out."

I grimaced at the word harvest. I couldn't tell if it was a cold, impersonal military word to distance the mind from the grizzly reality, or just Jackson being ironic.

"You're not trained for this yet," Jackson continued. "You don't need to come. But the more people we have, and if you listen to me and Claude, the more chance we have of getting that kid outta there."

We were all in, of course. Young, invincible, scared but fearless at the same time, if you know what I mean.

"Jackson, we'd like to help too," Elizabeth Jenson spoke up.

"Yeah, I'm pretty good with a rifle," her husband chimed in.

"Thanks for the offer, Mr. and Mrs. Jenson," I'd never seen Jackson so polite! "But there's a reason we choose our Freerunners young. They don't have any families counting on them. Your boy needs you."

"I've got a favour," I said to Gabe. "I'd like to trade you your front tire and your helmet for those two horses."

Gabe stuck out his hand and I grasped it. "Done," he said.

I hurriedly scrawled out an introduction letter for the Jensons, squinting to see in the weak firelight. They'd switch their three bikes for the two horses, and head north toward Hockley at first light. I didn't know if they'd be gone by the time we returned, or if we'd even return.

We were going to travel light, only day packs with water and weapons. If we got separated, or if things went south, any survivors were to meet back at this camp in the daylight.

Silently, we mounted up and headed for the highway, single file. Jackson in lead as usual, Claude bringing up the rear. In the middle, we three newbies: Me, Bear and Hannah.

The early morning was still, quiet; but as we got to cruising speed, we generated our own wind chill factor, and I felt cold.

The water tower perched on a hill overlooking the town. It had been a large community when I was a kid, but now it was pretty small.

In the false-dawn glow, it looked like any preinvasion sleepy town, with light commuter traffic just beginning to pick up on the major roads in and out. But when you looked a little closer, the cars were oddly shaped, round rather than oblong; and they didn't move as fast as cars.

Bear was on his stomach beside me, peering through the field glasses. "Jesus," he breathed.

"Have you seen the spike-pods before?" I asked quietly.

"No, we were too far out in the country to see the invasion." He didn't take his eyes off of the macabre parade below us.

I couldn't make out the details in the dark without binocs, but I knew what he was seeing. The slow-moving tree walkers had herded the panicked townsfolk outwards, where the spike-pods waited. A pincer-move, Jackson called it. Bear handed me the glasses.

I fiddled with the focus, and the monsters jumped into my view. Silhouettes of giant, spikey balls, like massive sea-urchins washed inland by a tsunami. Most were taller than a full grown man. They sort of rolled, sort of undulated along, faster than a person could walk. Because of their size, they appeared almost lazy, their movements random, sometimes rolling straight, sometimes veering off at an angle.

But I knew it wasn't random. They were seekers, gatherers. No eyes or ears that could be discerned by us humans, yet they could sense, somehow. They sought the bodies of dead or injured, and collected them on their spines.

75

Jackson pulled us back on the lee side of the hill, still under the imposing height of the water tower. He debriefed us in a low, steady voice.

"The main street has an old-fashioned layout, with a lawn in the centre, around a water fountain. See that line of taller buildings?" He indicated the main drag, off to the south, a row of four and five storey flat-topped buildings marching up a low hill. "Those buildings lead to the centre square, and the alien ship." He looked at our newest member. "Hannah, you wanna fill us in?"

She took a deep breath, and let it out in a rush.

"Okay, market day was yesterday, so everyone from the outlying farms was in town. The aliens came in around lunch time, so most people were in the food stall area or the shady spots." There was a catch in her voice, an emotional hiccough as she remembered the previous day's events.

"Sorry. I was killing time, waiting for the meet with you guys, so I had wandered into the deserted parts of town, was just cruising the old subdivisions.

"I stumbled upon a cluster of the spike pods totally by accident. They'd been hiding, waiting for the ship. I was racing back to the square when the ship came in, low and fast. Everyone scattered outwards, towards me and the pods. They must have dropped them off the day before, or even grown them out there. I don't know."

"This is a standard tactic they use with groups of people, or even herds of large animals," Jackson spoke up. "The spike pods are only effective in towns and forests; they're easy to avoid in open spaces.

"One of the reasons Will and Bear's people were able to repel the initial attack is because they chose the battle ground, kept it in the country."

I had to give it to the guy: he had just fought our elders to steal our youth, he had bad-mouthed my mother, father and whole community, but he gave credit where it was due, and didn't try to claim his people had won that battle.

Claude had been quiet till now. "Large animals," he began thoughtfully. "Hannah, where are the animals kept on market day?"

"In the soccer field by the old high school. It's maybe a half-k from the town square. There's usually sheep and cattle, and a few horses stabled there." Her voice was getting less wobbly. The men's factual, steady voices had that effect. They made the whole thing like a mental exercise, like a hypothetical: *If you were on a deserted island, and you could only bring three books with you*...but instead, it was *If you were rescuing a person from a town full of hostile aliens, how would you...?*

"Sarge, do you think the aliens have harvested the animals yet?" Claude asked.

"No, they'll gather all the stray humans and the bodies, then hop the ship over." We had just watched the parade of pods with their grizzly cargo headed toward the town square. Jackson picked up Claude's train of thought: "You thinking we create a diversion?"

Claude's silhouette shrugged in the moonlight. "Or we could wait them out. When they hop to the animals, Scott can just walk out."

Bear and I had been silent until now. He risked an opinion:"Hey, I made my stance on horses clear, but if we can free the livestock, it's a small blow against the aliens, right? We deprive them of an easy meal, make them work, and get our guy."

"We're not here to fight the enemy, just to extract our man," Jackson admonished Bear, back to his old self. "But I don't like Scott's chances if we leave him up there. Once the pods sweep the ground, the demon trees will vine the buildings, inside and out.

Hanna and Jackson gave a brief layout of the town, and then Jackson and Claude moved away to discuss strategy quietly. Bear, Hannah and I took the opportunity for some food, to recharge the reserves.

Hannah was wary with us, or maybe just with life. She'd had a bad couple of days.

"You like your Bianche?" Bear asked her.

She seemed startled by the question. "My bike? Yeah, it's solid."

"You work on it yourself? I noticed it's pretty stripped down."

"Yeah, I've been fiddling with the weight, got rid of the bullbars and stuff. My brother and I have a trials course at the farm."

I tuned out, and let the white noise of normal conversation wash over me. I should be feeling the old adrenaline rush, like before a Race, but I was strangely calm. Maybe my body just hadn't had a chance to produce any more yet.

The men came back to us and Jackson doled out the assignments. "Hannah, you're with me. Bear and Will, you two are going to free the animals, make as much of a fuss as you can, and get away fast. Claude will go for Scott."

He sought out my gaze, and held it. "Here's your chance. Don't cock it up."

Claude had more specific advice for us. "The demon trees' canopy of leaves is a solar collector on the silver side, and that's also its shield. The coppery side seems to be like a radar dish. They will turn the silver side to the morning sun; that is the blind side. Approach with the sun at your backs." He grasped each of us by the shoulder for a moment, then moved off into the gloaming.

Jackson took Hannah on their bikes around to the north and then west, taking a long circle around the deserted suburbs. They would start a car fire as a distraction on the far side of town.

Bear and I were to be in position near the livestock. Once we heard the explosion, Bear and I would release the animals, and get them headed toward the north side of town, into the direction of the forested parkland if possible.

Meanwhile, Claude would do his parkour thing, try to get onto that rooftop and guide Scott to safety.

10
Curly the Cow

No packs, no bikes: just our blades. We slunk through the darkness, down the hill, toward the town proper.

As we neared where the highway became a street, the long grass concealed more and more obstacles: bits of garbage, loose boards, and sheets of mangled tin roofing ripped off barns by time and wind.

We moved gingerly in the dark, side by side with a bit of space between us. Bear was quieter than I; I was used to speed, not stealth, and I'd only been an average stalking hunter at home.

We found the main road, and jogged parallel to it toward town. We were nearing the alien traffic, the spikey pods whose mission was to collect the bodies of the dead and dying, and move them back to the transport ship.

What had looked like slow moving cars from up on the hill gradually took clearer form: six or seven feet tall, undulating spheres of black spikes so numerous I had no idea of the size of their actual core. They moved in a nightmare herky-jerky motion, never perfectly round, like a partially inflated beach ball with a bit of water sloshing around inside.

The pods traveling outwards were creepy; the ones traveling back toward the town square were horrifying. Like a snowball rolling downhill gathers more snow, the pods gathered bodies. The multitude of spikes impaled the flesh, and as the creature rolled on, gravity assisted, pulling the corpse toward the middle of the pod more securely.

We moved on, shadowing the alien procession.

We were amongst the outer buildings of the town now, and cover was sparse. Crouching between two blocks of townhouses, we took stock.

"Look," Bear whispered. I followed his gaze to a pod larger than the rest.

In the dim light I could almost make out the shapes of bodies attached to it, and a loose arm flopped limply as the beast rolled on. The giant pod must have been eight or nine feet tall, and as it advanced its far side rolled into view. The remains of a pig, a big brood sow, or maybe a boar, came into view. Its big round head and stubby snout were clearly outlined against the lightening sky. Its weight was too much- it must have been a 700 pounder- and it slipped off of the spikes, and hit the pavement with a sickening wet thud.

The pod paused, backed up and rolled back over the dead pig. It kind of shivered, wriggling its spikes in deeper to the pig flesh, and started moving again. This time its cargo stayed secure, and it joined the loose line of its fellows bringing their harvest to the waiting ship.

"Jesus," I whispered, sickened. The larger implications dawned. "Shit! Do you think they've already attacked the livestock?"

We had an important role in the rescue operation; if we couldn't cause some havoc by chasing off the animals, more of the demon trees, and more of the spike pods, would stay near Scott's hiding place.

"I don't know. Let's move," and we were off again, heading toward the high school quicker than before, taking more risks.

The deeper we got into town, the more pods packed the road. "There's gotta be a demon tree around here, controlling the pods" I whispered. We wouldn't be able to cross here undetected. I remembered the stories; the pods were mindless, drones that were set to tasks by the intelligent walkers.

"Should we move back out of town, and circle around?" Bear asked quietly.

"No, man- we'll lose too much time. Let's wait for a gap, go for it." I was getting nervous that we hadn't seen a walker yet.

"Easy for you to say: you're faster than I am." We were crouched behind a derelict car in a short driveway. The pods shuffled by, not fast, not slow, just constant. We waited.

"There?" Bear asked as a gap appeared, but in the space of his asking it, a smaller, faster pod rolled outwards, in search of more fodder.

"We're just going to have to go... "

"Ah, man..."

A random gap appeared, and "Go go!" I hissed. We scooted through the traffic, like kids playing tag amongst stacks of hay; but this hay moved, and had pointy bits.

The pods slowly veered toward us as we raced passed, like iron filings pulled toward two fast-moving magnets; but once out of their sensory range, they readjusted their destination back to the ship, and lumbered on.

We hit the opposite row of houses in about eight seconds, breathing heavily, elated.

"That was awesome!" Bear gasped. "Wanna go again?"

I gave him a playful shove, and we were off through the backstreets, zigzagging our way toward the high school soccer field.

We skirted around the sprawling high school, staying close to its brick walls. We were unused to such a large building, and I was strangely intimidated. The sun was making a yellow glow behind us, and I prayed Claude was correct about the blind side.

Through cracked parking lots, around a greenhouse with no windows left intact; past rusted out skeletons of cars and pickup trucks near the school's auto shop, and down a slight incline to the sports field. We carefully hopped a rusty chain fence that ran the length of the school, just a single strand of links draped like a Christmas garland through posts set along the back parking lot.

Grass, a gravel running track, and more grass with animal pens in the centre. Several dark patches against the animal pens were probably spike-pods. The sun glinted off of the silvery leaves of a demon tree.

We lay in the overgrown field and considered the situation.

"There's no cover," Bear whispered.

"We'll have to belly-crawl. But get ready to run; I don't know how far away they can sense us. If it turns, it'll pick us up."

The grass was cold and dewy as we crept along. The track was a dirty scar in the green grass; we'd have to move quickly across it, totally without cover. We kept as low as we could, and duck-walked across the pea gravel, crouched over, heel-toe to try to minimize the crunching sound.

The animal pens were a make-shift affair, a large corral subdivided into smaller, animal-specific pens, that took up maybe two thirds of the soccer field. We could hear the animals: restless morning sounds, bleats and lows and that chuff noise that horses make when they blow out their nostrils.

All the livestock was at the southern edges of their pens, as far from the alien as possible. It was as still as a real tree, stationed at the northern end, its canopy spread to absorb as much of the bright morning sun as possible.

It was really quite beautiful. I'd never seen one in the daytime before. It stood over two meters tall, with a lean black and- green mottled torso that ran right down to its spidery rootlike feet. Feet that were embedded in the carcass of a calf. It was feeding from its roots as it recharged in the morning sun.

I couldn't see its front. Actually, I knew it had no front; but a rippling cascade of metallic leaves was spread out to catch the early morning golden sun on our side, the side that I thought of as the back. Only one alien. Another was probably near, with a small transport vehicle.

We crouched against the sheep pen, peeked through the slats. The sheep bleated and shifted. Slowly, using the cutters on his Leatherman tool, Bear began snipping wire. He quietly crept to the cattle section, while I stayed and twisted some cut bits together to keep the fence upright until the signal. I peeked up: the demon tree hadn't moved.

"Will," Bear hissed. I crept over to where he crouched near the cattle. There were perhaps 30 head, plus a handful of calves grouped on the other side of the fence.

Immediately I could see the problem: the fence itself was much sturdier here, to keep in the larger animals. Green-painted steel, five rails high, and spot-welded in place. We could never move or break this. I rose up above the fence and risked a look. A curious momma cow chewed her cud at me, appraised me with her liquid brown eyes.

"Hey girl," I whispered. I peeked around her. As I'd feared, the small cluster of horses was in the same enclosure. The goal was to create a distraction, but I wanted to save the horses from being alien food.

"Will the sheep and pigs be enough to create a diversion?" Bear asked.

I shook my head no. "Leave it to me. You be ready to release the sheep and pigs, I'll get the big animals."

He looked a question at me, then shrugged. "Don't do anything *too* stupid."

"Wait-" I stopped him, "How stupid is too stupid?" And I crawled through the metal rails, and in amongst the cattle before he could answer.

There are a few things about farm life that city people don't get. One is that the smell of cow and horse manure isn't that bad. Don't laugh, but I kinda like it, as long as it's outdoors.

Not pig shit though- that's one of the worst smells known to human kind. See? We say cow manure, and pig shit. That sums it up.

Anyway, it was almost comforting, creeping around the cattle. They seemed even bigger because I was keeping low. It was the warmest I'd been all morning, in amongst those massive bodies. They took little notice of me, but they were nervous because of the alien presence stationed at the far end of the enclosure.

I got bumped pretty hard a couple of times, almost fell. I got almost parallel with the demon tree, on the periphery of the inner dish of its canopy. I was counting on it not detecting me among the press of large animals.

I worked my way to where the cluster of horses were milling. There's a pecking order in the animal kingdom, and horse trumps cow every time; there was no water left in the trough, but they were stationed near it. From there I was able to spot the gate in the corral. The demon tree was sunbathing right in front of it.

One of the horses stepped on my foot, just caught the toe. I stifled a curse, and leaned into the horse's shoulder. It side-stepped to regain balance, and the pressure on my toe released.

Jackson and Hannah would be setting their fire soon. If I could subtly steer the horses and cows toward the gate, maybe I could unlatch it without being detected...

I moved among the horses, trying to shift them in the right direction. They were reluctant, and shied from the alien beast, tried to keep their butts pointed at it, in order to kick back in self defence. I started to feel the pressure of time.

Finally, I just grabbed a mare by the mane, tried to lead her to the gate, all the while staying low and slightly behind the alien's canopy. Full morning sun was upon us now.

The mare resisted, swung her big head at me. It was a casual blow, but it knocked me on my butt. I landed near another horse; this one shied away, kicked out. *Duck and cover!* I thought, and kissed dirt as a shod hoof whistled over my head.

Chain reaction: the horses spooked, and that got the cows going. The corral wasn't big enough for this much panic, and the space became a tempest. I was somewhere in the middle. I got to my feet, as massive bodies kicked, trotted and lumbered around me.

A metallic noise, like a hundred ball bearings dropped on a concrete floor. Through the chaos of cows and horses, I saw the demon tree's underside, the radar side, focused on me. It suddenly angled its canopy south, toward the downtown, and I knew it was transmitting a message to its fellows.

Well, we wanted a diversion.

"Heeyaw! Get!" I heard Bear yell somewhere behind me. The demon tree's attention shifted as Bear scattered the smaller animals. I leapt toward the gate, unchained it and shoved it outward. The demon tree blocked it, and its sinewy vines wrapped about it. I wasn't going to win this shoving match.

But the animals in the pen sensed the opening. Heads tossing wildly, the horses bolted. I threw myself over the metal bars and held on as they shoved gate, alien and me, forcing the opening wider.

Its attention was now on the cows, still in the pen. Its job was to guard the 'harvest', but the harvest was escaping. Ignoring me, it shuffled its way into the pen's opening, and unfurled its canopy and extended all its vines in an attempt to intimidate the skittish cattle.

Another misunderstanding about farm animals is that only the bulls grow horns. Not true. Horn growth has to do with breed, not gender. There were no grown bulls in that enclosure, but most of the cows had a wide spread of horns.

In these uncertain times, it was wise to breed cattle that could defend themselves.

Presently, the herd settled a bit, and the mommas got their babies behind them. They formed a wedge, like a blunt arrow, with a big Herford at the front. She was big and tough, with horns that curled oddly in front of her big head.

She huffed, pawed the mud. The alien sent a vine searching for the gate. It snaked near me, and I sliced at it with the kukri. It recoiled.

I didn't see the signal Curly Horns sent, but the rest of the cattle did. They charged as one, with Curly Horns in the lead. She got her head down.

The alien shuffled, much too slow. Curly Horns got under it, tossed her head up. It went up like a tree uprooted by a tornado, vines flailing. It came down in the middle of the little stampede, and didn't get up again.

I chased the cattle for a minute, and Bear joined me, making sure they kept running. The horses were long gone.

We went back to the corral cautiously.

"Reckon it's dead?" Bear asked.

"Dunno. I've only heard of fire killing 'em," I replied.

The beautiful canopy looked like scrap metal, the trunk like so much kindling. One of the vines twitched. Bear approached it cautiously with his hatchet out.

Thwack! His first swing just buried it in the earth, and it took two more to sever it. He hooked the limp vine on his weapon, still not touching it directly.

We peered at it, like two kids examining a strange bug in a jar. It was about as thick as my wrist at its widest, tapering to a finger's width. Short, sharp thorns just like the kids back home had theorized.

"Huh," Bear grunted.

"Yeah," I replied, "huh."

Again we heard the sound like cascading steel. We instinctively jumped back from the alien corps, but it was still.

"There!" Bear pointed in the direction of downtown. Two creatures, low to the ground like dogs, but much bigger...silvery manes, like metal satellite dishes. They would have looked a lot like lions, but there was no head, just that thick circle of metallic petals.

"What the...?" I asked. The new alien creatures trained their circles of metal leaves on us and began to run toward us, quickly, on four legs.

"Shit, that's just not fair," Bear said. "They're supposed to be slow, Will!" I had no explanation for him. I'd never heard of a fast-running alien either.

Just then, the world to the south went boom. The two strange aliens paused a hundred meters from us, and looked back at the huge plume of smoke that was unfolding over downtown Caledon, very near the alien ship. Jackson and Hannah's 'distraction'.

Ignoring us now, the aliens ran at frightening speed toward their ship. Bear and I ran the other way. And we ran, and ran.

Back at the water tower, Hannah and Jackson sat silent as stones. Claude still hadn't come back. We waited.

It was full night when the small Freerunner snuck in to camp, alone. Hannah held back a small sob. The rescue mission had failed.

11
Training

We arrived at Runner's Haven in the middle of the night two days later. There was not much to see in the dark, even under the night light of the aurora borealis.

We ditched the bikes in an outbuilding, and entered through a labyrinth of dark tunnels into the base. I had an impression of vast space, and our footsteps echoed. Claude led me and Bear to the boys' area; Jackson took Hannah in the other direction. No one had enough energy for a 'good night'. I could hear Bear shuffling around in his cubby next door. I awkwardly climbed into my hammock, and slept forever.

A long time later, I followed my nose to the kitchen. It was a large room, with too many tables and not enough people eating at them. Bear and Hannah were already there, eating porridge and unleavened bread. They waved me over.

"Morning sleepyhead," Hannah teased. "Or should I say afternoon?"

I grunted in reply, and they directed me over to the self-serve table. I could tell from the soft light filtering in from the high windows that it *was* still morning. A few other young people were finishing up breakfast, and most nodded and smiled at me.

I scarfed down some hot food while my friends discussed what was ahead.

"My whole body hurts." Bear complained. "Do you think we'll start training right away?"

"I think we'll get some info first. Maybe a tour of this place."

I was curious about our new home, too. It was a great facility, unlike anything I was used to on the farm. It was so shiny, and open and modern.

Claude had told us it was a former outdoor adventurers' co-op. He'd first seen it as a kid. "It was great, boys!" He'd told us on the ride south. "The future of retail. State-of-the art energy-efficient design for the building. There was an indoor rock climbing wall, and all the gear I needed for a reasonable price. At fifteen, I was a member, so a part-owner. I was there with my parents when the invasion happened."

I was picking at crumbs when a clean-cut young man came to get us from breakfast.

"Hi everyone! I'm Ollie, chief medic and tour-guide extraordinaire." He gave us a big smile. "Welcome to Runner's Haven."

We introduced ourselves, and he gave us the quick tour. The place was impressive. The store shelves and merchandise were long removed, and an intimidating obstacle course has been added. Playground equipment, a tangled rope course, sand pits and even a series of trapezes hanging from the steel girders three stories overhead. And of course the giant rock wall that Claude had gushed about.

The curtained off sleeping cubbies, guys on one side girls on other, were tucked into the back, where the storage had once been.

One wall in the training room was decorated with a wild assortment of small paintings. A wolf's head; a plummeting eagle; the silhouette of a barn swallow. A couple dozen small images, all painted separately, but working together in an artful collage. And it wasn't just animals, either. A skull and crossbones, a dragon, a raised fist. Even the words 'For Mom' decorated the wall. Ollie didn't explain the wall, and none of us asked

"Okay, we're going to get you some new shoes if you need 'em, then we'll meet your first instructor, and the recruits that got here yesterday," Ollie said, and led us back to the kitchen area.

For some reason, I'd been expecting we'd learn in an old-fashioned classroom like when I was a kid. Instead, there were ten other kids about our age settling into seats where we'd eaten breakfast. Six guys, and four girls. We had quick introductions, a flurry of names. I caught Hazel, Adrian, Gemma, Sneezy, Bashful, Doc... I'm bad with names at first, but I did take notice of a big guy named Geoff, and a girl with him named Dominique. Some people look for trouble. Some people, like these two, wear trouble like a suit of armour.

Geoff was about my overall size, but bigger; not work-on- the-farm big, but work-out-in-the-gym big. And his shirt was just a bit too small. Dominique had spikey dark hair, and would have been pretty, but she checked me, Bear and Hannah out with a sneer that looked permanent. Most of the others were keeping a bit of distance from the pair already.

Jackson was there too, standing like a 4x4 post, in grey camo that suited him much more than casual biking clothes. He introduced our first instructor, then he and Ollie left.

Our instructor was a middle aged woman with salt and pepper hair, leaning more toward salt. She had that 'thinker' look about her, like my dad did. I liked her right away.

"Hi gang, I'm Dr. Botsworth-" wow, even my dad wasn't geeky enough to say 'gang' "-and this is Alien Theory 101." She smiled like she'd made a joke. I smiled back at her, but I don't think anyone else did.

"All right! I'm going to give you some information that we know, and some things that we think we know. But there's much more about these creatures that we don't even know that we don't know." The little smile again, and I did laugh this time. Geoff sneered at me.

Dr. Botsworth continued: "What we know: five

years ago, solar flares knocked out electronics. We expect them to start working more often again, because the intensity of the northern lights is gradually diminishing." Well, I didn't know that last bit. "Now, did the aliens cause the solar flares, or know they were coming, or just capitalize on a natural event? That, we don't know."

She looked around at her group of students, to make sure we were following along. "What else do we know? They use organic technology, a nice oxymoron." The proud smile again. "They grow their ships, their weapons, everything. Quite remarkable, actually."

"You sound like you *admire* them," Dom quipped from the table she shared with Geoff.

The doctor seemed to miss the sarcasm. "Oh, indeed, in a way I do;" and she paused, thoughtfully. "Just how I'd admire the speed with which a rattlesnake strikes," she said directly to Dominique, "but that doesn't mean I would want to be bit by one."

Dr. Botsworth filled in some cracks on stuff I already knew. The aliens and their ships were a type of highorder plant. As a result, they needed solar energy, but also protein rich 'bio-fuel'. This is a scientific term for dead bodies. Where most plants native to earth wanted bio-matter that had been broken down by time, or processed through animals, like manure, the aliens craved something...fresher. The human scientists theorized that most of what demon trees and spike pods collected was to fuel, or grow, their main ship, which has been parked for five years at the domed football stadium. "I haven't been near the site myself since the Argos won the Grey Cup there in 2012, but apparently the smell now is quite terrific," the good doctor informed us.

Some other interesting facts she gave us were that New York had at least four alien ships, Washington DC had one, and Ottawa had one that also collected human bodies from Hull, Quebec. Apparently, the aliens were unaware of inter-provincial distinctions.

"All in all," she informed us cheerily, "we assume there are hundreds on Earth."

Even Dr. B started to notice that her students were losing interest. We were unused to lectures; even when my dad got going on some obscure information, he'd keep challenging me with questions to keep me interested. Besides, we knew most of this stuff.

"All right class, on to what we've deduced." Dr. B singled a boy out at my table. "Matt. What is our biggest advantage over the aliens?"

Matt didn't need to think. "They're slow. We're fast."

"Good," she looked around, "Now, why are they so slow?"

That was like asking *why is a turtle so slow?* Or *why does a fish like to swim?* We weren't sure what the question was leading to.

"Okay, we've got an evolved species, one that seems to cultivate all of its technology, including its space ships, from plants. It is a plant itself. But it has a major weakness. It is slow." She had our attention again.

"We've surmised that they've been a few generations in space, so the design of their bodies is good for limited gravity, but not for Earth." She cast her professorial smile upon us again. "Fairly short root-like legs and feet for feeding, or grasping surfaces in a confined environment; but long tentacles, which can grasp in any direction. Has anyone seen a demon tree move?"

Several of us put up our hands: me, Bear and Hannah; Dominique, but not Geoff; one other girl and two boys; surprisingly, the shy girl named Gemma raised her hand high.

The doctor nodded. "Then you know, they are not

suited for gravity. So we've deduced that they travel for long distances, and then 'park' and build up their reserves for a while before moving on again." She met each of our gazes.

"But we've long wondered if they plan on being here long enough to adapt to our planet. To cultivate the next generation. How will they progress?" She might have been talking about introducing a new breed of rose into a different temperature zone.

Her pleasant gaze found me and Bear. "Now, thanks to recent information we've received, we believe they are cultivating the next generation to mimic successful earth creature designs, such as wolves or big cats." That pleasant smile. "Bear and Will? I'm sure we would all be fascinated to hear about what you saw in Caledon."

At lunch the thirteen of us got to hang a bit. I was very aware of the two missing recruits. Scott and Evelyn. Fifteen was such a nice, neat number. We'd lost two of our number to the aliens before we'd even begun training.

I liked most of the others right away. Hazel was the oldest at eighteen. She was straightforward, and acted like a mother hen without being obnoxious about it.

Hazel touched Hanna's arm lightly and said "Hannah, your cubby is next to mine. I heard you come in last night. Let me know if you need anything." Hannah smiled and nodded, a bit taken aback. I was getting the idea she was unused to being around other girls.

Adrian was pretty small guy, Vietnamese background. He was shorter than Bear by a good ten centimeters, and a lot lighter. He had a habit of lifting his chin a bit, like it would make him look taller. But he moved with a lithe confidence that told me he was a good athlete. He smiled a lot, especially at Gemma.

Gemma was cute. If she were more assertive, or fierce or something, she might have been beautiful. But she came across as shy, hesitant, and …well, cute. She had trouble meeting anyone's eyes for more than a moment. I found myself wanting to protect her, and I wondered what made her or anyone think she could make it as *coureur des bois*.

Ollie came to get us again at the end of lunch.

"Okay, you've all taken your first step to becoming *coureurs des bois*!" Ollie exclaimed. Gemma opened her mouth as if to say something, but Ollie continued. "So let's meet the guru of Freerunning! This way!" We all jumped up, and whatever Gemma was going to say got lost in the excitement.

12
Parkour

I was surprised that Claude was our next instructor. He seemed so young, and so immature. Not the right word...carefree? Yeah, he was child-like, but not child-ish.

"Okay, we are going to begin our study of Parkour," he began, his accent barely noticeable. The thirteen of us were lounging on the padded floor of the obstacle course area. "Parkour is the art of body displacement. How do we get from point A to point B? How do you do it with the most efficiency? With the least amount of lost energy? That is the study of parkour."

I had to interrupt. "Hold on Claude- I've seen you run and move- are you telling me that those flips you did over the fences in the Race were the most efficient way to get over?"

He laughed. "*Bon pointe.* Will is right. Now I'll be honest. I am not a purist. I prefer what is called Free Running. It has many of the same elements...but is more...flamboyant. But when you are running for your life, to deliver a message that is life and death for dozens of other people, flamboyant is not necessarily your best option."

The mean-looking guy, Geoff, whispered something at the back of the group, and the girl Dom sniggered. I think it had something to do with 'flamboyant'. I guess if I was questioning Claude's ability to teach us, what would these people, who had never seen him in action, feel? His youth and easy-going attitude were working against him.

"Okay, I want you to move through the obstacle course. Try not to touch the mat. Let's get used to our bodies moving above the ground."

There was some milling about, a lot like those cattle in the pen. What exactly were we supposed to do? Hannah shrugged and started to climb up some monkey bars. The rest of us each found an access point on the apparatus, and started to hesitantly climb.

I started up the rock wall, with my eye on an elevated beam that came near it about four meters off the ground. When I got to that height, the short space to the metal beam gaped like a chasm, and I hesitated. I held my breath and stepped across the distance, arms outstretched for balance.

The beam was solid, and as wide as two hands beside each other, but everything is relative. I told myself I could walk this beam if it was on the ground, no problem.

From my perch, I took in the scene. Hannah had jumped from the bars to a loose rope net on the other side of the space; Bear was swinging up an ascending set of parallel bars, catching the next higher one with the underside of his knees; city thug and girl thug had climbed the monkey bars, and sat chatting.

"Come on, Geoff and Dominique- let's see you move." Claude encouraged.

"What's the point? Isn't an obstacle course supposed to have a start and a finish?" Geoff challenged.

"Perhaps," Claude conceded, "But this is not an obstacle course. These are not even obstacles. They are opportunities."

Even I thought that was a bit corny, but Geoff was totally fed up. "Fuck that, Yoda," the big jerk said, "You're the instructor; so instruct us. "

Claude refused to rise to it. "Very well. Some specific instructions." Claude called to us from below the monkey bars. "Everyone, come on down here, *sil vous plait.*"

I cautiously made it down to the padded floor. Geoff and Dom made a show of taking their time.

"Okay. Some instructions." Claude looked up at the bars. Like a playground set, but more industrial, and higher and about twice as long. Two vertical poles up at each end, connected by two horizontal beams. Short bars to swing from marched across the whole structure. I remember swinging like Tarzan at recess when I was a kid.

Claude began, "Parkour is about transferring your body efficiently from one place to another. Bear, could you traverse the bars?"

Bear climbed the bars, and swung as I did as a kid, but skipping every other bar.

"Okay, now Matt, but you must do it in a different way," Claude directed. Matt held the side bars, and swung along awkwardly. Hannah was next; she stood on top, and lithely cat-walked across the rungs, her twin braids barely moving. Each person after had a greater challenge, as another method of crossing was removed. I couldn't see the point, but I was intrigued by the challenge.

Claude chose Geoff to cross. As we all predicted, Geoff crapped on the exercise. "There's nothing left. This is bull."

"Okay, how about you, Will?" Somehow I knew Claude was going to pick me to prove Geoff wrong. My pleasure. But what *was* left? I stared up at the bars for a moment. So far, everyone had chosen a pattern: one way across, repeated. Could I combine several?

I started swinging in the monkey way, then shifted to hanging from the sides; then I muscled my way up, and walked the last few meters as Hannah had. Just to show off, I jumped from the top and absorbed the impact with bent knees. It didn't impress anyone though.

"Thank you, William," Claude said formally, an inside joke from the fight in the forest.

"Real cute," Geoff challenged, "But again: what's the point?"

Claude kept his calm. I wondered why he didn't just dazzle us with some of his crazy parkour moves, or challenge Geoff to a race, then make him look like the chump he was.

"When you are Freerunning, you must get from one place to another quickly and efficiently. But there is another challenge." Claude was in full instructor mode now, meeting each set of young eyes in turn. "The aliens look for patterns in our movements. Then, they wait. Or set traps. If you cross the same space two times in the exact same way, they will anticipate you. They will catch you, kill you, and feed on your corpse." He finished as calmly as he had begun the lecture, eyes locked on Geoff.

"Now Geoff. Please go get that net bag, and I will continue to instruct you." Geoff did as he was asked, not quite meekly. Claude reached in the bag and pulled out a plastic Frisbee. "These discs represent an alien's tentacle, or a trap. If they touch you, you are dead."

Claude dragged the bag of disks to a duct-tape strip ten meters from the monkey bars, and motioned us to reach in for one.

"One disc in the air at a time please. Let's start slow," and the old shit-eating grin was back. "Now, Geoff. Could you please traverse the bars? Any method will do."

Okay, Claude didn't try to hurt Geoff with the Frisbees, but I'll admit I threw harder than I needed to. Geoff was competent on the bars, and refused to stop or even grunt when struck by a flying disk. He was a bit too bulky to really fly across the rungs like Bear had done, but he adapted quickly, changed direction often.

Adrian volunteered to go next, and he was like a greased snake through the bars. No one hit him on the way past; when he got to the end, he taunted us with "Come on, people! My grandma could throw better than you, and she's dead!" He traveled back toward the start again, and swung the normal way just to rub it in. When a disc came close, he'd pull himself up flat, parallel under the bars, and hold on with hands and feet.

Hannah hadn't thrown for a bit. When it was my turn, she said "Will, throw low, get him to tuck up again." I zinged one in fast, and up he tucked. Before my disk landed far beyond him, Hannah tossed an easy one up. It floated gently, gently, and settled through the rungs and right on Adrian's legs. A cheer went up from the throwers. Adrian dropped to the ground with a grin, the disc held between his knees. "Okay, Hannah, but you had to have two discs up to hit me," and he gave her a low-five.

Hazel suggested we break into smaller groups and do the exercise on other apparatus. Claude was quiet, and seemed pleased to have the group running in a new direction with the exercise. He quietly stepped back and the room quickly filled with acrobats and flying discs.

I had trouble focusing at first with all the chaos. When it was my turn to climb the rope nets, I got pegged early and often. I kept ducking at shadows from other groups' discs, and not anticipating my own groups'.

I was almost to the platform at the top when a jolt like a brick hit me in the back of the head. I lost my grip for a moment, and hung by one hand before I could pull myself up. I looked over my shoulder to see Geoff grinning at me from the floor. He wasn't even in my group. I pulled myself up, and flipped him off.

13
Haven

We broke for some free time before dinner. I felt like my body had worked out a lot of the stiffness from the past few days.

I had worked up a good, clean sweat and followed some of the others out back to clean up at a rain barrel. It had been hot for a few weeks, so the water level was low. I thought about my dad's system of rain catchment off every roof on the farm; I'd mention some ideas to Claude later.

"Where're you from, Will?" Hazel asked as I shook off my wet hands.

"North a bit. Hockley Valley," I responded. "You?" Hazel rolled her eyes. They were very bright eyes, not quite brown and not quite green. She was very tall. "Everywhere. Mom and dad ran the blacksmith shop at Pioneer Village when I was a kid. When the invasion came, we went on the road, town to town, teaching people how to do metal-work old-school." She smiled with lots of teeth, unself-conscious and totally confident.

"Hockley Valley, huh?" I didn't need to turn around to know it was Geoff who'd spoken, so I didn't. Hazel and I started to walk back in for lunch, mutually ignoring the asshole behind us. "Thought I smelled cow shit," Geoff added to my back.

The thirteen of us settled in the kitchen at a long table for rice, sandwiches and raw veggies. Geoff and Dominique were near the other end.

Real Freerunners, support workers and even a few military people sifted in for dinner. We got a few 'Welcomes' and pats on the back as they made their way past us to the buffet. It was pretty easy to spot each occupation. Freerunners wore athletic clothes in shades of brown and grey, but had the most extreme hair and facial piercings I'd ever seen. The military wore camo in the same muted tones, but were such a stark contrast in their short hair and stiff bearing. The support staff, medics, trainers and scientists were a jumble of different clothes and ages. I mingled a bit with all the other recruits, but Bear, Hannah and I automatically fell in with Hazel. Gemma seemed a bit worshipful of her, and Adrian was all moon-pie over Gemma, so we kinda became a group.

"What was that 'cow shit' crack about anyway?" I asked Hazel quietly. "Doesn't just about everyone do a bit of farming these days?"

Hazel shook her head as she chewed a carrot. "Nah, there's a whole sub-culture of urban dwellers in some of the smaller cities. Adrian, you're from Mississauga, right?"

"Yep. Born and bred." Adrian talked like he moved, fast and precise. "We call ourselves Traders, but we're expert scavengers, really," he smiled, "But don't tell anyone I said that. There's a professional pride in finding a good cache, like a small warehouse that somehow hasn't been looted yet, and trading up-up-up for other stuff. Kinda like what you boys must feel when you muck out a stall really well."

I chucked a cherry tomato at him, which he caught in his mouth. He tilted his head toward the other end of the table. "Geoff's from a small Trader group in the east end of the city. They're tough, good traders. His folks probably sent him here so Haven would trade with their group." He lowered his voice, "But there are rumours that they deal with raiders a bit too often, stolen goods and all that."

Gemma was a farm kid like me. I tried to get her talking about home, but she was hesitant, shy.

Hazel came to her rescue. "How about you, Bear?" Hazel asked. "You don't seem to smell like 'cow shit' as much as these two do." I laughed, but Gemma's eyes widened and she looked down. Hazel put her hand over Gemma's to show her it was a joke.

"I'm a little bit country," Bear said with a grin. "We'd just moved out of the city before the invasion, so my family was a bit out of its element." He nodded in my direction. "The people of the community helped us out, basically kept us warm and fed that first year." Huh, I hadn't known that. "Mom was a nurse, dad had been an accountant. It was weird. Mom was suddenly in high demand in the area. Dad went from tax returns to chicken farming."

Hannah got up and cleared away our trays before we could get to her. Bear watched her go, uncertain if he should follow. There was some big hurt that Hannah was carrying. She hadn't let us in on the ride south, so she wasn't going to open up in front of the whole group.

After dinner, I figured we were done for the night, but Orienteering was next. I thought I'd be good at that, being a country kid and all. Turns out I was really bad at it.

We had five instructors, each one a bona fide Freerunner like Claude. They parcelled us into small groups. Five instructors would have been right for 15 recruits, I thought, again mourning the two kids I didn't get a chance to meet.

"Okay! This is Orienteering! Or Babes in the Woods, as we like to call it!" yelled a lean girl with blue dreadlocks. "Gemma, Will and Dominique, you're with me!" The other Freerunners called their groups, and we split up.

"Hi guys, I'm Skeet, and I'm going to help you out this week." It was hard to tell Skeet's age. Her face was weather worn and tanned, but framed by those youthful blue dreads. She was muscular, not skinny, with no body fat at all, as far as I could tell. Her face looked a bit gaunt, dehydrated or something.

"Here are your compasses," Skeet handed out the small plastic discs on carabineers. I'd played with Mr. Nelson's compass as a kid and knew the general idea: the needle points north. Our instructor continued, "Five years along, and we are still working through the Co-op's supplies, like these compasses. But the stores are running out: treat them kindly."

Skeet took us to the parking lot behind Runner's Haven where there was a simple orienteering course, a couple of acres of dead vehicles and lamp posts. After some basic instructions, Skeet gave us a sheet of coordinates, and a place to start. Dominique and I struggled, but Gemma was a natural. The other groups scurried around from different starting points. The sky was clouding over, cooling things off. I was happy to be outdoors.

Gemma got us to the third control, a blue piece of yarn on an old GMC truck. I couldn't help thinking about the yellow markers in the Race back home.

"Gemma, put your compass away. The other two are leaning on you a bit too much," Skeet commanded, and Gemma blushed at the compliment.

I looked at Dom and forced a smile. "Okay, what's our next instruction?" I asked.

Without Geoff around, she was almost pleasant. Almost. "Uh…" She looked at the sheet, and at the compass she was holding flat on top of it. "Uh, 15 degrees east…"

I couldn't figure it out either, so I stalled. "Hey Skeet," I said, "Is it true there's going to be a party tonight?" She was easily diverted. "Yeah! Lots of us just came home from long tours with the squads, plus we've got to welcome you slugs in style."

We heard some whoops from the other end of the parking lot. The rain had started. A visible wall of downpour was marching toward us. Instructors and recruits ran for Runner's Haven, laughing and yelling.

Dom and Skeet headed in. Gemma started to run with the others, but looked back at me hesitantly when she sensed I wasn't with them. I'd been two days on the road, shot at, attacked with an axe handle, almost killed by aliens and a herd of cows, all right after the big race. Rain was *good.*

"C'mon, Gemma!" Adrian called from the entrance. She smiled and ran off. I looked up at the sky, and let it pour over me as I walked slowly toward my new home.

"William!" I heard Bear's voice call through the rain's white noise. He, Hannah and Hazel were up on top of a defeated BMW sports utility vehicle. Bear had his shirt off, and Hazel was down to her tank top, both sitting on the hood. Hannah was lying on her back on the roof, eyes closed. Bear's brown skin was like double-double coffee; Hazel's tan lines were cream on gold. Each of them offered a hand, and hauled me up between them.

We sat shoulder to shoulder to shoulder, enjoying the cool, cleansing deluge. Two days ago, I didn't know these people. Now we shared a home. A haven.

The party was starting up when we came back in. We went to our respective cubbies to dry off and change. I checked to make sure the kukri was in the bottom of my pack where I'd left it.

I also found a leather wine skin my mom must have snuck in there. It sloshed as I read the note she'd attached: *For Oliver. Cheers to old times. Your friend, Laurel.* Curious, I unstoppered the skin: fwew! There was no mistaking Mark Nelson's 180 proof moonshine. I'd have to find this Oliver and deliver the goods before someone else got a hold of it.

Bear poked his head through the curtain. "Let's go, Will!"

"Coming," and I followed him out to the sounds of the party.

The training apparatus was hung with lanterns and torches, even though daylight still trickled in from the high windows. A stab of nostalgia poked me in the heart and I thought of the barn party back home. Was it really just a few days ago? But the lights were the extent of the similarities. Maybe fifty partygoers filled the space, and there couldn't have been more than ten over the age of thirty. Bear and I paused and looked at each other. His face broke into a wide grin. He clapped me on the shoulder and waded into the crowd. Someone, I don't know who, handed us each a beer.

I searched for familiar faces as we cruised through the party. There were a few of those military haircuts among the crowd, but not many, and the soldiers were dressed in casual clothes, not camo. There! I spotted Claude near the rock wall and worked my way over to his small group. Bear moved off in a different direction.

"Will! This is Myles, Kat, and I think you met Ollie." We all touched bottles as greeting and we each drank.

"So Will, how was the first day?" Claude asked.

"Good, good," I answered. "But did you have to make me even more of a target for that Geoff asshole?"

Claude laughed his big laugh, and cheersed my beer again. I was trying to go slowly on the alcohol, but when I didn't drink, he told me a rule I didn't know: "You clink, you drink, *mon chum!*" So we drank.

"Hey Ollie," I asked above the din, "How come you don't Freerun anymore? Claude says you two started out together."

"Had to give it up a few years ago," Ollie replied. "Got caught by a rose bush trap on Bloor Street. Nasty little creeper vine with thorns." Ollie lifted up a pant leg. From ankle all up his muscled calf was a mess of scars. "Just about severed my Achilles."

Myles jumped in. "No drugs at the Haven that week, so Ollie was totally feelin' it while they stitched it up!" He raised his glass in another toast. "He was so fascinated by the process, he took up medicine! Now he's our resident doctor!"

We saluted Ollie's misfortune, or his change of career, and drank. Man, these guys would make a toast to anything. If I'd held my glass up and said, "To healthy bowel movements!" everyone would have drank with me happily.

My head was already starting to swim. Somewhere behind me, someone started up with some bongos, and a shrill pipe or flute wove a fast melody.

I remembered the flask on a strap over my shoulder. "Claude!" It was becoming necessary to yell above the music. "Do you know a guy named Oliver?"

Claude nodded to Ollie. "Ollie is Oliver, and so is his dad," he shouted back. "Oliver senior is the manager of Runner's Haven. Ollie's parents started the co-op when Ollie's was a kid." Ollie was only a bit older than I, so I was guessing the booze was for his dad.

"My mom sent this for your dad! Is he around?" Ollie took the wineskin and read the note. A mischievous grin passed between him and Claude. "Your mom was a great Freerunner!" Ollie shouted. "Now, are you sure this is for Dad?" His grin got even bigger, and he showed the note to Myles and Kat. I took a sip of my beer, surprised to find it had been replaced with a full one. Myles opened the skin and sniffed much as I had done, and let the others have a whiff.

"No no no!" the girl named Kat yelled in mock severity. "Ollie, your dad is getting old! Very poor health! This can't be for him!"

I was just drunk enough to play along. "Maybe if we lightened the contents just a bit?" I suggested. "You know, control the portion he gets? For his health, of course."

Kat held up the moonshine and made a toast. "To Oliver Senior's health!" She exclaimed, and took a drink. Her face went purple, but she held it down.

"To Oliver's health!" Myles toasted and drank, then Ollie, then I took a shot. The burn started up my nose and travelled all the way to my gut. I almost sprayed, but then a warm glow replaced the burn.

Claude grabbed the skin and yelled "Santé!" He hung the skin around my neck. "Keep a hold on this, William. I think you will be very popular tonight!"

I don't know how we got to the dance floor (I don't even know where the dance floor was), but I found myself in a press of moving, sweating bodies, and the bongos were my heartbeat.

I was singing along with the rest, *500 Miles,* and then the Irish Rovers' *Wasn't That a Party?* and Bear, Hazel and Adrian were jumping with me and singing at the top of their lungs. "Coulda been the whiskey! Mighta been the gin! Coulda been the 2-4, six-pack, I don't know, but look at the mess I'm in! My head feels like a football! I think I'm gonna die! Tell me me-oh-me-oh my! Wasn't that a party!"

Claude called it right, and word spread about the liquid gold around my neck. People were introducing themselves and taking a shot; then they weren't introducing themselves and taking a shot; and the flask never left my neck, and I never stopped dancing.

Full night had fallen, and the lanterns made streaks through my vision as my muddled brain tried in vain to keep up with my eyes. I found myself kissing someone fully and passionately, and slow dancing to a woman singing *Subversives* by The Lowest of the Low. It was my parents' wedding song. Mom used to sing it to dad while they washed dishes or weeded the garden.

Time jumped, and I was being helped into my hammock. "*Bon soire, mon chum,*" someone said, and I heard him stumble out of my cubby. The hammock swung gently like a cradle, and I drifted off into drunken slumber, alone.

14
Death Run

"Wake up people! Toxic Death Run time! Whoo-hoo!" some maniac was yelling, and beating a pot. The pot-banging person was summoning me to hell. Every strike pounded the inside of my delicate skull.

I struggled to work some moisture back into my mouth, but couldn't do it.

I heard a death moan from the cubby next to me, "Uhng..."

"Bear?" I croaked. "Are we dead?"

"God, I wish I was," came the disembodied reply.

"Toxic Death Run, kids! Get your gear on! Woohoo!" came that evil, chipper voice.

"Bear? Will you help me kill her?" I begged.

"Yeah. I hate people who 'woohoo'."

One by one we stumbled into the main building. All thirteen recruits, and close to twenty Freerunners and a few of the GI Joes who stayed for the party. We were all in various stages of being hung over, except for Gemma. She seemed as fresh and healthy as on any fine morning. Claude and most of the other experienced Freerunners were red-eyed and slow moving, but they didn't moan and complain like us young guns.

"Smoothies in the kitchen, kiddies, then we run!" Pot-banger yelled. I forced down some kind of green concoction that smelled like grass. I almost barfed it right up, but once it was down, I felt marginally better. Then the Toxic Death Run began.

The chipper 'woohoo' girl led us out into the gloomy morning. She was a compact Freerunner named Fee, I think short for Fiona. For all her happy yelling, she looked pretty green in the face too. But she damn well didn't stop running, or talking. "Heading north, kids! Into the safe zone!" She took off at a good pace, and we stumbled in her wake, a brood of damaged chicks chasing a perky mother hen.

We jogged through an old commercial-industrial zone. Long, low warehouses intermingled with the occasional storefront. In the first k we crossed about four train tracks, or maybe the same ones several times. This would have been a low-population area of the city, so the aliens would have left it alone.

My hangover was further clouded by guilt. I was sure I'd been kissing someone last night on the dance floor. Thoughts of Magda kept sneaking in to my head. I checked to make sure I was still wearing the leather bracelets, my little links to home.

Once the warm up jog was over, Fee yelled "Fartlek! Follow Wings!" I learned later that a fartlek was a run where you took turns torturing your group with a variety of exercises. I learned quickly that Wings was a tall lean guy with a sick sense of humour.

He stopped jogging and squatted down on his haunches. "Frog hops to the next telephone pole! If you can't do it, you're on dishes! And remember, first person to puke digs the new latrines this week!" And we all started to hop.

The hopping killed my thighs, but the real worry was my stomach. Hunched over, popping up and down, I could taste that grassy smoothie at the back of my tongue. *Don't puke don't puke...* this wasn't about latrines or dishes I was realizing; this was about pride.

We all made it to the pole, then jogged for a bit more. Wings picked another Freerunner, who made us grapevine for 100 meters, where you run sideways, crossing your legs over front and back; then jog, then another runner picked another exercise. I jogged with Hazel for a bit. We were both recovering slowly.

"Good night last night?" she asked wryly.

I grunted in reply. "Sleep okay?" I asked.

"I don't know if a coma counts as sleep, but..."
Someone yelled out "Claude's up!" and a collective groan
went up among the Freerunners.

We all followed Claude off the street, toward a
deserted rail yard. Jogging fast, he headed for a line of rusty
Canadian Pacific rail cars. In typical Claude fashion, he
ignored the ladders, and instead used his hands and feet to
create pressure between two cars to climb up. We followed,
as best we could. Our pride insisted.

Up on top, he led a game of follow the leader,
hopping from train car to train car. The gap wasn't that big,
but we were all exhausted, hung over, and I couldn't keep
my mind off of Magda. We didn't have a promise between
us or anything, but-

"Will!" Hazel yelled from behind me, just as I was
about to run off the end of the car I was on. The people in
front of me had hopped to the next car. Hazel grabbed my
shirt and pulled me back from the drop. To cover my
embarrassment, I muttered "Thanks" and quickly jumped the
gap.

We'd gone about three k, in all manner of styles, and
no one had heaved. We'd almost circled back to the start,
and I was sweating out the toxins. I was feeling almost
strong again, my head a bit clearer. We were running
through fields, coming up on a low hill. The group had
bunched up, joking around and getting friendly; Freerunners,
recruits, military...we were bonding through mutual
suffering.

The lead runner yelled out "Adrian! Finish us off!"
From the top of the hill we could see Runner's Haven, just a
few hundred meters away.

Little Adrian stepped up with a mischievous grin.

"Okay everyone, the last leg of the Death Run! Roll
down the hill!" He lay down, and, like a little kid, log-rolled
down the short slope. We followed.

111

The world spun sideways, sky-grass-sky-grass- and the laughs, shrieks and groans of the group filled my ears. My stomach started to argue with itself, and the world wouldn't stop spinning, even though I had come to a stop. A body bumped up beside me and I heard a grunt. Hazel crawled up to me, groaning, laughing. Her bright brown eyes were inches from mine.

"Gonna puke, Willy-boy?" she taunted.

"Not before you!" and I tickled her hard in the ribs. She doubled up, and for a second I thought she was going to lose breakfast.

"Good to have you back," she said when we'd settled down. We lay side by side at the bottom of the hill. "You were pretty deep in thought for a lot of the run. Wanna spill it?"

All around us, people were lying where they'd stopped rolling, enjoying being still, enjoying each other's company. I thought about Magda back home, and then about the trust I already had in these new friends: Bear, Hannah, the rest; and Hazel, right here.

"There's a girl back home," I confided. "Not my girlfriend or anything, but... I don't know." I finished lamely.

Hazel tickled me back. "That's cool! So what's the problem?"

How could I explain the guilt I was feeling? "I think I kissed someone last night!" I blurted, "When I was really drunk!"

For some reason that sent Hazel into wild spasms of laughter. Was it so hard to believe someone would want to kiss me?

"What?" I demanded.

She was laughing too hard to breathe now, but she was trying to explain.

"That was-" giggles, "-you were kissing-" giggles-

"What? Who?" For a moment I thought of Claude making sure I got to bed- *naw*...

"You were kissing *me*!" She forced out, and the laughter got the better of her. She puked green smoothie all over me.

"We have a winner!" Fee yelled, and everyone cheered.

15
Interlude

Splash! Bear cannonballed off the grassy bank, sending diamonds of cool water all over me. The girls shrieked, and I protected my novel from the worst of the shower. His dark face surfaced, split by a white grin. His black hair was as sleek and glossy as a muskrat.

Hannah threw a fistful of mud at him from where she sat on the bank, and he ducked under.

We had a rare afternoon off. Claude had worked us on the course all morning, and I'd been craving sun and fresh air. Farm life didn't have a lot of indoor summer activity, and I felt the day pulling at me. A picnic lunch, a few old blankets by the creek were perfect.

Hannah and Adrian were walking upstream, trying to catch little water creatures in an old pot. Most of the girls were dodging clouds on the shore near me, only going in the water when they needed to cool off.

I'd splashed around a bit, and was just getting into an old Lee Child adventure novel one of the kitchen staff had leant me when a very wet Hazel sat down on the edge of my blanket.

"Scoot over, Will. Gimme some real estate here." I scooted, pretending to still be into the book. Hazel stretched out beside me, her tanned body dappled by water.

A cloud passed over us and I felt a bit chilled. I glanced up from my book; not a shadow, a person. An outline of a person, with large, round shoulders and a thick neck. The contrast with the bright blue of the sky behind him made him seem less like a presence, and more like an absence, a cut out of where the sky should have been.

"What's the deal, Geoff?" I kept my tone carefully neutral. We were going to have it out one day, but I didn't really want it to be now. The afternoon was too fine to spoil with playground crap.

"Oh, sorry there, Will!" he said in a mock-polite voice. "I just thought you'd feel more comfortable, since you're used to being in mommy's shadow, and all."

Before I could reply, Hazel jumped in. "Why don't you kiss my ass, Geoff?"

"Oh, no thank you, Hazel. I'm into girls. You're a little too butch for me." I started to get up, furious, but Hazel held me back, and Geoff walked into the stream ungracefully, like a draft horse through deep snow.

"You're an asshole, Geoff!" I called, and he just raised his middle finger without looking back.

The real target of my anger gone, I snapped at Hazel, "Why do you do that? I can look after myself just fine!"

Hazel's green-brown eyes widened in hurt surprise. "Sorry, Will. It's automatic. It's just a reflex."

"I don't need you to defend me," I said, and thought *but I'd like the chance to defend you*, but I didn't say it.

"I'm not defending you," she replied, "Or, rather, I'd defend anyone. I just hate bullies."

"Then why did you hold me back? I'd like to beat his head in for what he said to you."

"What? That I'm butch?" She gave a big laugh. "I've been made fun of for worse than that! Besides, have you seen the size of my shoulders, Will? I'm a blacksmith. I'm a bit butch."

"You are not," I said earnestly; then more quietly, "Your shoulders are perfect. There's nothing wrong with you."

Her face was close to mine. There were little sunkissed freckles on the bridge of her nose than I'd never noticed before.

I hesitated, and she prompted me. "I'm not perfect. My knees are funny."

"They're lovely, like a colt." I inched closer.

115

"My nose is crooked."

"It adds character."

We were moving in, closer...

"Can I play?" Bear interrupted from the water. "You ride a bike like a girl!"

Hazel and I locked eyes for a moment, inches apart, then she shouted back to my (former) friend, "Good! Hannah's a girl, and she's ten times the biker you'll ever be, Bear!" She stole a quick kiss from my parted lips, then jumped up and threw herself into the water on top of Bear.

"C'mon, Will! I can't drown him on my own!"

16
History Lesson

The next week progressed in a blur of training and workshops. I helped Hazel with the latrines (it was partially my fault she puked) but we didn't discuss our drunken make-out session again.

Claude continued to teach the parkour sessions.

"Not bad, Will, but you need to slow down a bit."

I was lying on the mat on the floor where two walls met at an inside corner, right where I'd fallen. Claude was being patient with my lack of progress. I wasn't climbing the wall, I was attempting to run up it, like the birches back home.

There was a metal bar hanging from a girder about four meters up. By running at the corner, and converting my forward momentum into upward momentum, I should be able to run up: hit one wall, push off the other, and eventually push out to the hanging bar.

"I don't want to slow down," I complained from the floor. "I need speed to reach the bar."

Claude reached down and pulled me up. "There's a balance to find," he said, one of his favourite themes. "Speed and power, versus control and finesse." He held his hands out like he was weighing two objects.

"Will, you can beat anyone here in a flat run, at just about any distance under a klick. And that will save your life many times." He looked at the bar, back at the wall. "This time, don't take such a big run." The small Quebecois drew an imaginary line on the mat with his toe, just a few meters from the wall.

Before I could protest that it was too close, that I needed a bigger run, he took off. Four quick strides to the wall, then *boom boom boom*, and he was dangling from the bar like a cartoon monkey.

I looked up at him and made a face. "Claude, how do you say 'fuck off' *en francais?*" I asked.

Before he could reply, I took off too, following his steps. *Boom boom boom!* I hit the wall three times, spun in ungainly flight, and grabbed the bar awkwardly.

I'd done it!

Claude, dangling beside me, said through his laughter, "The phrase you're looking for is *esti calisse, baise-toi.*"

"Well then, *esti calisse, baise-toi,* asshole."
We dropped to the ground, and wandered over to a small table where cool herbal tea sat sweating in a glass pitcher. I sometimes dreamed of truly cold food, like ice cream or a coke right from the fridge, but when you were working out, anything colder than your own body temperature was amazing.

Claude pored for us both. As he poured, I noticed he still wore the three leather bracelets from the Race back home. *Courage, Will, Strength,* all tangled on his wrist. He saw me looking.

"Why are you wearing those still?" I asked. I'd been wearing my own proudly, but it was a tradition of my own community; and even to me, compared to the trials I faced out in the war zones, they seemed a bit…innocent? Trite, even?

Claude rolled his wrist, made the leather loops turn.

"Do you know poetry?" he asked out of nowhere.

"A bit, I guess." I was getting used to Claude's roundabout ways of answering questions. "My dad tried to get me into it. I like the story poems, *Cremation of Sam Magee* 'n stuff." I thought for a moment. "And Robert Frost is good. He makes sense. *'Two roads diverged in a yellow wood, and I took the one less travelled by,'*" I misquoted, feeling kind of proud of myself.

"Good!" Claude encouraged, supressing a smile.

"Do you know Tennyson?" I shook my head no. He recited,
"I am a part of all that I have met,
Yet all experience is an arch wherethrough
Gleams that untravelled world, whose margin fades,
For ever and for ever when I move."

He gave me time to think about it, then continued, "Your community...your mom, the race, and now you, *mon chum*. You are all part of my experience. I may never return to Hockley Valley, but you are a part of me, who and what I've met. The bracelets remind me of that."

I nodded, and thought about the untraveled world ahead of me. I took a sip of tea.

"I'm heading back out for a tour tomorrow," Claude said casually.

"Oh," I replied, "I thought you would keep training us." I felt an unreasonable stab of fear at being left without him, way more anxious than I'd felt leaving my home and family.

"All the Freerunners will take turns with that, while we're at the Haven for rest and recuperation." He grinned his grin. "Can't say that our adventures bringing you back here from the farm were restful, but it was a lot more fun than Freerunning in the hot zones."

Crap! How many times had I almost died on the way here? Five? Six? And that was more fun than Running? I drained my glass, refilled for both of us.

"You've done a lot for me, Claude." I said earnestly. "I'm going to miss you, man."

"*Salut*, Will." We clinked glasses, a sober echo of that crazy party night a week ago. "See you when I get back, *mon chum*."

Claude couldn't tell me which squadron of soldiers he was Running for. He bid us all goodbye like it was no big thing, and he passed us off to the Freerunner named Wings. I wished him *bonne chance*, and didn't know what else to say. We'd been through a hell of a lot in a short time, and now he was going out into worse.

Wings was a big, lanky guy with tattoos of wings on his ankles. His training was really helpful for me; we were both taller than most, so his tips for transferring weight and balance from obstacle to obstacle were more geared to my body type.

"Stop trying to be Claude, and do what works for your body," Wings advised. "We're both half a foot taller, and neither of us will ever *twitch* like him; we've gotta twitch like ourselves." I knew what he meant about twitching; Claude's body operated at a different frequency or something.

On a break, I asked him about his tattoos.

"Like 'em?" he asked. "Hermes was the messenger god on Olympus, had these magic winged sandals." He displayed his body art for me and the other trainees. "When you slugs finish your first real Run, you earn your tats. Talk to Ollie, he'll help you design something."

Training continued. Adrian was a natural at freerunning, Bear was competent, as were a few of the girls.

Hazel had the female version of my body, tall and broad shouldered, and she struggled along with me and gentle Gemma. But we were all getting good.

I got better at using a compass, too, and really enjoyed the orienteering runs. They were part conditioning, part parkour, and all dictated by the control markers that our trainers had set up for us. Even though we were in a safe zone, we had to travel in packs of two or three. These runs were free, and exhilarating, and social.

Pretty soon, rumours started up about a renewed military push against an alien stronghold in downtown Toronto. It was a hot spot, an area where Freerunners had gone missing before. I tried to find out if that's where Claude had gone, but that information was classified.

I was worried about him. One evening after supper, I decided to ask Oliver Sr., maybe play on his friendship with my mom, see if he could tell me.

Ollie's dad was once fit, but going soft as he got older. He had an office where he spent more time than he wanted to, organizing food and supplies for his Freerunners, liaisoning with Jackson and the other military contacts, and scheduling Freerunners with squadrons. In the week I'd been at Runner's Haven, he'd done quick 'inspections' of our progress, offering encouragement but not staying around long enough to give real advice. He was kind of an absent father figure, respected by all, and treated with detached affection by the athletes.

I rehearsed my arguments for breaking the 'classified' rule as I approached his office. I paused outside the open door, hung back. There was already an argument going on inside.

"I'm sorry, Skeet, but you can't go back out yet," Oliver's voice was firm.

"I'm ready, Oliver! I'm rested, I'm fit." Skeet argued. "I'm getting stale in here!"

"Look at yourself, Skeet! You're skin and bones! How many k did you run out there in your last week? One fifty? More?" I'd just assumed Skeet was always this lean; I hadn't thought of the toll a long tour would take on a Freerunner.

"You need to rest up, and get some calories into you."

A voice I hadn't heard much this week spoke up. "We need a Freerunner, Oliver," Jackson said. "The 23rd is manoeuvring blind, and we've got big shit going down in the next few days."

"C'mon, Oliver," Skeet implored. "I'm ready."

Oliver hesitated. "Sorry, Skeet. You're strung out, you're scrawny. It's too soon, your body is already starting to burn muscle. You go out there now, you start making mistakes. I can't let you go."

There was fat pause. I held my breath. Should I speak up, volunteer like I did back in the barn? I knew I was far from ready, and I didn't know those downtown streets. I waited.

Suddenly Skeet stormed out of the office, almost knocking me over. Jackson followed, slowly, ramrod straight. He paused when he saw me, and gave me a knowing look.

"Don't even think about it, Dunmore. You're fast, but you're not there yet." He nodded once, almost respectfully, and marched off.

I waited a beat, and knocked lightly on the office door.

"Come in," Oliver said tiredly. "Hey Will, what can I do for you?"

"I'm trying to find out where Claude's been sent," I said, forgetting all of my schemes for weaselling the info out of him.

He smiled, and leaned back in the creaky chair.

"He's in the thick of it, Freerunning the downtown corridor." He saw my surprise, and said "I don't see what all the secrecy is about. We may as well know where our friends are."

"Is he going to be okay?" I asked.

Oliver spread his hands. "Who can say? Claude is about the best of us." He said *us* not like he himself was a Freerunner, but like it we were all a family. "But there are no sure things out there." He sighed.

"Oliver," I hesitated. He waited patiently. "Oliver, why do Jackson and my mom hate each other so much?"

Oliver leaned forward in his chair and rested his arms on the big scarred desk.

"Well, Jackson is military. He was an army brat growing up, so it's all he knows." He paused. "How much do you know about how the Freerunners started?"

I admitted I didn't know much.

"Well!" He slammed his hands down on the desk and stood up. "It's time you knew the story. All of you. The rain has passed, it's a nice night, and I've been chained to this desk long enough.

"Tell the others to grab some warm clothes and meet me upstairs." He looked back over his shoulder, and waggled his eyebrows. "I just wish I had some moonshine to share around!"

"Wait!" I chased after him as he marched toward the training area. "We have an upstairs?"

'Upstairs' was a rooftop garden. Runner's Haven was a large building, and as Claude had said, it was designed to be state-of-the-art environmentally friendly. This included a 'living rooftop', a flat roof that was designed to hold gardens, even trees. The root system and soil acted as a water filtration system, so what rain and snow melt wasn't used up by the plants was funnelled into the building's reserve tanks in the basement. The garden insulated in the winter, kept things cool in the summer.

As we all climbed up the spiral staircase that evening, we were astonished to find ourselves amidst neatly planted corn rows, berry bushes, tomatoes, and even carefully pruned fruit trees.

Most of the seasoned Freerunners had gone to bed early, so Ollie led us up and over to where his dad had started a small fire going in a brazier. The smell of herbal tea drifted out from a large pot handing from a tripod over the coal flames.

Ollie and Oliver handed out mismatched cups, and we all settled onto logs and old lawn chairs. There was a seat open beside Hazel on a small bench, but I intentionally ignored it and sat down near Hannah and Dom.

I still had some issues to sort out on that front.

"C'mon, Will. I won't bite," Hazel said playfully.

"Maybe not," Bear put in, "But you might puke on him again. Hey, that's got the makings for a new saying! Once puked on, twice shy."

Hazel laughed with everyone else. I loved that about her: the joke was totally on her, and she enjoyed it more than anyone.

But I couldn't allow myself to get drawn into that confidence, that aura that surrounded her. Her whole persona shone with strong greens and blues, like the lights that played peekaboo behind the scudding clouds over our heads.

Oliver Senior accepted a cup of tea from his son, and began his tale. "Ollie's mom Helen and I had taken the biggest risk of our lives opening up the co-op. It was called *Adventurer's* Haven then, and if you were into outdoor activity, we wanted this to be the place.

"Rock climbing gear, and a free wall; camping gear, mountain bikes… Ollie was sixteen and into skateboarding, and he opened his own skate shop on site, and was going to run it on weekends himself. Helen had taken a leave from teaching, and we invested all of our savings in this place.

"But we were scared. What if no one joined the co-op? What if we were too far out from downtown to attract customers? I hadn't slept in weeks! The alien invasion put our fears in perspective, let me tell you.

"It was the grand opening week, and we were hosting local bands in the climbing room to attract young people on summer break.

"Man, what a scene! Rich kid rock climbers were hanging with Ollie's skater crowd, and a bunch of bike couriers from downtown had come up to support one of their friends who played bass in a metal band.

"When the power went down, the musicians went unplugged, and we jammed for hours before anyone knew that the world was ending just down the street.

"We all have our survival stories from those first weeks, and ours is little different from all of yours."

Oliver got up from his seat and poured more tea all around. I took some gladly and warmed my hands. The night was getting cool. I noticed Geoff was in a t-shirt, and pretending not to be chilled.

Oliver continued, "But the co-op became a safe place, and the aliens ignored us. The demon trees hone in on large groups of humans or animals." He gestured in the dark at the rooftop paradise. "We often had dozens of people down in the co-op, but we think the gardens saved us from detection. The gardens became our shield.

"Anyway," he continued, "we were surviving, little more, when Jackson and Will's mom found us." He nodded in my direction; even in the dark, I couldn't help but notice how sharply Geoff looked at me.

"They'd heard rumours about a group of young people, athletes, who grouped together. And they had an idea," Oliver finished.

Ollie Junior picked up the story for a bit. "Dad and mom had been telling all of us to lay low, but look who they were talking to? Thrill seekers, extreme athletes, adrenaline junkies, well...teenagers!" He got a few chuckles.

"Skaters wear scars like freakin' badges of honour, and the bike couriers had been risking their lives in the concrete jungle *before* the invasion.

"And let me tell you, an angry BMW driver could run you down faster than any alien! "

Oliver took over again. "Claude and his parents were often here, too. He was just a kid, the same age as Ollie, but he'd been freerunning with his dad for a few years, and they had a lot to teach us about avoiding becoming mulch.

"Anyway, no matter how hard Helen and I tried, we couldn't keep the kids away from the aliens. Fire bombs, road blocks with derelict cars... they had a little guerrilla movement going by the time Jackson and Laurel found us.

"Will, do you have anything to add?"

I had embarrassingly little to add, but I tried to play it cool. "Mom was a great athelete, and when our little community managed to stall the aliens, Jackson recruited her. They knew the army couldn't coordinate without radios, so the squads couldn't manoeuver in concert. So I guess they hatched this plan," I finished lamely.

"Exactly," Oliver continued, leaning forward and putting his hands toward the little fire. Thirteen teenagers were listening intently. "Here were all these willing people, young athletes who longed for a chance to fight back, to be a part of a bigger plan. But Jackson and his superiors wanted to..." He searched for the right word, "*absorb* us. They thought they could make us military." He barked a laugh. "The kids who hung here had been, by and large, voluntary exiles from society! Even Helen and I had raised Ollie to ask 'why' before doing what a teacher asked him to do! And she was a teacher!"

Ollie took that as his cue to take over again. "But Laurel, Will's mom, stood up to Jackson. If she was going to be involved, she argued, the *coureurs des bois* had to be an independent agency. We wouldn't live with the military, and we wouldn't be trained by them. We wouldn't *answer* to them, not ultimately."

Ollie looked over to his dad in the firelight. "Lately, we've been debating whether or not to accept soldiers *here*, to train with *us*. There are some great athletes in camo out there, and our numbers are low."

The mood took a sudden nose dive. Hazel tried to recapture the campfire story atmosphere by asking, "Oliver, why exactly are we called *coureurs des bois*?"

"It was Helen's idea, actually," Oliver immediately warmed to the topic. "My wife was a grade six teacher, and she loved Canadian history. The early explorers like

Champlain, Cartier…but she loved the unnamed heroes the best.

"The *coureurs des bois*, the runners of the woods. It's a romantic name, isn't it? A group of adventurous young men, mostly French, who acted as liaisons between the natives and the Europeans, trading furs for muskets and knives.

"They were renegades, often loners. They learned forest craft from the natives, explored where no Europeans had dared set foot." He sighed, and looked up at the heavens. "The *coureurs des bois* were both feared and celebrated by the people of New France. They would be out in the wild for a year or more, then return with a small fortune in beaver pelts. They would drink and gamble most of it away, and happily return to the wilderness to start afresh."

"The only real difference I can see," Geoff said unexpectedly into the silence, "Is that none of you are making any profit."

The spell was broken once again, and gradually the campfire group broke up and we headed for our hammocks.

As we were descending into the Haven again, Oliver called out, "Anyone from north of here, a supply cart is due any day now. If you want to get letters home, they should be able to deliver within a week of leaving."

Sleep took its time coming to me. I turned over Oliver's stories in my mind happily. As sleep finally settled over me, I thought of how Geoff still didn't consider himself *coureurs des bois*.

17
Fight in Training

Training. Summer heat, summer rain, summer humidity, and training.

Wings went back out in the field, to be replaced by another tired Freerunner on leave. Skeet began teaching us the layout of the city.

We studied old maps, memorized the names and order of streets that most of us had never seen: Dufferin, Bathurst, Avenue, York, Bay, and Yonge all running north to south. And St. Claire, Dupont, Bloor, College, Dundas, Queen, east-west. Skeet assured us we'd never get as far south as Queen, it was too hot with alien activity. The bastards were planted in the domed stadium way down on Front Street, close to the shores of Lake Ontario.

"You've got to know where you are and where you're going at all times," Skeet informed us.

We were grouped in front of a big wall map of Toronto, a colourful poster designed for tourists. She pointed to a spot in the north end of the city, crossed with open spaces and railroad tracks.

"This is us, Runner's Haven." Her lean finger slid a few centimeters east, and down. "This is the main military camp, known as John A, after John A. Macdonald, Canada's first prime minister.

"To the east and north, in what used to be North York, we've got John B. Around the bottom of the Horseshoe," she slid her finger in an arc left and down, following the shores of Lake Ontario, "is John C., the last of our permanent military camps. We haven't heard from them for a few weeks."

That sank in slowly, and Skeet gave it time before she resumed.

"When you're in the city, some of the street signs are still standing, but you can't count on it. And if you need to detour to outrun an alien, you've got to know how to get back on track."

Weapons training wasn't what I'd expected. First, Jackson picked out blades for those few trainees who didn't bring their own.

After a few sessions where we learned basic dos and don'ts (*do* cut away from your body; *don't* slice your femoral artery), Jackson challenged us to do "every damn thing for three days with your blade in your hand; then another three with it in the other hand; even, and especially, going to the bathroom."

For a week we ran with our weapons in hand, ate with them, trained with them. After the six days, he asked to see the worst of the cuts we bore.

I had a few deep ones on my forearm, and my pillow would never be the same, but overall the exercise was effective. I was totally and unconsciously aware of the kukri, on my belt or drawn, the same way you're unconsciously aware of your thumbs. You don't really think about your thumbs, but you rarely poke yourself in the eye with them either.

After that week Jackson got a bit more serious. He had us all draw our blades, and place them in front of us. I gently set the kukri down. On either side of me, Bear placed his hatchet, and Hazel put down her weird blade, like a short machete, but thicker and heavier.

Down the line, all the recruits put their weapons down for the first time in a week. Jackson walked the line, nodding to himself. He stopped at Hazel and picked up her blade. He examined it closely, turning it, weighing it against some invisible scales in his mind. He swung it experimentally.

"This your work, girl?" he asked. Hazel nodded.

"Explain it for me." There was respect in the order, but it was still an order.

Hazel seemed impervious to his tone. She explained the knife casually, enthusiastically. "Well, my parents have been working on this design since they learned I wanted to be a Freerunner. They call it a hybrid; part KA-BAR, part machete." I know now that a KA-BAR is a combat knife; I didn't know it then. "It's got the heft of a machete, so you can slice a vine just as well; but because it's shorter, it's more maneuverable in tight quarters, and easier to sheath. On your back, or conceivably on your hip."

She held her hand out, and he gave it back to her, hilt first. With a deft movement, she slipped it smoothly into the sheath at her back, with the hilt pointing down for easy access. She drew it again, flipped it and handed it back to the military man.

"May I?" he asked. She nodded again, looking pleased. Jackson retrieved a length of nylon rope from the ropes corner, and had me and Bear hold its ends, leaving a droop of slack between us.

With the cobra-fast movement I'd seen at the bridge ambush, Jackson swirled Hazel's blade in a complicated pattern, then sliced cleanly through the rope. I didn't even feel a tug.

Jackson gave Hazel an appraising look, nodded, and lay the weapon gently back on the floor. He turned back to the group as Bear and I coiled our bits of rope.

"Today!" he said forcefully, "You will train with someone else's blade! You will be forced to improvise in the field, and you must not become dependent on one style of weapon. If you can't adapt, you die. Go ahead and choose."

He grinned meanly at me as he said it. He knew the kukri was my baby. I mean, it's not like I gave it a name or anything, but it was *mine*. And I bet most of the others were just as possessive of their own weapons by now.

There was a bit of milling about, people making a show of window shopping the selection of weapons. No one wanted to be the first to infringe on someone else's territory. Gemma came over to Hazel. "May I?" she asked tentatively.

"Of course," Hazel said with a warm smile. The hybrid blade was far too heavy for Gemma, and she examined it with two hands.

That got people moving, and everyone started choosing each other's weapons. Bear nudged me; I looked up and saw Geoff walking over, eyeing the kukri. Bear knew how I felt about it. Quickly, just before Geoff could grab it, Bear got his toe under the hilt, and flipped the kukri up in the air. Geoff had to lurch back or get hit by my knife. Bear caught it deftly by the hilt, and said, "Thanks, Will! I'll treat it right." Geoff eyed Bear, actually looking him up and down. Bear was probably thirty centimeters shorter, but just as strong. Bear eyed him back.

"Well, would you look at this," Geoff said in his pretend-nice voice. He bent down and snatched up Bear's hatchet. It was a cool little axe, a one-piece design, a nice brushed finish. The small but wicked moon-shaped blade was balanced on the back side by a heavy square of metal for hammering. Geoff held it by two fingers, as if it were a toy. Bear tried hard not to react, but his dark eyes narrowed to slits.

"Bit of a cliché, isn't it?" Geoff asked. "An Indian carrying a tomahawk?" The big oaf actually patted his open hand against his mouth and did a war whoop. Bear didn't react. No one did, but I was furious. But it was Bear's play; I'd follow his lead.

"Actually, I'm Mohawk, not from India," Bear said in a tight voice. "Indians are from the other side of the planet, you see," he continued, as if explaining to a child. "I think *you're* the cliché, my friend: big and stupid."

Geoff's face got meaner, but he kept control. He'd been poking at me for weeks, but Bear had always been so happy and goofy. This angry Bear was an unknown element to him. He decided to keep pushing.

Casually, the bully reached around behind himself, and used the blunt side of Bear's hatchet to scratch between his butt cheeks.

"Ah, that's better," he sighed with an evil grin.

Bear took a step forward, and Geoff turned sideways in a fighter's stance. We all took a step back, giving them space.

"Stop!" a voice commanded with such force that the combatants did. Jackson stepped forward. I breathed out, relieved. But I was premature. Jackson held out both hands, and said, "Weapons." After a moment's hesitation Geoff and Bear both surrendered the blades, my kukri and the hatchet.

"Now, you may proceed," Jackson finished politely.

The two faced off again, and some of the fire had gone out of Bear's eyes, replaced by a steady intensity.

Suddenly Geoff rushed in, a mountain charging at an outcropping of granite.

Bear, expecting him, crouched a bit; Geoff's big fist pulled back. Instead of retreating, as both Geoff and I expected him to do, Bear leaned forward, and suddenly he stood up straight, using his powerful biker's legs to propel his body up like a spear. He came up inside of Geoff's charge, and as the big man's wild swing came around uselessly behind Bear, Bear's head connected with Geoff's face.

Geoff rocked back on his heels, blood leaking from a gash on his cheek. Before he could recover, Bear stepped in with left and right-handed jabs.

Geoff got his meaty forearms up to protect his face from further damage, and managed to shove Bear back. He shook his head to clear it. Little drops of blood splattered like rain on the training floor. He got his fists up again, and eyed Bear with wary respect. Then he came at him again, more slowly.

Bear mimicked his opponent's sideways stance to make himself a smaller target, and managed to block the first few powerful punches. Geoff was fighting slower and smarter now, using his longer reach to keep Bear from landing any more blows.

Bear was faster, but I knew he couldn't take many direct hits from the bigger man. He lured Geoff in by dropping his hands as if exhausted; Geoff took the bait, went for another big, finishing roundhouse. If it landed…

Instead of moving inside the punch like last time, Bear ducked it at the last second. Geoff tried to correct, managed to clip the top of Bear's head; but he was off balance now. Bear stood up and delivered three fast jabs under Geoff's rib cage. Geoff swung back with the fist that had just missed, and backhanded Bear. It caught Bear in the ear, and he went down hard.

He was up in a second, but wobbling. Geoff was clutching his side, and sucking wind in harsh gasps.

Jackson stepped between them. "We are done here," he declared. He looked each of them hard in the eye, one then the other. Bear nodded; then Geoff. There was no clear winner, and I think Jackson planned it that way when he intervened.

I just about fell over when Geoff reached out his hand to Bear. My friend clearly thought it was a trick, a ruse… all of us did. I saw Hannah actually reach down slowly to pick up her machete from the floor.

Bear took a chance, and shook Geoff's big hand. Geoff grinned, a horrid sight with the blood between his teeth. Bear shook his head, and couldn't help but smile back. What the hell.

18
Brothers on a Beemer

The rotation of experienced Freerunners continued through the Haven, and I started to get to know them and their specialties.

The bike crew were a wild bunch who considered themselves purists. A lot of them were the original bike couriers from before the invasion. They saw little difference between delivering legal documents from law firm to law firm, and delivering battle plans from one squad to another.

Skeet said they acted all insulted when asked to fill in for a running Freerunner, but she assured me they were fast enough.

"They don't burn out as fast as the rest of us," she told us trainees. "They do the longer Runs on the highways, where there's less alien activity, fewer traps. They're vital for keeping the larger bodies of the military connected to one another." Bear made efforts to talk to these guys and girls; Hannah eyed them with a competitive look.

There wasn't a lot of downtime for socializing during training days, but inevitably a bond grew between all of us recruits, even with Geoff and Dom. I'd been trying to keep that bond fairly loose with Hazel, and it didn't go unnoticed. Bear approached the subject with his usual tact and sensitivity.

"What's the deal with you and Hazel, anyway? She's totally into you."

I looked over at him. You could barely see the shiner against his brown skin in the dark. I pretended indifference. Training was done for the day, dinner had been eaten. We were lying on top of the BMW again, just the two of us, enjoying the moist night air.

"What do you mean?" I asked. "There's no deal."

He chuckled into the night. "Don't bullshit me, Will. Is this about Magda, back home?"

I sighed, decided to be honest with Bear and with myself too, I guess. We'd been through a lot in the short time we'd been friends. "Yeah, it's about Magda."

"Okay, that's cool. I don't know Magda well, but she seems great. Really pretty, kind of an earth-mother vibe." I'd never heard Bear wax philosophic before.

"So is she expecting you to stay faithful and everything? Have you guys fooled around 'n stuff?" That was more like Bear.

"Naw, it's not like that," I tried to explain. "There's just this unspoken understanding. We've always been neighbours, we've always been friends. I guess there's just always been this expectation that we'll end up together."

"Expectation from who?" he asked. "Do you expect it? Does she?"

It's dumb, but I hadn't narrowed it down so finely before. "I dunno," I stalled, "Just an expectation. From our parents, from the community." I shrugged uncomfortably. "You know, in a small community, things just go a certain way. We're the same age, there aren't many other kids around..."

Bear turned to me in the dark. I could see his face by the light of the ever-present northern lights.

"In case you hadn't noticed, Willy my boy, your situation has changed." He spread his arms wide and looked up to the heavens, almost knocking me off the beamer.

"Look man! There are nothing but kids around!" He exclaimed, as if we were surrounded by young women in the empty parking lot. "You're not in Hockley anymore, you're in the Haven."

He sat up and pointed to the building. "There're more eligible girls in the recruits than there are in the whole community back home, and don't discount the Freerunners, either. Most of them are only a few years older than we are, and every one is wild."

"I don't want wild," I replied, semi-truthfully. "I've always had this picture in my head, of a calm life with a calm woman who I'm in love with."

Bear made a gagging noise. "You're sixteen, man! And you are almost officially a *coureur des bois*, a freakin' Freerunner! There is nothing calm about any of this life!" He swung his legs up and sat crossed legged on the hood, facing me, looking like wise Buddha on the mountain.

"Look, Will; Hazel is here. Hazel is now. Once we get out there, Freerunning for the military, all bets are off. You're better off cutting Magda loose now, rather than crushing her heart if you don't make it home."

Not making it home hadn't really occurred to me. I mean, the thought was always there, but it was abstract, an idea, not a reality. I didn't like this conversation anymore.

"What about you?" I challenged. "You're not living the wild life, chasing a different girl every night." I gave him a poke with my finger. "But I see you all moon-pie eyed when you look at Hannah."

Bear lay back down with his hands linked behind his head. I'd been trying to lighten the mood, but it backfired.

"Hannah is Hannah," he said cryptically, seriously. "I'm not trying to get with her, Will. I mean, I really like her, and we have a lot in common, like bikes and all." He paused. "Right now, Hanna's hurtin'. She's blocked off."

He paused again, for so long I thought he was done. Then, "I just want to be there for her."

"That's good, man," I said. I worried about Hannah too. Practical, competent, strong...and damaged, delicate somehow. But she'd punch you in the face if you said so.

"Well, you keep being there for her, and I'll keep not being there for Hazel." But even as I said it, I felt the lie. I'd be there, at least as a friend, for Hazel. This world of danger and training we'd entered was so vivid, so alive. It consumed you. Sometimes, when I was drifting to sleep in my hammock, I thought of the farm fondly, but I didn't think of it that much. Mom, Dad, Magda, Mr. Nelson...their images were fuzzy in my mind, like old photos carefully kept, but age-worn nonetheless.

That night, in my cubby, I wrote letters home. The candlelight flickered and danced across the page as I struggled to capture my new life in a few words...exciting, intense, new. Mom would understand. Dad would be happy for me.

I wrote a few lines for Mr. Nelson about my training with the kukri, about how it was becoming a part of me, of my new identity as a Freerunner. I thought he would be pleased with that.

I started a separate letter to Magda. *Dear Magda...* what should I say? *Things are going well here...* (I barely miss farm life at all) *I'm meeting a lot of people...* (like a girl who I may be falling for)...*training is challenging* (but it may not be enough to save my life)... I tore the letter up. Instead, I opened up the note to my parents and jotted at the bottom: *P.S. Say hi to Magda for me.*

One night in our third week at the Haven, enough Freerunners were home that another party picked up. I shared a drink with Myles and Kat, Claude's friends.

"Any word of Claude?" I asked. Adrian, Ollie and a Freerunner I didn't know were jamming quietly with acoustic guitars nearby.

"Saw him for a bit at John A last week," Kat said. "Said he's doing recon for the army. No regular Freerunning at all."

"Recon?" I asked. "What's that mean?"

"Reconnaissance. Scouting," Myles put in. "I heard he's been all the way to the dome."

"Shit," I said. The dome, where the mother ship was parked, where the vast majority of the dead were taken, to fuel it.

"Yeah," Kat said, "Shit."

The party was a lot quieter than the last one. It wasn't just that the thirteen recruits had learned a hard lesson last time, either; there were fewer Freerunners, and they'd all been doing longer tours. There was an air of relief, rather than festivity. Then Oliver stood up near the musicians, and motioned with his hands.

"Friends, quiet please." There was a seriousness in his voice that settled everyone immediately. "Some of you already know the terrible news I'm about to give." I didn't, but Myles and Kat stood soberly beside me. Whatever it was, they knew.

"I'm sad to inform you that we lost a good Freerunner this week," Oliver continued, and I panicked. *Claude*, I thought, but if Myles and Kat knew that, they'd have told me.

"Elliott Walters, also known as Wings, died while Freerunning yesterday," Oliver said, and I added my shocked gasp to the others.

Ollie stood up, and said formally, "Did he deliver his message?"

"He did," Oliver replied, and it had the air of ritual about it.

"And did the enemy harvest his remains?" Ollie asked.

"They did not," Oliver said with satisfaction, and as one, the experienced Freerunners raised their glasses. I raised my own.

"To Wings," Oliver said loudly, and we all echoed, "To Wings," and everyone drank to a lost friend.

Then, among the Freerunners, some *serious* drinking began.

19
Run Into the Danger Zone.

For the next week, they kept mixing up our running partners. While sometimes uncomfortable, I knew it was a good thing. It was too easy to become reliant on Gemma, with her compass skills, or Adrian, who was a city kid with an instinctive understanding of urban layout.

Ollie spent an afternoon painting an exact replica of Wings' tattoo on the art wall near the obstacle course. I stopped my training for a bit to watch. He had a steady hand, and was so focused that he didn't notice me watching him.

Or so I thought.

"Twenty-three Freerunners," he said suddenly, not stopping his art.

"Huh?" I must have said.

"Twenty-three dead Freerunners. Twenty three tattoos I've transferred to The Wall."

I looked at the wall with new eyes. *The Wall*, not the wall. A memorial to fallen comrades.

I thought of my mother's tiny tattoo: a simple band around the ring finger on her left hand, because she couldn't stand exercising or working with her wedding ring on. How easily that small circle could have adorned this wall.

It was a Tuesday or a Wednesday morning when I was hooked up with Geoff. It was supposed to be recruits only, but Skeet surprised us.

"I'm coming along, boys. I need a run." She had her blue dreads tied back in a red kerchief. "Got your blades?"

The question wasn't necessary: once weapons training had started, we'd been taught to carry them if we so much as went outside to pee.

"Okay, go get a light pack, water and field glasses. We're going on a longer run today."

We got our gear, did a bit of dynamic stretching, and were ready. "Geoff, set a bearing for due south," our blue-haired Freerunner instructed. "Our first control is The Hudson's Bay store."

"A store? Not a marker?" Geoff asked.

"You've got your goal-" her tone was tighter than I'd heard before-"So let's go. You set the pace."

Geoff didn't need to consult his compass; the streets were set up in a north-south grid. He shrugged and took off. It was a fast pace for the start of a long run, and I knew he was challenging me. I relaxed my stride and sat off his right shoulder. Skeet trailed a few meters behind, keeping up easily.

I hadn't been south of the co-op yet, and I'll admit I was on edge. Vigilant, not nervous. I kept scanning, scanning: alleys, buildings, behind vehicles; the road ahead for debris, quick shoulder check on Skeet, make sure she was with us. She jogged smoothly along, the hilt of her short samurai sword poking up over her shoulder. Geoff never checked back.

We were cruising down Allen Road, four broad city lanes, mostly cleared of cars.

Geoff kept us to the middle of the road; if there was alien activity, we wanted as much room around us as possible. Dr. Botsworth believed the small ships used a lot of biofuel, and rarely went out unless a large animal population had been detected, so if we had an encounter it would probably be on the ground, not in the air.

So just how did the aliens detect these populations? There were theories of intelligence-gathering spores or seed pods, that travelled on the wind and somehow reported back... but we should be safe if we kept moving.

Industrial land quickly eased into apartments and malls, Jiffy Lubes and Wendy's burger joints. It was desolate. Only birds and small animals inhabited this area of the city. At one point a fox examined us curiously as we jogged by. It was totally unafraid.

By 9:00 am the big Bay department store appeared on the right, a flagship establishment with a mall's worth of smaller stores in its shadow. Geoff started toward the parking lot, but Skeet had other plans.

"This way. I'll lead for a bit," and she took off at an even faster clip, heading east on a side street. I was supposed to lead next, but I didn't say a word.

Skeet was in a weird mood. I was starting to think this run wasn't sanctioned. The thought made my heart race, and I calmed my breathing. An illicit run into the edge of a hot zone? This was cool.

I snuck a glance at Geoff; he raised his eyebrows in a challenging way, as if to say "Are you going to wimp out?" He was so macho and aggressive, I knew he'd be good to go for this. I wondered what it said about me that I was pumped for it too.

Skeet slowed us to a jog as we neared a residential area. There was a cluster of highrise apartments coming up. Skeet pulled us to the side of the street, still moving, her eyes coming back to the apartments periodically. From this distance, the four large buildings looked fuzzy, without the clean sharp lines you'd expect from a large man-made structure. I was trying to figure out what was wrong with them when Geoff interrupted.

"Okay Skeet, you know we're not going to rat you out," Geoff said. "So let us in on the plan."

We stopped in an alley between townhouses. Skeet looked at me, got my nod, and explained.

"All right boys. I thought you'd be in. There've been reports about one of the new breed roving this area. The fast aliens. I wanted to see if I could sneak a peek."

So that's why I'd been included; Bear and I were the only ones at Runner's Haven who'd seen the new, faster variety of alien, and Bear was better on a bike than on his feet.

Geoff rolled his big shoulders. "Cool. So what's the plan?"

"We get a perch in one of those apartments, look around. If we don't see one, we go home, no problem."

"And if we do see one?" I asked.

"Then we see one. We go back with intel, and some Freerunners live a little longer than they would have."

"Sounds good to me," I said. It sounded a bit less than good, but I was all in. I was ready for a bit more action.

"Fuckin' A," was Geoff's response.

We scooted house to car to tree, working our way to the apartment complex. If one of those running trees, as I'd started to think of them, was in the area, keeping to the middle of the street was no longer our best option. I knew the lecture: in an open space you could outrun a demon tree, and they'd lose interest in you.

But could you outrun a running tree? I thought of those four long root-legs, that fluid, feline movement. Avoiding detection was our best defence.

It didn't take long for me to realize why the apartments looked funny. They'd been vined. I'd never seen it before. You ever see an old farmhouse with ivy growing up it? And in the winter, the leaves are gone, but the stems twist and curl over the whole structure, like a black spider web? Picture that, but on a thirty story building. On four thirty storey buildings.

We paused again, crouched behind a redbrick gatepost, the entrance to the apartment complex.

"You ever see a vining?" Skeet asked us.

I shook my head no, but Geoff said, "I've salvaged in some vined buildings, but never seen it actually happen."

In a low voice, Skeet painted a picture for us. "The demon trees circle a big building like this, set off these seed pods. It's like friggin' Jack and the beanstalk or something.

142

The vines just *grow,* like they're on speed. Cover the inside and the outside in just a few minutes."

So that's why the buildings looked blurred. Skeet continued, "Anything organic, the vines just immobilize, don't even kill it. Then as soon as the vine stops growing, it dies, poof, like that." She snapped her fingers. "Then the aliens can shuffle in, slow as you please, and harvest."

She pointed to the pavement parking lot. "Chuck the poor suckers right out the windows, living or dead, to be collected by the spike pods."

"And we're going *in* there?" I asked.

Geoff clapped me on the shoulder, too hard. "Come on Willy; you aren't scared are ya?"

"Fuckin' right, I'm scared," I replied incredulously. "If one of those running trees is actually in there, we're mulch." I knew I looked like a wimp, but sometimes the thinker part of me, from my dad, surfaces.

Skeet grinned. "Running trees, huh? Like it. But why would they be in there? They go in to harvest, they don't come back. Been five years."

"How about to 'get a perch, look around a bit'?" I threw her own words back at her.

"You're welcome to stay down here, on your own?" A smile was playing at the corners of her mouth. She knew I was going with them.

"Ah, geez…" I suddenly grinned back. "Let's go. The faster we move, the quicker my pants will dry."

Geoff laughed, and we sprinted for the building. Just to show I wasn't a wimp, and to be a prick, I turned on the jets and beat them both to the entranceway.

Stupid male pride.

20
Encounter

The dead vines held the glass doors wide open. It was like entering a cave: the sun was dimmed, the walls were organic, indistinct.

We crept along through the foyer, but there was no way to move quietly. Every step crackled; it was like walking on the skeletons of little birds.

This had been low income housing, so the halls were narrow, ceilings low, and made lower by the veiny pattern of dead vines. Skeet took the lead again, and we began to climb the stairs. Intermittent windows allowed some light, and the stairwell felt open compared to the oppressive confines of the hallways.

At the landing for the fourth floor, Geoff asked "Can we get in there and look around?" I guess the scavenger part of him hated to miss an opportunity. Skeet said no, and we kept climbing.

By the tenth floor, the tension had left me, replaced by boredom. I know I'd resisted this climb, but I still craved a bit of adventure. "C'mon Skeet." I said. "Let's go through here. We can scout just as well from the tenth floor, and we'll have better cover from the apartment windows than from the roof. "

Skeet hesitated, then relented. "Okay; but we stick together," she shot a look a Geoff. "We're not here to loot." Geoff held his hands wide, gave her a 'who, me?' look.

Back into the cave we went. The vines had pulled all the apartment doors off their hinges, so there was a fair bit of daylight sneaking into the corridor. The floor vines were thicker here than in the stairwell, and the toe of my running shoes snagged a few times. If we *did* have to move quickly in here…

Skeet consulted her compass. "We want the southeastern most apartment. See if it has a corner room, windows facing two directions." I checked my own compass. "Will, you good to lead?"

I nodded, and headed east down the hallway. The last apartment in the row, 1012. I drew my blade, and crept through the open doorway. Listened. Nothing. Something tickled my neck; I mule-kicked instinctively, made contact with something, and spun with the kukri ready to slice.

Geoff was holding his stomach where I'd kicked him, and laughing. A thin length of broken alien vine dangled from his hand.

"Enough, boys." Skeet said. "Let's have a look around. "

A small apartment, with cheaply made furnishings. Normal, except for the creepers that covered everything. They were heavier on the couch, on the beds, places where people spent a lot of time. Did they smell living organisms, or sense them some other, more alien way? I'd wondered the same thing with the spike pods.

Skeet and Geoff moved to the back bedroom. There were indeed two windows, with a great bird's eye view, south and east. The glass was still intact on the south side, but the east was just an opening. Maybe a kilometer or two away, the high rises of downtown Toronto dominated the skyline. They appeared dull, rather than shiny, because they too had been vined. In contrast, behind them the sun glinted cheerily on the waves of Lake Ontario.

Skeet set up with her binocs facing south, and I took the opening to the east. Geoff said he wanted to "poke around a bit."

"Stay on this floor," Skeet cautioned. I scanned the surrounding side streets. A strip mall, a big playground and empty community pool, parking lots. Nothing moved below us. A fresh morning breeze, gentle even ten storeys up, kissed my face. My mind wandered, and I looked over at

Skeet. She was intent on the cityscape below. She was small, with ropy muscles. A small, simple tattoo of a mosquito decorated her right calf muscle.

Oh, Skeet, I thought, *short for Mosquito*. I refocused on the streets below.

I'd been scanning for movement for about fifteen minutes when I spotted the fox again, or probably a different fox, I guess. Just a small streak of reddish brown, rushing from some evergreen bushes.

I tracked it under a van, then it rushed out again in a different direction. It reminded me of Claude's parkour training tips: change direction often, unpredictably; transfer energy smoothly... *wait, the fox hadn't been afraid of us. Why was it running now?*

I backscanned with the binocs. There! The long, low slung body, the silvery mane, trained on the fox's path. "Run little fox," I whispered, then a bit louder, "Skeet. Just south of the playground." I impressed myself with how calm I sounded. "Got it." She had joined me at my window.

"Well I'll be damned. Looks like a skinny lion, but..."

"With no head," I finished.

"And three or four tails," Skeet added. "Okay Will, we keep still, and we just watch. Pay attention to how it changes direction. Where does its power come from: front or hind legs? Observe."

The running tree stalked the fox, and we watched. I knew a regular *walking* tree would never bother itself with such small prey, mostly because it could never catch it.

As the alien slunk along, periodically it used one of its tail-tentacles to reach under its mane. The tentacle would come out with something too small for me to make out, and then place it carefully along the ground, next to the obstacles the fox had hidden behind.

"It's placing traps, probably puff-balls," Skeet whispered. "They trigger when you come near, sending noxious spores up in your face. They'll blind you temporarily, disorient you, make you cough... If you ever trigger one, close your eyes, hold your breath, and get the hell away."

The alien wasn't far from our building now. I'd lost sight of the fox.

"Check this shit out guys!" Geoff burst into the room, arms loaded with loot.

"Shhh!" Skeet hissed, but the damage was done. I watched through the binocs as the running tree stopped, and trained its mane of satellite receiver leaves up, up to our window.

"Ah, geez, Skeet," I whispered. "What do we do?"

"Stay still, and watch," she commanded. "If it's coming up, we need to know how and where."

I remained as still as I could, but my gut was screaming for me to *move*. Behind me, Geoff was protesting, apologising. Skeet told him to be quiet. The alien stayed focused on our position for a moment, then suddenly it was in motion. Damn, it was fast. Would it circle around to the front entrance of the building on the west side? No...

"It's climbing the building, Skeet! Up the vines!"

"Okay, let's move!" And Skeet was headed to the hall.

I threw my field glasses in the pack, and buckled it on. Kukri in hand, I followed them out. Ahead in the gloom, I could see Geoff had dumped his haul and had his machete out, but Skeet hadn't unsheathed her little samurai sword. The vines crunched under our running feet as we raced along.

I gripped the railing in the stairwell to stop from tripping on the vines. We were moving too fast for stairs, but not fast enough for my liking. We were making too much noise, crunches and echoes, and I knew we had to get into the open. Two flights down I paused on a landing. I heard something above.

"Stop!" I hissed. "Stop for a sec," and my companions paused mid-stride. I sheathed my blade.

We listened.

Above us, that sound like a cascade of ball bearings, as the alien's metallic hood zeroed in on us.

"Go!" I shouted, and we were off again.

21
Out the Window

I was picturing the alien bounding down the steps above us, like I'd seen them bounding down the hill back in Caledon.

I felt my chest tightening, restricting breath and movement. Heard my mother's voice, coaching me to relax, breath, run freely. If we could make the ground floor, we had a chance.

I don't know how many flights we'd come down when I finally started to think. I could hear the thing maybe a floor above us, and gaining. *Think*. Skeet had wanted me to watch the alien, analyze it. I knew from Dr. Botsworth's lessons that the aliens were creatures of habit, and expected us to be as well. It was one of a Freerunner's advantages that we mixed things up, while the aliens repeated patterns.

"Skeet!" I shouted down. I was picturing that morning at the corral with Bear. "Skeet! They hunt in pairs!"

"What?!" She yelled back, and more clearly I heard Geoff repeat it, "What?" just ahead of me.

"They hunt in pairs! Don't go through the front door!"

I heard obscenities from below, then I collided with Geoff who'd stopped abruptly on a half-floor landing. He had just collided with Skeet.

"Back up! Back!" She screamed. "We're at the bottom!" And we heard that dreaded clink-clink-clinkclink-clink. From below us.

We scrambled to the floor above. Looking up, I glimpsed a whip of vine-like tail flash out above the railing, then we were back in the gloom of the second storey hall. I was in the lead again.

I ran blindly right, with no plan. Was there another stairway? Cheap housing, maybe not. If it was a government building, safety first and another set of stairs, maybe. Maybe not.

I ducked into the next apartment, heard Skeet and Geoff right behind me. Hurdled a coffee table and vaulted off the back of a vine-covered sofa. Thank God- the picture window was blown out...no balcony. I didn't hesitate.

*Out the window! Reach with right hand for the vines. Swing out. Worst-case scenario, the vine breaks and I fall, only one storey. Best case...*the vine held, and I monkeyed down, fought gravity, hand-to-hand to gain control, bits of dried alien vine spitting in my face.

Geoff came out right behind me, mimicked my move. He was a fair bit heavier, and his vine didn't hold. I watched him drop his machete and scrabble with both hands for a grip. He slowed, free-fell for three meters, hit the ground and rolled like he'd been taught.

Skeet swung out the window above me, and was violently jerked back. "Fucker!" she screamed.

I watched helplessly as she dangled upside down, a tentacle wrapped around her ankle. Her dreads hung like a blue mop. She reached for her short sword, drew it. She hesitated.

If she chopped the alien limb, she would fall head-first. Upside down as she was, even a one-storey fall could be fatal. But if she didn't chop...

"Hang on! I'm coming!" I screamed. I started to climb. She was suspended, but the creature didn't seem quite strong enough to dead-lift her up.

I was only a meter away when a faceless ring of silvery leaves appeared out the window. *Click-click-click* as it focused first on Skeet, then on me. It turned to its companion that faced the other way, holding Skeet with its tail. Communication seemed to pass. It, too, turned, ready to help haul her up.

I reached toward Skeet's outstretched left hand. Above her, a second and then a third tentacle appeared through the opening.

"Cut it, Skeet!" I shouted. She trusted me and swung, up at her feet. *Thwack!* A woody noise, but a clean cut, and Skeet fell. Our fingers touched, hooked…held. Her body swung around the axis of our linked hands, and she was below me, mostly right-side up.

With a sickening tearing sound, the vine I clung to with my left hand ripped from the wall, and we both fell.

Skeet hit hard and screamed, and screamed louder when I landed on top of her.

Geoff was there in an instant, and hauled me to my feet. I was disoriented, but intact. Skeet was not intact. She'd landed hard on her right shoulder, and it was out of line with her body. It was dislocated, maybe broken.

"Fuckfuckfuckfuck!" she said through gritted teeth.

"Can you move?" I asked her desperately.

"*Fuck,*" she said with emphasis, which I took as a no.

"Gotta pop it back in," she managed.

I looked at Geoff; he looked at me. He said, "I've seen it done, but never done it."

I looked up. One of the aliens was cautiously heading head first (mane-first?) down the side of the building, a lot like a cat trying to un-tree itself. The other must have been taking the stairs. I looked back at Geoff and said, "Do it."

He nodded, grabbed Skeet's arm, and put his foot on her chest. She started to scream again, and he hesitated. "Just do it!" she said through the agony. He pulled, the shoulder popped in, and suddenly Skeet went slack. Out cold.

"Pick her up!" I yelled. "I'll rabbit, draw the aliens the other way!"

Geoff picked her up in a fireman's carry over both shoulders. He looked at me and hesitated again. "Go!" I urged. "You're stronger, I'm faster!" And he moved off toward the redbrick gate, travelling quickly considering the deadweight he was trucking on his shoulders.

22
Be the Fox

I circled around to the front entrance as well, staying closer to the building. The alien coming down the stairs had to see me before it saw Geoff and Skeet, or it would pick them off easily.

I saw a flash of movement in the lobby, waited for the creature to detect me...and I took off full speed. I could hear it running behind me.

A low hedge encircled the apartment complex, maybe a meter and half tall. I couldn't jump it. I rounded the north side of the building, looking desperately for an opening. Was it some instinct, or Claude's training that made me make an unpredictable turn toward the hedge? I don't know, but just after I veered, the other alien came around the building toward me, its vine-tails thrashing angrily.

The hedge was a green wall that was getting closer and closer. Remember that campfire game? *Can't go over the mountain...can't go around the mountain...* I shortened my strides and pumped my arms to accelerate, ducked my head- and crashed through the mother.

Teeny sharp branches scratched every bit of exposed skin, and I sprawled onto the pavement on the other side, getting terrible roadrash on both forearms. I scrambled to my feet and looked back as the first monster followed me through.

Well, almost through.

It must have folded its leaves forward like the cone of a plane, but its root-like front legs had too many little edges and little branches. Imagine trying to pull a Christmas tree tip-first through the bush to get it home. The creature was neatly wedged in the hedge, like Pooh Bear in the tree.

I fought the urge to moon the bastard where it was, but took the high moral ground and decided to run for my life instead. As I turned to go, the other alien leaped over the hedge.

Unpredictable turns, no patterns...*be the little fox*, I thought to myself. But the fox used cover. I needed obstacles, or *opportunities*, as Claude called them. The playground!

Zigs and zags, moments of full speed, the alien on my heels. It scrabbled on the pavement and lost momentum, but made ground over grassy surfaces. I glimpsed the bright primary colours of the playground through the trees.

It was like playing with a home field advantage. The playground had everything that Runner's Haven had: monkey bars, net ropes, even a little climbing wall. Oh yeah, and some things we didn't have, like slides and tunnels and swings and other fun stuff.

I hit the monkey bars full tilt, and swung up as a tail vine scratched at my ankle. I'd been practicing some of Adrian's moves, so I tried them out.

The problem was, these monkey bars were a lot lower to the ground, and now I knew these new aliens could jump. I stood up on the bars, took a few quick steps along the rungs and jumped...over the creature as it leapt up, trying to grasp me with its front limbs.

I hit the top railing of the main playground structure, (which was designed to look like a cool pirate ship), and used my momentum to propel myself over the far side, hit the woodchips on the ground and rolled like I'd been practicing. Now the bulk of the pirate ship was between me and the running tree. Its leaves made the clinking sound as it tried to zero in on me.

I stayed still for a moment, considered my options. Could I get it wedged into one of the tunnels? Probably not, they were too smooth. And that reminded me, the other creature had probably freed itself by now. I remembered being chased by a big kid in the playground when I was in grade two or three. A quick little guy can avoid getting caught on a structure like this indefinitely.

But with two bullies, your chances dropped drastically. I needed to use the playground to stall until I had a plan, then try to get a head start.

For a few minutes, I *parkoured*. Rope nets to crossbars of the swings, roof of the pirate ship, change direction off one foot-spin-back to the rope bridge. I don't know if alien trees have emotions, but I think the thing was getting frustrated. It was chasing me around like a dog trying to herd a flock of birds. The other one hadn't caught up yet, but I had to get away soon.

I thought about the surroundings I'd viewed from above. The empty pool? No, that would be an advantage for the flesh-eating aliens. The strip mall? Maybe. A short sprint away, and there had been a mom & pop hardware store there. If it hadn't been looted too badly, maybe I could find some weapons, or at least barricade the door, then get to the roof, or sneak out the back.

I lured the running tree under the pirate ship again, reproducing a series of moves I'd done a minute before. If I could use its expectation of patterns to my advantage, if I could make it anticipate my next move...

I couldn't see it under there, but my next move should have been to slide through the short blue tunnel and pop out near the little rock wall. I feinted that way, saw a flash of movement between the boards under me, rushing toward the blue tunnel. I scrambled the other way, no fancy moves, just speed.

I was only two meters above ground, with soft wood chips to land on. I sprinted toward the ladder, intending to leap, hit the ground running, and not look back until I was at the strip mall.

Pfoott! A noise like an air rifle, just as I was taking off. What the? Puff-balls! I was in the middle of expelling my breath, so my lungs were spared the worst of the noxious spores, but my eyes were less lucky.

Cayenne pepper couldn't have been more painful. Bee stings on the eyeballs might be about right. I shut them tight instinctively and cried out in pain, forgetting I was flying through the air. The weeks of training saved me from broken legs, and I rolled along the wood chips, and was on my feet and running blind.

Fight the panic...fear is the mindkiller... I sprinted full out, arms pumping, without vision. I knew there was a swing set nearby, a few trees...and a running alien or two on my tail. I thought I might be going in the right direction. The tears were doing their job, but I could only sliver my eyes. Light and dark, then shapes. And the strange feeling of running without seeing where I was going.

I could see shapes a bit, but my eyes were so sensitive that the pain of daylight was making me whimper. The alien could be right on me. A vague shadow to my left: a tree? A sign post? I deked before it, just clipped it with my elbow, and it sent me askew. A tinkle of metal hitting metal behind me as the alien hit the sign harder than I had.

Still I ran.

Across the gravel-strewn pavement I deked and dodged, almost blind, using my superior cutting to advantage. The alien scrabbled and scraped across the small rocks, and I widened the gap. The world still swam through my tears, and I could feel twin lines of snot bouncing all the way to my chin.

I hit the hardware store with a few meters' grace. A cute little tinkle bell above the door signaled my entry. I shoved the glass door closed and fumbled with the little latch. That wouldn't hold for long.

The dim light was a blessing on my eyes. A small store, with a bit of everything. It was too close to the hot zone to have been looted. The bell tinkled again as the running tree hit the door. Its fan of metallic leaves filled the glass, gently contracting as it focused on me, just a meter away.

I wiped my eyes, and desperately began to pile large items in front of the door. A garden bench, rakes, heavy paint cans...I threw them haphazardly in a jumble. If either of the creatures carried the seeds for a vine attack, I was screwed. I finally just knocked an entire metal shelf into the doorway, and moved back into the gloom.

A bit of everything...but what could I use? With a laugh totally inappropriate to the situation, I went and browsed the gardening section. If Claude were here, he'd undoubtedly find a joke about gardening, or weed control. Okay, pruning shears? Hedge clippers? An electric chainsaw...if only there was electricity.

Axes! I grabbed a shiny red wood splitter. Could I take on the monster with an axe? I was doubtful, but it would be better than the kukri in a stand up, knock 'em down fight.

The beast was still rattling at the door, but I hadn't heard glass break yet. The little bell was dingling frantically. My mind was working just as frantically. I rushed through the other aisles. Electrical, plumbing, tiles and flooring. At the back of the store I found the emergency exit. I could hear the second creature scratching at it.

Ropes and chains on massive spools caught my attention. If I could set a giant snare, or get one of the monsters tangled up for a time, it might give me a chance to escape. I knew how to snare rabbits with fishing line and a bent-over sapling, but there were no convenient flexible trees in this particular hardware store. Maybe a lasso? I measured out a good length of thick cotton rope, more than I'd use to rope a calf, and sliced through it with the kukri.

My fingers fumbled while trying to fashion the loop, and the work pulled at the painful cuts on my forearms.

I moved cautiously through the gloom toward the front where the first alien was pounding against the glass door.

I waited.

How long till it broke through? How long till the one at the back door gave up and joined its friend at the front? I couldn't handle two at once. I stood with the lasso coiled in my right hand, the axe in my left, and listened to my doom scratch at the doors. Decision time.

Slowly and deliberately, I leaned the axe where I could reach it quickly. I readied the lasso, and shoved some metal shelves away to give me some swinging room.

Then I started moving the junk I'd piled up away from the door.

23

It Worked on Mustard Gas

Darkness. Darkness, and my own moist breath in my face. The Darth Vader sound of my own breathing through a painter's mask. And the sour smell of urine. Yeah, my own urine.

But I was alive.

I wasn't sure if the running tree was. Alive, that is. And I was too scared and tired to check. So I sat in the darkness. And breathed. As best I could.

Tinkle tinkle. That damn cheerful bell over the door. That damn second alien, trying to get in.

Mother of pearl, I thought, for some reason using one of the Widow Cox's favourite expressions. Wow, I'd gotten into a situation where swearing wasn't even effective. I had to use an old lady's words to really capture the situation.

And it was a situation. I was covered in snot, blood, alien tree sap, and paint. Crispy Lettuce Green, the Behr can said. I was jammed inside a metal locker, in the back of the hardware store, wearing swimming goggles to protect my eyes from the alien pepper spray, and breathing my own pee through a painter's mask, because I'd once heard Mark Nelson say that's what soldiers did in World War I when the Germans bombed them with mustard gas.

One alien was out in the main store, swinging from the girders by a lasso. Its tail tentacles had been pruned, thanks to me and my axe, so I didn't think it could get itself down. It too was covered in its own sap, and a lot of Crispy Lettuce Green paint. Probably a fair bit of my blood and snot, too. Man, we'd had a battle.

And now the other one wanted in. I didn't have anything left. No fight, no flight. So I sat, in my locker, like a sad little mushroom. In the darkness.

Tinkle tinkle. And then the sound of shattering glass. *Mother of...*

"Will?" Bear's voice.

"Will!" Hazel's voice. And others, adding to the chorus.

"In here!" I shouted through the mask, through the locker. I struggled to rise, but my legs had cramped. So I pounded on the thin metal with the butt of the kukri. "Here!" I screamed, my voice hoarse from the noxious puff ball spores.

The locker door ripped open, and I looked up at my friends. Bear, Hazel, Hannah, their mouths and noses covered by kerchiefs, like modern day bandits. And behind them in the office doorway, Adrian, Gemma, and even Dom and Geoff.

Bear pulled me to my feet, and wrapped me in a big man hug. Hazel stood there with tears in her eyes, probably from the spore fumes that saturated the entire store.

"You okay, Will?" Hannah asked me gruffly, and I nodded. "Then let's get the hell out of here."

Bear helped me through to the store. The carcass of the alien creature dangled from the steel girders, like a mutated piñata with all the candy beaten out. Its thorny tail tentacles lay strewn about. The once beautiful bouquet of metallic leaves were dented and misshapen, and splattered with green paint. Several lay on the floor.

Hazel bent to pick a couple of the leaves up, tapped one lightly with the tip of her machete. It sounded like tin from a barn roof. Thoughtfully she turned Hannah around, and slipped it into her backpack.

Hannah eyed the gently swinging monstrosity cautiously. She gave it a poke with my axe.

"You did this, Will? On your own?" She asked.

I nodded yes. I was too exhausted to be proud.

"Good job," she said, and swung a mighty two-handed chop

160

with the axe, embedding the blade deep into the alien's wooden trunk.

Fresh air and sunlight. I sat on the hot pavement while my friends clustered around me. Someone handed me water and I dumped it all over my head, scrubbed at my stinging eyes.

Geoff was quiet, and he shifted his weight from foot to foot.

"The other one?" I choked out. "Is it still around?"

"Saw us coming, took off south," Bear said.

I struggled to stand. My legs were still cramped from being jammed in that locker for so long. "It'll be back. With reinforcements."

I looked to Geoff. "Is Skeet okay?"

He nodded, and Adrian jumped in. "You shoulda seen this beast! He jogs in- *jogs* in- to the Haven, Skeet on his back. He lays her down after running with her for 6 k, whips us all up into a posse, and gets on his bike and leads us back here. We could barely keep up." Adrian clapped the much bigger Geoff on the shoulder. "You're a fuckin' superhero, man!"

I did some quick math. 6k here, 6 back with Skeet, then on the bike and 6 more at a fast pace. A hell of a triathlon. Now we had to get home again safely. 12 running and 12 biking.

Wow.

I gave Geoff a hand clasp, with linked thumbs, like guys do when they don't know how to express emotion. "I owe you, man." I said quietly.

"No, Will. You don't owe me nothin'."

"Come on guys," Hannah broke in, ever practical. "We've gotta jet."

I looked around. Seven people, six mountain bikes. Aliens coming any second.

161

"You can stand on my pegs," Bear said, "Although you smell like piss." He rummaged in his pack and pulled out little chrome pegs that could be clipped onto his rear axle.

"Or you could ride with me," Hazel suggested. "I'll ride fast enough that I can't smell you."

"No offence, Bear," I joked wearily. "I'd rather hold on to her waist than yours." Truth was, I wasn't sure how well I'd be able to hold on to anyone. I had the shakes pretty badly.

The pegs were quickly clipped to Hazel's bike, and we took off. The roads were smooth, but my legs were wobbly. I did end up leaning into Hazel's back, and her hair whipped in my face.

I closed my eyes, and breathed her in.

Before I even washed up, I rushed to sickbay to see how Skeet was doing. Ollie was puttering with supplies outside of a curtained area. I raised my eyebrows at him in silent question.

"Go on in, Will," he said softly. "She's fine."

I poked my head through the curtain. Skeet was propped up in a hospital bed, white sheets tucked tightly around her thin frame, like a large linen napkin around a desert fork.

"So this is what you gotta go through to get a proper bed around here, huh?" I joked. "Move over. Sleeping in a hammock is killing my back."

Skeet gave me a tired grin. "The pain killers are even better than the bed," she replied in a hoarse voice. "Thank god you're okay, Will."

I sat on the edge of the bed, handed her a water bottle. She sipped through a straw.

"You alright?" I asked.

"Yeah, just feeling stupid." She sighed. "I should be up and Running in a few weeks. Sorry I put you guys into that situation."

"Hey, Geoff and I are big boys. We each made our own decision. We wanted the action as much as you did." No way was I going to bring up the fact that I almost backed out. She didn't need that, and what I'd said was true: no one became a Freerunner without being able to make their own decisions. I could see that clearly now.

"How the hell did you get away?" Skeet wanted to know.

"You up for the long version, or just the dirty details?"

"Just the details for now," Skeet closed her eyes. "These drugs are kicking my skinny butt."

I gave her a quick sketch of how I made it to the playground, then the hardware store.

"So, I figured I had to take at least one of them on, and I made it on my terms," I continued. "I managed to get a rope around it, hoisted it up, locked the door again.

"Man, it was pissed! It chucked every puffball it had at me, so I raided the hardware store. Mask, goggles, leather gloves. I even threw a can of paint at it. And then I just started to hack away. With it tied up, it was almost a fair fight," I finished, trying to keep it light. To not reveal the terror, the chaos, the agony in my eyes and lungs.

"I'm gonna drift off in a second, Will. So tell me: did we learn anything? Was this all for nothing?"

I nodded, and patted her hand. "I learned a lot, Skeet," I said honestly.

"Good. Take it to Oliver." And she was out.

I washed the paint and stink off in the rain barrel, and Ollie looked after my scrapes and wounds. It hurt like hell when he used tweezers to pick little rocks out of the road rash on my forearms, but I tried to put it all in perspective of the day's events. I was alive.

Dinner was a strange affair. Skeet had been the only Freerunner left at Haven, because Oliver's fear of her burnout; now even she was absent. It was just the thirteen recruits and a few support staff, and loud-mouth Geoff was pretty quiet. Everyone was pelting us with questions.

"Is it true they scream like a rabbit when they die?" young Matt wanted to know.

"Adrian said you were covered in alien blood. Did any get in your mouth? Is it sweet like tree sap?"

"How fast are they? How high can they jump?" Gemma asked quietly, the first sensible questions, in my opinion.

"Actually, those are things I'd like to know, too." Everyone fell silent. Oliver stood at the head of the table, hands on his hips. Dr. Botsworth was a step behind him, looking stern. "May we join you all for dinner?" Oliver asked politely.

Hannah scooted down to make room for the two adults.

I suddenly felt like a little kid who's been caught getting away with something naughty. I started justifying to Oliver, to get Skeet off the hook. "Listen sir, Geoff and I were in on it the whole time. It wasn't Skeet's fault."

Surprisingly, Geoff joined my chorus. "No, sir; it was all my fault. I'm the one who put us in danger." He looked down at his plate. "If you want me to leave, I'll go."

Oliver looked at Geoff for a second, then he and Dr. Botsworth exchanged a glance.

"Let's get something straight around here, everybody," Oliver started, and I braced for a lecture. "Dr. Botsworth and I are not your mom and dad." Down the long table, we squirmed, examined our hands, our plates. "I am not your boss, either, and if anyone calls me 'sir' again, I'll throw a tantrum." This wasn't going in the direction I was expecting. "I am the manager of Runner's Haven, and I guess the owner, too." Oliver leaned forward. "While you are here, I will make sure there is food and shelter, and experienced people to train you for the dangers you will very soon face."

He examined me, a wry smile on his face. "Will, if I had known the three of you were going into the hot zone, I would have tried to persuade you not to. But I have no authority to have stopped you."

"But I heard you talking to Skeet. You wouldn't let her Run."

"In that, I do have some authority," Oliver sighed, and rubbed his eyes. "Truth is, Skeet could have chosen to go with Jackson. But she wouldn't ever do that against my wishes. That would open the floodgate, you see." I didn't, and he could tell. "If the military doesn't see us as an organization in some way…if Freerunners just start going hot without my say so… then this all crumbles apart. And that autonomy your mother and I fought so hard for is gone. You would just be another cog in the military wheel."

He focused his casual gaze on Geoff. "And Geoff. If you put Skeet and Will in danger somehow, that is between you, Skeet and Will." Geoff dropped his gaze.

"But it is not my concern unless one of you asks for advice, which I would gladly give. In the meantime, Geoff, if you do not learn from your experience, that is also your affair; but your life expectancy will drop dramatically." There was some of the steel in his voice that I'd been expecting.

"Now, Dr. B and I are going to go get some dinner. When we get back, perhaps Geoff and Will can enlighten us on this new generation of alien....I believe you're calling them running trees? And maybe we can all learn from this experience, and extend *all* our lives considerably."

He paused after a few steps toward the buffet table. "When we get back, let's have an intelligent discussion, fifteen adults, about the new threat that we all face."

Having the two *real* adults narrowed the questions down considerably, kept things a bit more sensible. But it was really hard not to feel like a kid. Skeet, Geoff and I had done something stupid, and it was somehow worse not to get reprimanded. Maybe it was even harder to accept the responsibility with no punishment.

I though back to the Toxic Death Run. Had anyone made us run? Was the run some kind of punishment for drinking in excess? No, it was a self-imposed consequence, one that all the Freerunners participated in by choice. But maybe it was more than pride, or the camaraderie that comes from shared misery.

Dr. Botsworth pulled me back to the present. She had a plate of food, and ate daintily. "Will? This is your second encounter with the running trees. Analysis, please."

166

Okay, think. The doing is done, I thought to myself. The experience was so fresh that I hadn't had a chance to sort out individual things. I didn't know quite where to start.

Surprisingly, Gemma was the one who helped get me focused. "Will, why don't you begin by comparing the new aliens to the old. That will give us all a frame of reference."

"Okay, yeah," I started. "Well, the obvious difference if the old ones are upright, the new ones are low, four legs like a dog."

Dom broke in impatiently, "We know this stuff-" Gemma held her hand up, silencing the other girl. "Okay, Will, " Gemma encouraged, "So what are the end results of this difference?"

"They're faster, obviously," I said, "And..." I thought back to the run-in Bear and I had at the corral, "...and the new ones have a front and a back. The old ones could shift their shield around, so any side could be the front, any side the back." I didn't know how useful this was, but it was something.

"You know..." Geoff broke in slowly, "Will's right. And I think when they gained speed, they gave up some, whaddya call it, versatility." He looked down again, embarrassed by the positive attention he was getting. I warmed up to his train of thought.

"Geoff, when you were on the ground, and Skeet 'n I were hanging..." I said.

"They couldn't see you! They couldn't see you and grab you at the same time!" Geoff was excited.

"Yeah!" I exclaimed. It seemed like no one else was in the room for a moment. It was just me and Geoff, hashing out significant details from our experience. "It looked at us, or whatever, then turned around and had to sort of grope with its tail to find us!" I looked at Gemma, became aware of our audience again. Gemma smiled encouragingly, then looked at Dr. Botsworth.

167

"A design flaw," quiet Gemma said, with confidence. "They can't see behind themselves very well, where their vines are. It would be like us having our eyes looking forward, but our arms reaching backward."

"Also," I said more thoughtfully, "Their leaves or manes of whatever, don't protect much of their bodies. When I was hacking at it, it folded them back, but most of the wood body was unprotected."

"That's something," Oliver put in. "You'd never kill a demon tree with an ax. It would simply enfold the shield around itself."

The adults had some more questions, and Geoff and I found ourselves talking over each other excitedly. It seemed we had a fair bit of information to share: the running trees could jump a two meter hedge; they were probably faster than a human, a thought that sent a shiver through all of us Freerunners-in-training; and paint on their canopy of leaves seemed to hinder their perception.

"I splashed it on maybe one third of its leaves," I estimated. "It made the thing, well, frustrated, I'd say."

"Elaborate, please," Dr. Botsworth instructed me.

"Well, it was hanging up at that point, trying to grab me with its vines." I thought for a few seconds. Was it frustrated, angry? Or was I attributing human emotions to a plant, that had no emotions? We knew they were intelligent to a point, but at what point did really good survival instincts end, and actual intelligence begin?

I decided to stick with what I actually saw, and leave the conclusions to the botanist. "When the paint hit the radar dish, it kinda turned in on itself. On the paint side. Like it was lopsided all of a sudden." I'd tried to attack from that side, swinging the ax with tired arms, ducking the frantic swipes it took at me with its tails and legs.

"Maybe the army's been going about things all wrong, fighting them with bullets and grenades," Bear put in. "Maybe they need paint ball guns."

Gemma smiled, and spoke again. It was weird how she was acting, all calm and in control, all un-Gemma-like. "Dr. Botsworth, has your team ever studied a live specimen before? I've never heard about a captured alien."

"Certainly not one of the new breed, they're too new," the botanist responded. "And the demon trees, when captured, fight vigorously for a short time, then when they conclude there is no escape, they release a corrosive mold, and self-destruct. Within minutes, there is little more than a gelatinous goo to study." Dr. Botsworth seemed to notice Gemma for the first time. "Gemma my dear, where *would* you have heard of what my team has and has not studied?" She peered at her sharply, her scientist's brain almost clicking audibly as she made connections. "Gemma, what is your surname?"

Gemma looked down, all shy-Gemma once again. "Hoffman," she murmured.

Dr. B tilted her head, bird-like. "Dr. Adrianne Gugleti-Hoffman and Dr. Robert Hoffman's daughter, perhaps?" Gemma nodded slightly, eyes still downcast. "Good heavens, child!" the scientist exclaimed. "We've been wondering when you would arrive! What on earth have you been doing, playing at being a Freerunner!"

The whole bunch of us looked from Gemma to the scientist and back, silent in our confusion.

Oliver laughed out loud, and explained. "Freerunners, I'd like you to meet Gertrude Hoffman, daughter of two of the best analytical minds to survive the invasion. She is here to assist Dr. Botsworth in the lab, and to work on her own PhD."

Oliver turned his bemused gaze to the quiet girl we were all staring at. Adrian, always a bit in love with her, looked at her like a pagan worshiping an idol come to life.

"Why didn't you tell us, Gemma?" Oliver asked gently. "Why have you been training with the Freerunners?"

Gemma shrugged, and mustering up her courage, raised her eyes. "At first, everyone assumed I was a Freerunner recruit, and I was too shy to speak out." She shrugged again. "But I was enjoying the training so much, and I've never really been around kids my own age, I, well, I didn't want to miss out."

Hazel reached out and grasped Gemma's hand.

"Well Gem, you're a sight better at Running than any of us would be at botany." Hazel looked at her friend thoughtfully. "So you study plants, and I'm a blacksmith. And our little alien friends are plants with metallic leaves." She looked over to Hannah. "Hannah, you still got those things in your pack?" Hannah nodded yes. "You want to do a little cross-curricular project, Gemma? I've got some ideas."

The three girls took off to the women's quarters, and gradually lunch broke up.

Oliver put a fatherly hand on my shoulder, and told me to rest up a few days. "Take some time to think, and jot down anything else that comes to mind. Anything at all," he urged. "What you have to say could change the course of this war."

25
Friends Weeding the Garden

Okay, maybe I was milking the alien encounter a bit. Hey, I was pretty shook up and sore as hell, but did I need a few days of rest and recover?

Maybe. Not.

But Olivers senior and junior ordered it, and I was happy to oblige. We'd be sent on our first real Runs soon, and the rest would do me some good.

Anyway, I was hiding out on the rooftop, lying between rows of young corn, back at that adventure novel. The protagonist was nothing like me: he's this huge, 250 pound ex-military dude, who wanders around getting into trouble. He's a great fighter, and a slow runner, the total opposite of me.

But where it matters, I could relate. The guy is set in the 21st digital century, but he shuns material possessions, and only lives for experiences, for the adventure.

And what was this new life I'd chosen? Living for now, for the thrill of the Run. The essence of freerunning, meets the thrill of danger.

What did I see in the eyes of the exhausted Freerunners who came limping back at the end of a tour? Relief at the rest, relief at still being alive and in good company; and an urgent desire to get back out, to fire up the adrenal glands for another 'near-life experience'. We weren't risking our lives to save beautiful women in distress like in my novel, or to bring back a fortune in furs, like the original *coureur des bois*; but the desire to experience life was the common thread.

I was deep in these thoughts when I became aware of people nearby, in the vegetable patch. The sun snuck through the young corn stalks, and from where I lay, if I squinted my eyes, they seemed like towering plants, tickling the sky with their silky threads.

"Well, pick a row. I'll start on the cucumbers." Hannah's voice.

"I'll go at the onions," Bear replied. "Do the marigolds really keep the slugs away?"

I tuned out my friends as they weeded the veggies. I closed my eyes, the book open on my chest. Their low voices became part of the ambient sound, like the insects droning, and the breeze in the corn stalks.

Some change in tone or timbre of their voices roused me. An urgency, or an intimacy perhaps, a subliminal message that this wasn't for my ears. So of course I held still, and listen harder.

"Sorry, Hannah. I know it's not my business, but-"

"No it's not," Hannah's voice was sharp, then she softened. "Sorry Bear, you've been so nice to me but..."

"No, no! It's really not my business. But it might help to talk about it?"

Should I announce my presence with a discreet cough or something? Or keep playing possum? Bear had been hovering over Hannah for two weeks. If she was finally going to open up, I didn't want to interrupt.

There was quiet for a bit, just the sound of trowels in mulch coming from their direction. I was totally awake now, but didn't want to open my book for fear of making some small noise. Hannah spoke suddenly, quietly.

"When Caledon got hit..." Bear waited her out. "When the town got hit," she continued eventually, "I wasn't there alone."

"Your family?" Bear asked softly.

"It was my brother who got me into bikes. They're just transportation for mom and dad, but my brother and I have always been competitive with each other. So when he was eight and I was almost seven, he started doing tricks on his bmx, I tried to imitate him."

"You don't talk about him much. What's his name?" Bear asked. Hannah continued as if she hadn't heard him. "Anyway, soon it became mountain bikes, riding rails, stairs...we made a cool trials course in the barnyard.

"When I wanted to become *coureur des bois*, my parents were flat out against it." She gave a humourless laugh. "They said it was too dangerous, that I was too young, that the farm couldn't run without the whole family."

A grasshopper landed on my cheek, and I resisted the need to swipe it away.

Hanna continued, "So Scott said he'd go with me, look after me. We'd be Freerunners together, look after each other. My parents finally said yes." A small sob escaped as she finished, an animal-like noise from down in her throat.

Scott. A name I'd thought about a lot on the ride south from Caledon. A failed rescue mission. A young Freerunner who I never got a chance to meet. I thought back to that sleepless night, Jackson's words, '*the girl will want to come too*', as we set out to rescue the other recruit.

A shuffling noise, and I pictured Bear moving over to comfort Hannah; brave, stoic Hannah.

"Your parents?" he asked quietly. "Do they know?"

"They were there. At the market. They're gone too."

Her whole family wiped out. And she'd said nothing, the whole ride south.

Three weeks of training.

Not a word.

26
First Run

Twilight. A beautiful time back on the farm, with the soft evening air, the wet smell of freshly cut hay.

Not so beautiful in the city. We set out from John A with a dying sun at our backs, and the broken skyscrapers looking like jagged stitches on the purple wound of the sky.

The only good thing was the presence twenty meters off to my right, cruising silently in time with my own footfalls: Hazel.

A few nights before we were given our assignments, Jackson and Oliver had had one of their 'discussions'. Their voices echoed like competing thunderclouds through the closed door of Oliver's office. We weren't ready yet; the campaign needed Freerunners; these kids shouldn't be sacrificed, they were too green; they were ready, they were stronger and had better training than the first Freerunners five years ago; yeah, and how many of those originals were now rotting in the Dome... and on like that.

The really bizarre thing? Jackson was the one saying we weren't ready. Oliver argued we were.

The compromise was we'd Run in pairs for the first couple of weeks.

We'd done some night runs from the Haven, even some parkour. But that had been night in a familiar area, with familiar curbs, telephone poles and buildings. Their friendly shapes had been made socially awkward in the dark, but they were old friends nonetheless.

Nighttime downtown was different.

I was acutely aware of what I did and didn't carry. No pack, no food, no real weight. And more aware of what I did carry: a small water, the kukri, and the metal cylinder attached to a leather thong around my neck. Maybe fifteen grams, and the ominous weight of the knowledge that lives depended on me.

The farther east and south we got, the more desolate. There was barely a building that hadn't been vined, and after five years, many of the structures were crumbling, either from the vines themselves, or possibly from our own people. Huge chunks were missing from concrete office towers, exposing the steel skeletons underneath. I imagined grenades, high-caliber guns, maybe even rocket launchers; one of the early battles of human vs. the other. I thought of the tough, lean years my family lived through immediately following the invasion, and saw them in a new, gentler light.

While we sowed and reaped crops in warm months, and cozied up together in our snug homes in winter, the Royal Canadian Armed Forces battled here, and died here, hungry and cold.

A short whistle off to the right brought me back. Hazel was calling a halt. I trotted over to where she squatted against a delivery van. Her eyes picked up the last of the light, but the rest of her was in shadow.

"The streets look a bit choked with vines up ahead," she whispered. I peered through the gloom. Sure enough, black outlines of tangled vegetation filled the road a block ahead. "That should be Mavis Road. Let's cut south on a side street, circle around the mess."

"Let's check it out, first," I murmured back. "I'd like to see what it is while we're in control, in case we have to rush through it later."

Hazel nodded, and we crept forward, closer than before.

The fighting must have been fierce here at one time. There was evidence of struggle from both sides: the buildings and automobiles were scorched and crumpled, and thick, ropy vines snaked everywhere. They tangled the cars and streets, and rose in loops two meters tall.

175

We approached one of these loops. I could have walked through it without ducking. Thorns as long as my little finger sprouted at irregular intervals.

"These aren't harvester vines," I whispered, "These are traps, or maybe shields, like barbed wire."

"Think they're still alive?" Hazel wondered.   I drew the kukri, stretched as far as my arms would go, and touched the thick vine with the point of the blade. Immediately, the coil tightened. I drew back reflexively.

"I think let's go around," I said. Hazel nodded.

Hazel took the lead, and we jogged through the gloom, cutting down alleys and behind homes on tiny lots, the yards overgrown with regular earthling weeds. Crickets were loud, and a few mosquitoes irritated us as we ran.

When we'd covered a couple blocks of back streets, Hazel turned us back toward the main street. She stopped in the loading zone behind a store, waited for me to catch up. The thin moon played hide and seek amongst the clouds and northern lights, and it was now too dark to see clearly to the end of the ally, to see if we were past the growth of deadly vines.

Silently, Hazel pointed up to the flat rooftop of the store. Get a perch, check out the land. I nodded. She gave me a quick kiss, and took a run at the concrete loading dock. She planted her hands wide on the ledge, and she vaulted, legs swinging up between her arms as Claude has taught us. It was like watching water running uphill. She used a window ledge and a drainpipe, and then she was on the roof, crouching. I grinned in the dark and followed.

We lay flay on the pebbly surface while I caught my breath. I pulled her in close for a real kiss, but before I got there, she poked me in the nose. "You're supposed to mix it up, idiot, not do exactly what I did," she whispered. "They learn from patterns, remember?" I had forgotten, but I didn't care right then. We kissed, our first real kiss, alone and sober.

Duty called us back in moments, and we belly crawled to the edge of the roof. The main street was clearer than before, but thick vines still littered the pavement, like a loose parade of snakes, blacker than the sun-bleached asphalt.

"Let's keep to the back streets," I suggested. "60th Company should be only a few klicks away."

We free-ran back down, and yes, I took a different route. The backstreets ran clear and smooth in the night, and the city became gradually less menacing. We spaced out from each other, and took turns leading, so neither of us would get complacent or cocky.

I'm better at running with a companion. I don't know if it's the company, or that little edge of competition that inevitably sneaks in, but I'm faster and stronger and more sure of myself when I'm not alone. I thought of Claude, and his parkour philosophy, where it's about the thrill of the movement, and the freedom; and I get it.

But I am a competitive person, like my mother. And my thoughts drifted briefly to Magda, back home, running through woods and fields as therapy. She loved the freedom, but not the thrill.

We cruised the streets of a burnt-out Toronto, and I felt like an invisible elastic band of pure energy connected me to Hazel. We ran, we shifted position in relation to each other. We vaulted concrete rubble and car hoods and benches. We crouched behind bus shelters and boxes, avoiding broken glass and likely places for traps and vines.

We didn't speak, but we ran together, and we ran better for being together.

I was in the lead when I heard the whistle. As far as bird whistles went, it might have been a cardinal, maybe one with a cold. But cardinals are not night birds, so I slowed, and crouched. Off to my left, I was aware of Hazel doing the same. I whistled back.

From atop a first-floor awning, one shadow peeled off another, and gradually a human shape emerged. A hand raised, and I raised mine back. The shadow had a shadow helmet, and a shadow long gun. The soldier slid to the ground, landing lightly. My recent training said a roll would absorb energy better, but I guess you can't do that easily with a soldier's gear.

Hazel and I trotted over, and we clustered by the building.

"Freerunners?" he asked, and we nodded. "I'm Private Sleigh. I'll escort you into 60th Company's camp."

Sleigh was a young guy, maybe a bit older than us. But he had that awareness of his surroundings that I'd seen in kids who spend a lot of time in the woods, hunting and tracking, and he held his automatic rifle with easy familiarity.

He didn't wait for our names, and we let him lead off.

His pace was quick by other standards, but I was in the zone, and I had to force myself to go more slowly than my body wanted. Hazel and I cruised behind him; he took a convoluted little route that left me looking for the North Star to get my bearings, and suddenly we were in 60th Company's camp.

Immediately I felt a different vibe from John A's camp. John A had been busy, with the steady pace of professionals who know their jobs and waste no time doing them. In contrast, 60th's camp, though much smaller, was bustling with an urgency bordering on mania. Soldiers were running about, assembling gear, and shouting orders.

60th Company had a semi-permanent camp; I didn't know how long they'd been here, but they could pack up and leave with little notice. Private Sleigh led us to a large canvas tent and we halted.

"What's going on?" Hazel asked our guide when we halted. "Everyone's rushing around. Has there been an attack?"

Sleigh shrugged. "Naw, something big's been in the works for a few days, looks like it's finally gonna happen. But they don't tell me shit." He shouldered his machine gun, and adjusted his helmet. "Wait here. I'll let the brass know you've arrived."

So we waited, two civilian statues awash in a sea of military activity.

"Hey, Haze," I said quietly. "We've done it. Our first real run." She smiled, and moved closer, as if for a big hug. I felt this euphoria, pride and relief and some kind of victorious warmth. But we both hesitated; it would be weird to hug here, to show intimacy amongst these strangers. It'd be unprofessional or something. Hazel awkwardly punched me in the shoulder, and I punched her back.

The tent flap opened, and Sleigh motioned us inside. The soft kerosene light seemed harsh to our night eyes. Two men and one woman, all soldiers, stood around a camp table.

I don't know military rank or insignia, but one man was clearly in charge here. He had more silver than black in his hair, and his fatigues were both neater and more faded than the other uniforms. He walked toward us, as straight-backed as Jackson, with his hand outstretched. A patch on his right side read 'Leblanc'.

I was still riding the high of having finished my first Run, and I couldn't entirely wipe the stupid grin off my face. I stepped forward, and shook his hand.

"Good to meet you, sir," I said politely, "I'm Will and this is Hazel." He let me shake his hand, a wry look on his serious face. When I let go, he kept his hand out.

Hazel nudged me. "The canister, Will," she whispered.

"Oh! Right," I said, and undid the clasp that held the message tube around my neck. "Sorry, sir."

"That's fine, Will." He took the canister over to his colleagues at the table. Hazel and I stood there, unsure if we'd been dismissed or not.

The woman spoke. "Private, get these two some water and protein, and a place to rest." Then directly to us, "Don't wander off. We'll need you again soon."

Sleigh found an ammunition crate for us to sit on outside the tent, and went off in search of food and water. Hazel and I heard snippets of the officers' conversation just inside the tent.

"So the good doctor's done it," said the woman's voice. "But this doesn't mean we have to abort."

"We do, and not just because of the orders." That was Leblanc, the bigwig. "If Kordts somehow manages to blow that cesspool tonight, the enemy will be on full alert. It will make the real mission ten times as hard."

Private Sleigh arrived and handed us unopened Evian waters and Powerbars. We couldn't keep eavesdropping on his superiors with him right there, but I was plenty intrigued. The 'good doctor' must be Dr. Botsworth, but just what had she done?

Hazel was examining the package of her Powerbar in the flickering light of a disposable lighter. "Check this out. Expiry: January 2014. This thing expired *before* the invasion!"

"Should be still good," Sleigh said a bit defensively. "We keep a stock of 'em for Freerunners. No one's complained before."

"Oh, yeah," Hazel said quickly. She made a show of taking a healthy bite. "It's good. I'm starved."

It occurred to me that maybe ten year old protein bars would be a bit of a delicacy compared to ten year old army rations. I opened my own bar and offered half to

Private Sleigh. After a very short hesitation, he accepted and sat down with us on the wooden crate.

Food offered and accepted: we were all officially pals now.

"So what's this big deal going down?" Hazel asked. "There's gotta be some rumours."

"Two rumours, actually," Sleigh responded around a mouth full of Powerbar. "Lots of reported activity of the lion-trees near Fairview Mall. No civilians left down there since the invasion. I think maybe the weeds are growing a new ship or something."

"Like, space ship?" I asked.

"Naw, an airship, a carcass transporter. We took one of 'em down a few weeks ago, torched the mother," he explained with pride. "Anyway, a small detail, maybe ten guys, all specialists, snuck off last night. Word is they're gonna tear the new ship up by the roots."

"What about the other rumour?" Hazel asked.

"That one's a bit more out there," Sleigh conceded.

"There's been talk of a move on the dome itself. The mother ship."

Hazel and I exchanged a glance in the dark. This rumour fit with what Claude had said, about his tasks moving from Running to reconnaissance.

"That may not be that far-fetched," I confided. "These new running trees, the lion-trees as you call them, are changing the game. If we don't strike hard now, we might not get the chance to later."

The three of us sat silently for a few minutes, chewing our thoughts, chewing on those long-expired PowerBars.

Eventually, the woman officer opened the tent flap again and summoned us inside. "You too, Private."

The silver-haired officer, Leblanc, turned to us with controlled urgency. He addressed Hazel first.

"Young lady. Take this reply to Commander Barrett back at John A immediately." He handed her a message vial, then turned to me. "You, Will, have a somewhat more difficult Run ahead of you. Private Sleigh will escort you to the southernmost edge of our safe zone. From there-"

"Wait a second," I broke in. I heard Private Sleigh almost choke beside me. "Sir." I added lamely. "Hazel and I have only just done our first Run getting here. We're supposed to work together."

Leblanc made a visible show of being patient. I guess he wasn't used to being interrupted by teenagers.

"Hazel, is it?" he asked her. She nodded. "Will you have any problems returning to John A on your own? It is rather dark out." The sarcasm fairly dripped from his voice.

"No problem, sir."

"Now, Will." He turned rock-hard eyes on me again. "We've heard rumours of a young Freerunner of the same name who outran two lion-trees, and eliminated one of them, all by himself." The challenge was clear.

"Not just rumours sir." I forced myself to meet his gaze. "That was me. Sir."

"Well then. I'm sure with your track record, this assignment will be just fine to run solo." He turned back to Hazel, said, "On your way, Hazel," and she was dismissed. "Private, please secure two working bikes from the Quartermaster." Sleigh saluted smartly and left.

Before following him, Hazel gave me an ultra-professional nod, and held my gaze. I read a million things in that look: good luck, be safe, see you soon- and I'm sure there was some envy at the challenge I was being offered. I nodded back, and then Leblanc pulled my attention to the city map laid out on the camp table. Hazel was gone, on her own mission.

"We're here," the Leblanc's finger pointed to a green pushpin at the junction of highways 401 and 410. "Private Sleigh will escort you by bike to here," his finger slid a short stretch south on the 410. "This is the edge of the hot zone. Not a lot of alien activity, but no soldier activity either. From here, you can continue by bike or on foot- I won't tell you your business- to get here," a red pushpin at a large, irregular building on the map.

"Let me guess," I interrupted, a bit cheekily. "Fairview Mall?"

The three officers exchanged stern looks. I realized my cockiness may have gotten Sleigh into a bit of trouble.

"Fairview Mall, indeed," Leblanc said wryly. "We have a crack squad inching toward a hostile target in the atrium at the centre of the mall. The squad's goal is stealth going in, release all hell at the target, and get out any way they can." He looked up from the map, as if measuring me for a new suit, or a coffin. "Their ETA is 0500, less than two hours away. The problem, young Will, is the message you brought from John A." He indicated the tiny scroll lying on the map. *"Abort the mission at all costs."*

I looked for the scale on the map, tried to estimate distances and times in my head.

Leblanc already had the numbers figured out. "Nine klicks, at night, most of it through a hot zone. Traverse the mall to the centre, find the men. Abort the mission." He looked at his watch. "One hour and forty-seven minutes." He gave me that measuring look again, but it was tinged with something. Urgency? Challenge? Pity?

"Speed over stealth, I'm afraid, young Will."

183

27
Run to the Mall

I felt a jolt of adrenaline, and immediately started checking my gear. My shoes felt good, the kukri was at the small of my back where I knew it was, my daypack - The other male officer spoke suddenly.

"Slow down, son. I've got some intel that may help." I didn't take note of his name tag, but from his crisp, almost new fatigues, I figured he wasn't a field officer. "There's a nature reserve along here." He indicated a green and blue swath on the map, west and north of the mall. "Beavers have dammed this river up, so it's a small lake now. We've not seen much hostile activity here. The aliens largely ignore it. But it's got paved bike paths, so even though it's physically a longer distance, you might be able to get to the objective more quickly." He spoke precisely, like my dad; not like a soldier.

"Next. Take this." He handed me a short plastic tube on a thin string. It stirred a childhood memory. "Basic glowstick. Crack it, it gives off ambient light for a few hours. For some reason, the trees don't see the green ones. They're all over the red and yellow though, so if this pops up other than green, ditch it quickly."

I examined the tube. Cheap, smooth plastic, maybe 20 cm long. We'd played with them on Canada Day when I was a kid, running through the yards while the grownups set off fireworks. "We got lucky recently," the intel guy continued. "Found a Dollar Store warehouse full of them. It won't give off much light, but if other humans are near you, it might stop them from accidentally shooting you."

I slipped the thing into my pack, alongside my water and a crumpled city map. I rolled my head, and my shoulders. Maybe an hour and forty minutes, now. I was antsy to move.

"Last item." He put a hand on my shoulder, a strangely intimate gesture. "You probably haven't been in a mall since you were a kid." I nodded. "They're designed to keep shoppers *in*. Try to enter through a mall entrance, not a department store. The mall will draw you in to the centre: good.

"But getting out...there will be confusion and you'll be on the run. I remember trying to get my wife out of a mall before the invasion." He shook his head. "They're a maze, Will. A goddamn maze." I nodded seriously, unsure if he'd just made a joke or not.

Leblanc handed me the new message tube, and I slipped it around my neck.

"Okay, kid. That's it. Captain Kordts isn't going to want to abort. We've been planning this for a month. But the powers that be want that target untouched, for now. *Make him read the message*." I nodded again, my new and only response it seemed. "Sleigh will see you quickly to the hot zone."

Sleigh was waiting in the dark outside the tent with the bikes. I quickly adjusted the seat, a bit higher than comfortable as Jackson had taught me, for straight speed. For maneuverability, I'd want it a bit lower. Sleigh was saddled up, stripped of most of his gear, but the machine gun was slung on his back.

"You know the way toward the nature reserve?" I asked. He nodded. "Lead on," I said, and he did.

We cleared the bustle of the camp quickly, and hit the highway south. Four lanes in each direction, littered with cars like some giant child's discarded toys. Sleigh knew the road, and picked as straight a line as possible through the extinct metal dinosaurs.

The moon peeked through the northern lights, and we used its light to ride dangerously fast. Sleigh was a competent rider, and had obviously been briefed that speed was paramount.

185

He let me catch up beside him on a wide, swooping downhill curve. "Notice the noise?" he asked. I thought for a second. There was almost no noise, and I said so.

"Cool, huh? Stealth bikes." He looked down at his feet as we hummed along. "Nylon belt instead of a chain. Like a fan belt in a car." I looked at my own gears, couldn't tell much in the dark, but there was no rattle customary to geared bikes. "Trees don't pick up the vibrations. I was in on the field test."

"Any kinks?" I asked. My life would depend on this machine, at least for a bit.

"Don't run up and down through the gears too fast, tends to slip," he replied. "And rapid acceleration from a standstill is a problem. Once you're up to speed, though, they're fine."

"Huh," I replied, "Cool." Then there was no breath to talk as we came to an uphill.

There was nothing to indicate we were nearing the hot zone, nothing but Sleigh's increased vigilance, and a slight slowing of our pace. He led me to an off-ramp, and we cruised a smaller city street. The backs of townhouses butted up to the sidewalks, their dilapidated wooden fences throwing crazy moon shadows.

Another side street, a little catwalk that I would have missed in the dark, and we were on a paved bike path in a sparse forest. I stood up in the pedals to catch up again.

"Sleigh!" I whispered. "We've passed into the hot zone!" I couldn't make out his eyes under his military helmet.

"Yeah, but I know this area. You'll save time if I lead you through to the beaver pond."

"Not your job, man," I said urgently. I didn't want to be slowed down by this guy if things got messy, and besides, I liked him. I didn't want to be responsible for his death.

"We come here all the time when we're off duty, take a few deer to supplement the chow." I gave him a hard

186

look that I doubt he could make out in the dark, but he shrugged and said, "Balls over brains get you promoted in this unit, man." When I didn't respond, he said, "Just to the beaver pond."

I nodded, and we didn't talk any more. Sleigh took me through a labyrinth of leisure bike trails, and we made some serious time.

We cleared the trees at what had once been a picnic area. Now it was totally flooded. The northern lights danced really weirdly across the beaver pond, the slight ripples in the water going crosswise to the shooting streaks in the sky. We halted at the tree line. The beaver lodge was a dark hump out in the middle of the water. The actual dam was out of sight off to the left, I guessed.

"My stop," my military companion said. "Follow the path into the water, and there's a submerged bridge. You should be able to carry your bike through, water's about chest height. Or take the long way, adds about fifteen minutes, but you'll stay dry."

I didn't like the idea of slogging around in wet runners, but time was still tight.

"Where will this path spit me out?" I asked.
Sleigh pulled out a map, and I held my lighter over it.

"Residential area along Zina Street. Backtrack west about two k to King, then straight south to the mall." He checked his watch, a big clunky affair that must have been a wind-up to still be working amidst the solar flares. "If my eaves-dropping skills didn't fail me, you should have a spare half hour to actually find them in the mall." He looked back up at me. "Provided you don't get slowed down by any hostiles."

"Provided," I echoed, and gave my best imitation of Claude's shit-eating grin.

"Hey, I got a buddy runs a potato still back at camp," Private Sleigh said, and held out his hand. I clasped it. "You get back in one piece, drinks are on me."

I didn't turn to watch him pedal back the way we'd come. I had to stay focused on the path ahead, get back in my zone. I followed the path to where it dipped down into the lake.

The water was cold, but not unpleasantly so. The real thing that had my goose bumps out was walking through the water in the dark, on a path I couldn't see, over a bridge that I had to trust was really there.

The bike rested easily on my left shoulder; I kept my right hand free, for the kukri. The water was a bit deeper than chest height. The path was smooth asphalt, and I quickly got the hang of sliding my foot forward to check for obstacles. My eyes wanted to look down, but there was nothing to see in the dark murk. Besides, I needed to constantly scan the banks and the surrounding woods.

Movement at the edge of the woods. I froze.

At the threshold of the tree line, a deer stepped out cautiously. A good sized whitetail doe. There would be others behind. I continued my slide-shuffle, the bike becoming an increasingly uncomfortable weight, the wheels dragging in the still water.

A distant metallic rattle made me freeze again. I thought it was coming from the left, on the side of the pond I was heading to. The deer was looking that way, too. My right hand slipped under the water, and grasped the hilt of the kukri. Without moving my head, my eyes scanned to the left.

The noise again.

The acoustics of the open water were strange; I couldn't tell for sure where the sound was coming from. The deer was still looking east, her ears forward. A better barometer for danger than my own senses.

I kept one hand on the hilt, the other on the bike on my shoulder. I wanted to be free of the burden, to move quickly; but I couldn't risk dropping it and making noise.

A centimeter at a time, I sank into the water. Slowly, slowly…think glaciers, think sloths, think how time drags when you're getting lectured at by a parent.

Submerged to my bottom lip, I tried to remain still. The handlebars and maybe a bit of the bike seat remained in the air. I heard no further sound, but the deer suddenly bolted back for the shelter of the forest.

Just inside the treeline, a spidery shape dropped on the fleeing doe. There was a vague thrashing, shadows and indistinct forms in the dark, then a sickening snap. All was still.

My legs, half crouched in the cold water, were beginning to cramp. I remained still, eyes on the place where the deer had gone down. The metallic clacking, and a silvery lion's mane of alien leaves rose, sparkling obscenely beautiful in the moonlight. It made its silent communication, and off to the left, where the deer and I had first heard the sound, the second alien emerged from the shadows. It joined its partner, and together they lashed their tail vines around the carcass of the deer, and began dragging it east.

I forced even breaths through my nose, and watched the aliens melt into the dark with their fresh kill. I counted to one hundred, slowly, then continued my shuffle-slide step across the sunken bridge, shivering as my soaking body emerged into the pre-dawn air.

I didn't have a watch, but figured I'd lost most of the time I'd gained by having Private Sleigh as my guide. I pedaled quickly, to warm up as much as to make time, and soon my shorts and shirt were mostly dry. My shoes were still uncomfortably wet.

I rode without much caution, hyper alert only to low hanging branches on the overgrown bike path. The moon was almost down, and the forest around me was a wall of inky blackness. Even if I'd been careful, I doubt I would have spotted an alien before it was on top of me anyway.

The park fell away eventually, and I found myself in the residential area Sleigh had told me about. Huge city lots, with the empty shells of massive homes that could have housed three or four families comfortably.

Backtrack west on Zina Street, find the major artery south…there! A four-lane city street, littered with cars, locked in an eternal traffic jam as of five years ago. I slow pedaled through, but after getting clipped by a car's side mirror, I decided it was time to ditch the bike. I leaned it against a Bad Boy furniture delivery truck, as ugly and obvious a landmark as I could find, for the way back.

Time. Not enough of it.

The bike had helped, but it felt good to be on my feet again. I cruised and dodged through the cars, their proximity making it feel like I was going faster than I was.

Still no light to the north east, where the sun would be coming up soon, but time shifted, in my mind at least, and I was thinking that it was no longer late at night, but early in the morning.

Soon I spotted the first fading tourist sign, *Fairview Mall, .5 km.* I poured on the speed, making sure to vary my line, in case I was being stalked. Poor deer.

The mall came into view, and I saw the challenge *du jour:* the tangle vines.

I freeran car hood to truck hood to truck roof, and got a good vantage. Like a wall, the thorny vines stretched out left and right into the gloom, cutting the mall's parking lot in two: inside the perimeter and out.

If the running trees had a secret way in, I couldn't see it. I fantasised about getting a car into neutral and running it down the slight hill, crashing through the vines…but I'd never get enough steam. I was going to have to pick my way through by foot.

I didn't know why the military bigwigs had decided suddenly that this target needed to *not* get destroyed, but it never occurred to me not to try to get through. As I slowly approached the living security fence, I pondered why I was so willing to risk my life on this Run, to actually stop the good guys from blowing up the bad. Work ethic, instilled on the farm? Maybe.

Thrill, and the love of a good challenge?

More likely.

I cracked the glow stick. A sickly green light sparked, a cheap chemical reaction that seemed like magic in a post-tech world. I held it out left-handed, the blade in my right, and considered the deadly tangle in front of me.

The glow wasn't strong enough to penetrate the mass of vines, so I couldn't plan more than one step ahead. Deep breath. I picked an entry point, and delicately placed one foot into the mess, like a timid swimmer into cold water.

3-D Twister. That's the best way to describe it. Or maybe slow-motion breakdancing to no music, and following illogical steps that had no rhythm. Right foot over vine, duck down, head between your knees. Pivot, left foot up, tucked under your bum, swing through and touch pavement. Glow stick sweep; no path. Backtrack, left foot back, duck under the deadly coil, right foot pivot...and on.

In the thick of it, I realized I couldn't see any landmarks, and had to use the compass to make sure I was still heading generally toward the mall. I looked around me, and time got unstable again. There was only the menace of the spiked vines, the limited world inside the weak sphere of the glow stick.

A vague anxiety rose in me, starting in my gut and gradually moving up toward my head. My breathing became shallow and quick.

My pack scraped a vine, and it started to constrict. I panicked, lashed with the kukri, triggering more vines. I forced myself still, tried to normalize my breathing.

The vines settled, but closer than before. My mind wandered to a nightmare scenario, not one where I'd be late getting the message to the soldiers, or even one where I died in here, strangled by spiked creepers from a distant planet. But an illogical nightmare, one where I got lost in the maze forever, ducking and crawling in slow motion in perpetual night, lit only by the glow stick and occasional glimpses of the northern lights overhead.

In my little space, a closet of deadly plants, I forced another deep breath, filling my lungs right up to under my collar bones. I searched for my mom's voice, for a nugget of athletic wisdom, a training tip...but nothing came. An insect lighted on my neck and I jerked, panicked- the vines constricted tighter.

Surprisingly, it was my dad's voice that came to me. Not my logical, engineering dad, who could philosophise his way out of any problem. Instead, it was a version of his voice from my childhood. He didn't know any nursery rhymes, so when it was his turn to tuck me in, he sang obscure folk songs that he'd studied in university. Crouched and panicked in the moist dark forest, I heard one of his favourites.

I couldn't remember all the lines, but I heard him sing the first bit in a loop in my head: *The fox went out on a chilly night, He prayed for the moon to give him light, For he'd many a mile to go that night, Before he reached the town-o, town-o...*

My mind settled down, my breathing settled down, and I assessed the situation critically. ...*before he reached the town-o...* Indeed. The song kept playing, and I saw my exit, a small loop of vine...I carefully followed the glow stick, cautious, cautious...the rhythm came back, but now I was slow dancing to the song in my head, and I found some gracefulness...... *he'd many a mile to go that night...*

When I first glimpsed the hulking bulk of the mall again, I almost made a rush for it. Steady...slow...I stepped out of the tangle vines, and collapsed.

I sat on the parking lot pavement for a minute, just a few meters from the vine barrier, and sipped some water.

The water was cool, and there was some warmth coming up through the blacktop into my butt. I could have sat there forever. But there had to be some running trees patrolling this area, or maybe coming and going to check whatever they had growing in the atrium in the mall.

I heaved myself up, and got my shit together, as they say.

28
Body Soup

I avoided the Hudson's Bay entrance as I'd been told, and searched out a general mall door. The massive building would have been empty at the time the aliens landed, so it hadn't been vined. The glass doors were ripped off however, and entering had the feeling of entering a tomb.

And the smell...it was faint, but every farm kid knows that odour. The calf that gets lost, and found too late...the groundhog that the dog kills, and then rolls in...

The stench of rotting meat.

I stepped cautiously, keeping the glow stick tucked in my shirt to preserve my night vision. I didn't entirely trust that the trees couldn't detect its glow, and carrying it felt like waving a big "come and get me" flag.

The halls were broader than I'd imagined, wide enough to channel thousands of shoppers to their desired merchandise. I was a bit in awe of the whole building. How much energy had it taken to heat this structure during the harsh Canadian winters? To cool it during the humid summer months?

I crept cautiously along, occasionally using the stick to examine this store front or that display, the items and mannequins frozen in stasis for the last half decade. I was tempted to check out the Adidas outlet store when I came upon it (Blowout Sale! This week only! All items 20 – 30% off!), but the parable of Geoff's looting spree was fresh in my mind. Stay on task, William, I told myself.

Speed over stealth wasn't seeming like the best idea, especially since I had no idea where I was going. 'The mall will pull you to the centre;' yeah right. This ancient consumer world that I'd entered was as alien to me as the creatures that hunted its halls. I quickly lost all sense of direction. If only I had a map.

A map! I mentally slapped my forehead. Of course; there would have been a map at the entrance, one of those *You are here* displays. I'd probably walked right past it in the dark.

I took some risks, holding the glow stick aloft every few stores, till I finally found an overhead sign. Restrooms ahead and right, Food Court ahead and left. I picked up the pace to a quiet trot. A distant metallic rattle echoed the halls, plucking at my nerves like a banjo.

Light, or a darkness less dark up ahead. The smell of death stronger, so strong I could taste it when I switched to breathing through my mouth.

The corridor opened abruptly to a three story space. Twin escalators were like a frozen waterfall leading up up up. There was an empty wishing fountain on my floor; and a giant piece of abstract art, three columns of gracefully twisting iron stretching up toward the skylight.

My eyes adjusted to the dim light, and I could see another sign, indicating the food court was upstairs. And at the top of the escalators, as still as any real tree, one of the old-school walking aliens. After dealing with its running cousins, the larger, slower beast seemed almost like an old friend.

Options. I had to go up. Speed over stealth? How about both? Keeping the bulk of the massive art work between me and the alien, I climbed it. A faint, hollow boom echoed off the statue, but when I peeked, the demon tree remained still. The climb was simple after my training, and I didn't even hesitate at the three meter gap to the second floor railing. I landed hands-first on the rail, legs swinging between my arms, gently to the tile floor, and crouched in the gloom.

Predawn grey filtered into the mall through the skylights, and I knew the squad was going to attack the target any minute. Time for speed.

I simply stood up, and sprinted past the demon tree.

Can a rattle of metal sound surprised?

The stench of decay was thicker the closer I got, and as my lungs pulled air in deeper, I gagged a bit. Okay, shallow breaths, but keep running! The walker would have sent an alert by now.

Food Court, the sign said, and later on I would see it as a sick joke. Various food stalls and mini restaurants and chrome tables had been set up on the second floor of a giant, glass-roofed atrium, three stories high. I crouched under a table, and peered over the railing, down to the floor I'd just been on. It was like peering into the depths of hell.

Early dawn light revealed the space below me, perhaps a half acre, of total carnage. Dead bodies- human, horse, deer, and animals unidentifiable- lay in all stages of decay. Legs, hoofs, and massive cattle rib cages rose from the mess like dead tree limbs rising from a swamp.

And it was a swamp. The oldest bodies were liquefied, a thick goo that shimmered faintly in the dawn. From the fresher, more bloated corpses, gas escaped in obscene burps and wet hisses and farts.

I crouched behind the glass balcony and quietly puked up my Powerbar.

My shocked mind had barely even registered the aliens growing down below. Not a new transport ship, as Private Sleigh had guessed.

No, it was a forest of new running trees, hundreds of them, growing at regular intervals in the body soup, still and tall on their hind legs, metallic lion's manes reaching as cheerily as sunflowers for the rising sun.

There Were Sewers?

"*Hey, Freerunner!*" a voice hissed at me. I heard it, but I was transfixed by the horror below. I couldn't respond.

"Kid!" The voice was insistent, and suddenly a rough hand was shaking my shoulder. I turned to find a face, vaguely feminine behind the camouflage paint, inches from mine. "C'mon, don't look at it. Come with me," and I followed dumbly, imitating her crouched run.

I followed her behind the Lil' Miss Muffins stall, where two more soldiers were crouched, machine guns ready. All wore Dollar Store glow sticks around their necks.

I tried to shake my mind loose of the images that were weighing it down. A small part of me knew I could drown in those awful depths, and lose my sanity in the abyss.

A hand reached to me, and pulled at the message tube around my neck, snapping the leather cord. Moments later, I had the vague sense that a quiet discussion was going on, but I couldn't focus.

"What the fuck?" a male voice exclaimed. "We lose two good men sneaking into this horror show, now they want us to *abort*?"

"It's moot, Captain," the female soldier responded, "Too late. The charges are going off no matter what." That shook me out of the deep a bit. "Gotta abort," I managed. "There's something else big happening downtown, don't know what," I gasped. My mind was returning, as slowly but as surly as the daylight.

"Sorry, kid," Captain Kordts replied. He handed me the message tube back, broken cord dangling. "My explosives expert here says it's a go. You were about ten minutes too late." He reached around behind me, and I felt a tug at my almost empty pack. He shook loose about a meter of thorny tangle vine. One end had been neatly severed by the kukri, presumably in my thrashing panic. He held it up carefully so his soldiers could see.

"Christ, kid! Did you come through the vines?" I nodded. "You *coureur* are even crazier than they say. Didn't anyone tell you about the sewers?"

"Sewers?" I repeated, and sank back against the 'Lil Miss Muffins cupboards. "Fuck me."

The three soldiers had a quiet chuckle, then the woman checked her watch.

"'Bout sixty seconds, Cap," she said, and the third soldier poked his head above the counter, covered and uncovered his glow stick in a complicated dot-dash sequence. Morse code I figured. He ducked back, looked at me.

"Lots of alien activity, mostly the shufflers, maybe two lions. Freerunner here must've stirred 'em up."

"Go time," the woman said, and we waited. *One*, I counted in my head, *two-* I didn't make three before the world below us went *boom.*

The floor heaved and buckled, and a dozen geysers of alien, human and animal remains shot up from the floor below. Shrapnel fell, not really near us, but I instinctively covered my head. I peeked up to see the female soldier grinning through her grey grease paint. It was a strangely scary vision.

"Escape pattern Alpha," Captain Kordts yelled, "Keep the kid in the middle!" And we got up and we hustled away from the carnage. The three soldiers made a loose triangle with me in the centre. Their machine guns were up, and they picked out our escape along their gun sights. I felt trapped, in no way secured by their perimeter and weapons. Every instinct screamed at me to *move*, to run, to be an untouchable target.

We cleared the atrium, and the smell of cordite and decay immediately lessened. Another railing and a long one story drop on the right, stores on the left. The stores gave way to a corridor and the soldier to my left opened fire. I heard the hail-on-tin-roof sound of bullets hitting an alien's metal leaves. Kordts, at point, picked up the pace, and soon we were trotting through the mall, my entourage firing sporadically at shuffling targets.

Kordts led us to a glass elevator shaft, and the other two crouched behind concrete planters while their captain pried open the steel elevator doors. Nylon ropes dangled into the elevator box from the open maintenance hatch above. This must be how they entered in the first place.

"Here they come, Cap!" The female soldier yelled, and four more soldiers came running down the concourse. Two swift moving forms followed, vine tails lashing angrily.

"Two lion-trees in pursuit!"

"Can you cover them?" Kordts asked.

"Negative! Good guys are right in my line of fire!"

"Johnson, stay where you are! Meyer, you and the kid start up the ropes!"

It seemed like a good escape route, but I still didn't want to be tied to these slow-moving soldiers. I hesitated.

The four new soldiers were maybe twenty meters away; the running trees were gaining. In their heavy gear, the soldiers were losing this footrace.

"Can't they drop a grenade or something?" I asked frantically.

"Blew everything in the atrium," the woman, Johnson, said from behind her gun. "Army's on a bit of a diet, case you haven't heard."

"Let's go, kid!" Kordts yelled.

I was turning to follow orders when a new figure, dressed in shades of grey, emerged, sprinting out of the side corridor. He came out between the fleeing soldiers and the pursuing aliens, and paused as if taunting the fast moving trees. When they were almost upon him, he sprinted right, back towards the corridor.

One alien turned to follow; then in a move that looked effortless, the human figure ran up the glass front wall of a shoe store, tucked and back-flipped, landing behind the running tree that pursued him. It was a basic freerunning move that Claude had been struggling to teach me.

This pulled the first tree out from behind the fleeing soldiers; Johnson was able to hit it now, and she opened fire with her machine gun on full automatic. The tree spread its leaves, but they were inadequate protection for its long body. Johnson kept firing until its woody body almost tore in two.

One running tree remained, only meters from the desperate soldiers. It ignored the figure in grey and its own fallen partner, and kept pursuit. It pounced, slipping slightly on the smooth tiles. The trailing soldier went down. I heard a familiar *pfoot* sound, saw the toxic puff ball shoot its spores into the fallen man's face; he covered his face and screamed. The alien got over him, and wrapped a tentacle around his neck.

Johnson and I reacted at the same time, running for the fallen man. The three remaining soldiers saw us coming, turned to help. The mystery Freerunner reached the alien at the same time. The five of us fanned out around the alien and the thrashing soldier. If the soldiers shot, they might hit their man.

The beast crouched, rattling its fan. Two tail vines shot out, keeping us back. The spores were stinging my eyes, but nothing worse.

The kukri was in my hand. I didn't remember drawing it. The other Freerunner had a short machete. I sidestepped over to him and said, "Hey, Claude. How should we do this?" It had to be Claude. No one else moved like that.

He pulled the grey kerchief down from his mouth so I could see his face.

"Hey, Will," he responded casually. "We should do it *quickly*." He nodded down the hall, where a forest of slow trees were making their way toward us.

I nodded, and said to the group, "They're blind behind. I'll distract it," and before I could think better of it, I jumped at the creature's front, swinging useless but distracting blows at its shield of leaves.

It reared its claws at me, and swung its heavy metal front like a club. I got clipped in the elbow, and my arm went numb.

While I was switching knife hands, I saw Claude and two others at its rear, hacking viciously at the vine tails. They pulled the downed man free, and bodily picked the creature up, and heaved it over the railing. They dragged the man toward the elevator, but I could tell by the way his head lolled limply on his neck that he was gone.

We hustled into the elevator. Johnson got off a few more ineffective shots, and they forced the doors closed behind her.

A half dozen of the original aliens were slowly making their way toward us, broad silver canopies open, making them seem huge.

Kordts was up top of the elevator, and he reached down to pull us up one at a time till we were crammed in the glass chimney. The soldiers clicked into the nylon ropes with carabineers. They tied their dead comrade in a harness, and started hauling him up.

Johnson said, "One thing to die; another to become their fertilizer."

Captain Kordts started making a makeshift harness for me and Claude. Claude ignored him, and just started to climb.

"'S'okay, we're good," I said to Kordts, and I followed my mentor and friend, climbing the elevator's cables and struts like a little kid climbing a tree: instinctively and fearlessly.

"Fine kid, but don't land on any of us if you fall." Kordts called after me.

I think he was starting to like me.

30
Riding Double

We crouched on the roof of the mall in the hazy morning
light, six living soldiers, one dead, and two *courier des bois*.
Claude shook Captain Kordts' hand, old friends bidding
farewell.

"Sure you don't want to come with us, Claude?"
Kordts asked.

"*Non, merci,* Jay. I was just delivering the same
message as Will. You're to go east, where I just came from,
join the campaign there. Will and I will go back to 60th, get
some rest."

To my surprise, Kordts shook my hand as well.

"Guess they didn't trust you to get the job done, huh
kid?" he said. "Wait till they hear you got here *before*
Claude."

"Yeah, but neither of us was on time," I said
ruefully.

"Fuck 'em," Johnson said. "Did you see those new
trees they were growing?"

I hadn't really looked at them, I was so messed up
by the scene. She explained: "Full armour, small leaves
growing all along their bodies, and tentacles front and back."

I whistled. "They're fixing the design flaws," I said
in horror.

"Like I said, fuck 'em."

We said our good byes, and Claude led me west
along the rooftops.

We freeran, quickly and efficiently, along the
different levels of flat roof, and I felt alive. The panic of the
thorn maze, the nightmare of the body soup; they receded in
my mind, replaced by the joy of being alive, with a friend,
and moving swiftly under the power of my own body.

To my relief, we avoided the tangle vines by going through the sewers, dry, dusty tunnels that hadn't seen human waste in a long time. We popped up west and north of the mall, fairly clear of where Claude thought the aliens would be searching for the enemies who had destroyed their new crop.

We jogged to Zina, and stopped for water. "I left a military bike just down the way," I explained. "Should we get it? We can take turns, rest our legs a bit."

Claude considered, and nodded. He had bags under his eyes that I'd never seen before, and his cheeks had a bit of that hollow look that told me he'd been Freerunning too long.

We found the bike by the ugly truck where I'd left it. It didn't have pegs, but Claude said, "I'm not sharing," and told me he'd sit on the handlebars.

We laughed a bit, fumbling to get the bike balanced, and then Claude said, "Mush!" and we were cruising, like a couple of kids on summer vacation.

We didn't catch a single whiff of aliens on the way back, and Claude figured they were all gathering at the mall.

A scout picked us up in the safe zone, gave us the all clear, and we cruised into the military camp riding double. Soldiers we passed smiled and shook their heads, and one older grunt muttered '*Fuckin' Freerunners*' affectionately as we passed.

I think Claude had his eyes closed, and as I peered around him to see where I was going, I could make out the edge of his smile.

The camp was in full morning bustle. We were escorted into the command tent, gave a quick report, and were sent off for food and sleep. I crashed hard and slept the entire day.

Private Sleigh woke us for evening chow. I introduce him to Claude.

Sleigh gushed. "You're Claude? *The* Claude?"

Claude nodded, slightly taken aback. Sleigh shook the Quebecoise's hand vigorously.

"Is it true that you've been in the dome? And actually seen the mother ship?" Claude looked at me to save him from his adoring fan.

"Well, Sleigh," I joked, "That's classified. He could tell you, but…"

"Yeah yeah, he'd have to kill me," Sleigh finished. "Sorry I'm being an idiot, Will, but Claude is the *man!*"

We followed the private to the meal tent, and I quietly asked Claude, "Have you really been in the dome?" He smiled at me, and made a cutting motion across his neck. I shoved him, and used some choice French insults he'd taught me back at the Haven.

At chow, Sleigh showed Claude off to his buddies. They were all young, low-ranking soldiers, guys like me who barely remembered a world without alien invaders. The meal was hearty and filling, heavy on starch and unidentifiable meat.

After dinner, the guys (and a couple of girls, but you know, they were each just one of the guys) snuck us off to a barracks tent where they hid the moonshine and the potato still. We sipped it from a table spoon, lighting it first. The flame burned blue, which Sleigh said meant we weren't going to go blind from drinking it.

These were good guys, and the feeling was a lot like the camaraderie at the Haven. One of the girls asked us what the training was like to become *coureur des bois*. "They're asking for volunteers, you know," she said. "Soldiers to train to be Freerunners."

Claude nodded. "I'm all in favour of it," he said. The young soldiers leaned forward to hear the legend speak. "With the fast aliens, this war is going to change. We need a new partnership. And we need soldiers, trained in combat *and* parkour, to fight this new war."

Everyone had another little nip of moonshine, and then we drifted off to our own cots. I'd done about four hours of Freerunning yesterday: my easy Run from John A with Hazel; the tortuous Run down to the mall and all the chaos that entailed; and then the easy trip back here with Claude. I was beat.

Sleigh helped us travel the maze back to our quarters. Before I could follow Claude into the tent, Sleigh grabbed my arm. "Hey Will, do think I could make it?" he asked. I didn't know what he meant at first. "As a Freerunner. I mean, if I hadn't been in Air Cadets when the invasion happened, I probably would have tried to become a Freerunner in the first place."

"I think so Sleigh," I said honestly. "You handle a bike really well and all, and – well, I think so."

He nodded, pleased, and we said good night.

I stepped into the tent. Claude was already lying down on his cot. And sitting on mine was Hazel. She rushed to me, and we embraced.

Claude pretended to be asleep.

31

Visitors From Home

"Lose your fear, let it go! Trust me- I won't let you fall."

Sleigh took another run at the cinder block wall where Hazel was waiting to spot him, but he balked again at the last moment.

"Damn it, it's just unnatural," he muttered. He skulked back to his starting mark for another attempt.

Once Claude had left for the Haven for some well-deserved rest, I'd told the story of the escape from the Fairview Mall. The story got told and retold, and a few extra details got added with every telling. Now everyone wanted to learn the wall flip.

Haze and I were still on Freerunning duty, but there were no messages to carry. Alien activity in the area had ceased, and scouts had reported no movement at the mall. So the week passed in simple training, and teaching some of the potato-still gang the basics of parkour.

Sleigh took another short run at the wall, his face screwed up with determination. One-two steps up the wall- he abandoned his fear, and Hazel guided him with a hand under his back, and he landed it.

"Hell yeah!" he yelled. Hazel high fived him, and smacked him on the butt as he walked back to the start mark in triumph.

"Again," he said, and they kept at it. I wandered away to find some water.

"Will, got a moment?" a voice asked from the cool shadows of the command tent.

"Yes sir, of course." I'd had little contact with Corporal Leblanc since returning from the mall, but I was learning about him by his reputation. The soldiers respected him, and he was in the habit of rewarding bravery and quick thinking, not just "balls over brains" as Sleigh had claimed.

Now, he motioned me into the tent. I stood in the shadows with him. From this vantage, we could just see the munitions building where Sleigh and Hazel were training. "How's Private Sleigh coming along?" he asked. I was surprised he knew we'd been working with him.

"Good, sir. He's a natural athlete, and he's got good instincts."

"And the others? Anyone else got what it takes?"

"Yeah, two or three," I responded. "Van Horn is a quick learner; Connelly is crazy strong; and I think Ritz is teachable. He just has to unlearn a few things first."

Leblanc nodded thoughtfully. "How do you feel about this idea? Of training soldiers in the art of Freerunning?" He looked at me, ready to gauge my reaction. "I think your mother would have been against it."

I met his gaze, and thought before answering. "I think you're wrong, sir." I'd learned a lot about my mom's ideas in the last month, from Oliver and Claude. "She was against training Freerunners as though they were soldiers. I don't think she'd mind training soldiers to be Freerunners. Parkour isn't about exclusion, or elitism."

He nodded, and seemed satisfied. "You may be right. Truth is, there are fewer Freerunners than we need, and we're running low on professional soldiers, too."

He looked back toward where Hazel and Private Sleigh had moved on to simple methods of changing direction off of the wall. "Guys like me were trained to fight modern warfare against other men and their machines.

"Guess we're in a postmodern world, and young guys like Sleigh are going to save us, or not."

I nodded. I didn't know what to say.

He continued, "I'm sending you and Hazel back to Runner's Haven tomorrow. There's not much for you to do here, and I think we'll be pulling up stakes soon, to join the campaign downtown."

He paused again, weighing options. He made a decision, and said "And I'm sending Privates Sleigh, Van Horn, Connelly and Ritz with you."

I nodded again. I'd guessed as much. "We'll take good care of them, sir."

"Take care of each other, Will. I hope your generation does a better job working together than your parents' and mine have done."

He nodded respectfully to me once, and turned away.

The morning came early, as army mornings and farm mornings do. The mist was chest height as the six of us started off: me, Hazel, and the four army privates, all of us riding military stealth mountain bikes in camo grey.

We were quiet, Hazel and I happy with the prospect of home, the others nervous with a new venture.

We took the long way, north and around the area Hazel and I had travelled on our first Run. We made Runner's Haven by mid-morning. It was bustling, busier even than it was the night of our first party.

"What the hell, Adrian?" Hazel asked our Vietnamese friend when we finally saw a familiar face. Adrian paused, and gave us each a huge hug.

"Welcome home guys!" he exclaimed. Then he gave the bemused soldiers each a hug, too.

"What's going on?" I asked.

"Lull in the fighting, man," he explained. "Most of the Freerunners are home, arriving by the dozen. Hey, check this out!" Adrian turned his leg so we could see the new, scabby tattoo on his calf: writing in an Asian script. "It means *speed*," he told us proudly.

We promised to catch up on his adventures, and went off to find bunks for our soldier friends.

We heard all about everyone's first Runs over lunch. When you boiled them down, most were uneventful, but everyone tried to outdo each other with embellishments and close-calls that never happened.

I kept silent about the mall escapade, but Private Sleigh found his voice, and told the tale. He made me the hero, and tactfully left out the part about me puking my guts out, and why.

Some of the older Freerunners at our table listened in, nodding as Sleigh wove the tale. They'd already heard the story, and knew the gory parts. They gave me their respect with nods and hands on my shoulder, but they were too experienced to take it as entertainment only.

I helped clear dishes after lunch. The mess hall was almost empty when Fee, the *woohoo* girl from the Toxic Death Run, poked her head in the kitchen.

"Willy-boy?" she asked. "Supply wagon just came in from north. Guy asking for you."

Curious, I dumped my dishes on the counter and followed her out the loading bay door.

And there was Ace Mathews, unloading baskets of produce from the supply wagon. Old Mr. Scributan was up top, handing stuff down, his long rifle near to hand as always. Mr. S's team of grey horses were hitched at the rain barrel nearby.

"Need a hand, fellas?" I asked. In answer, Ace smiled and tossed me a haunch of salted pork. He wouldn't socialize till the job was done.

When the wagon was unloaded, Mr. S went off to find Oliver, and I showed Ace around the Haven. He was quiet as usual, stopping occasionally to examine the weapons rack and the strong nylon ropes. Good rope was in short supply back home.

A few people were casually practicing on the obstacle course. Ace watched their smooth maneuvers carefully, his fingers twitching as though he were mentally going through their moves with them.

"Wanna have a go?" I asked. He hesitated, and gave one of those small, rare smiles.

We worked at it for an hour or more, Ace learning difficult tricks quicker than anyone I'd seen. His moves were stronger than mine, too; but I saw that I was faster than him, more fluid.

We rested up on top of the climbing structure to catch our breath. I started a bit of a commentary on the people below to fill his silence.

"That's Gemma, the redhead. She's studying the aliens with Dr. Botsworth," and I pointed out the bird-like doctor. "And that tall thin guy is Ollie, our medic, a former Freerunner. His dad runs the place."

Ace nodded, but I knew he wasn't really taking it in. I changed direction. "So, like, what's new at home? Have you seen my parents much?"

"Yeah, Will; they're good," he replied. "I've got a package from them for you. Letters, some baking." He looked at me, sort of studied me a bit. "You've changed a lot, you know?" he said.

"Yeah, I guess I've put on that muscle my dad promised me," I said.

"No- well, yeah, I bet you weigh as much as me now- but-" he paused; there was something on his mind. He'd get to it, I guessed. "You're different, Will. In a good way." I guessed he was right, but I didn't feel all that different.

"So, Ace, how'd you convince Widow Cox and the council to let you come down with the wagon? You must be jumping with work this close to fall."

"I didn't ask her, I *told* her I was going," Ace replied. My eyes widened. No one *told* Widow Cox anything.

He saw my expression, and we both started to laugh.

"Okay, I begged and pleaded on my frigging knees," he confessed. It occurred to me that Ace never really swore.

"Will, I've got something to say," he began, more seriously.

"Yeah?" I asked.

"It's about Magda," he said, and I panicked for a moment. "She's fine, she's fine," he calmed me. "But, she and I, well, we've been hanging out a lot, and, well …"

I put my hand on his shoulder and rescued him, this man who could never find words. "It's okay, Ace. You have my blessing," I said, and I was happy for them.

"But Will, you came down here for me," he kept going. "And I repay you by-"

I interrupted him by pointing down at the floor of Runner's Haven. "See that girl? The one with the dark hair and the big shoulders?" I asked. He nodded. "That's Hazel."

Ace looked at me and nodded again. "She's real pretty, Will."

"Yeah, she is."

32
Tattoos

"Ta-da!" Ollie said, and swiped gently one last time at my leg with a cloth.

I struggled around to see. On my left calf muscle, in bold black and ochre, was the image of a little fox running.

Hazel and Claude made appreciative noises, *oohs* and *ahhs,* and Ollie told me how to care for it. "I'll cover it up for tonight, then you just need to keep it clean," he finished.

I didn't want to cover it up; I wanted to look at it, and show it off. I felt like a kid with a new toy.

"C'mon, Will," Hazel said. "I left your pal Ace alone out there with Geoff, and I'm worried Ace is going to kill him."

We headed out to where the party was starting. Claude called to us at the sickbay door.

"Will, Hazel; go light on the drinks tonight." He and Ollie exchanged a look. "Spread the word. Myles and Kat just got in from John A. "Jackson will be needing Freerunners. Soon." We nodded, and left.

The music was going, and the crowd was bustling. But as I looked around, the visiting soldiers and older Freerunners were holding drinks without actually drinking much from them.

We joined Ace and Geoff out near the ropes course. The others were there too: little Adrian, hanging close to Gemma; Bear, laughing at whatever Geoff was lying about; Hannah with an almost-smile on her face; Dominique, her hair a bit longer than before, framing her face more softly.

Geoff was telling Ace some outrageous story about finding a warehouse full of condoms, and how his dad had made a fortune from it. Ace had a slightly panicked expression, like a small animal with its foot caught in a trap.

"So Ace," Hazel interrupted, "Will tells me he kicked your butt in the big race back home."

"Hey! I never-" and the night went like that. I whispered Claude's message to the guys, and only Geoff kept on drinking. Hazel told the girls, but neither Hannah nor Gemma really drank anyway. We danced, and told stories and lies, and hung out with the other Freerunners.

The night wound down early, and soon just a dozen people were left awake. Ollie was playing his guitar quietly, and I sat on the gym mats nearby. Hazel was asleep with her head on my lap.

"Hey, Ollie," I said softly. "Do you know an old song called *The Fox and the Goose*?"

Ollie nodded, and asked Claude in French, "*Est-ce que tu souviens? Le Renard??*" Claude nodded back, and Ollie quietly strummed the opening chords.

To my surprise, it was Claude who began to sing.
The fox went out on a chilly night,
He prayed for the moon to give him light,
For he'd many a mile to go that night
Before he reached the town-o, town-o,
He'd many a mile to go that night,
Before he reached the town-o…

I drifted on the song, back to my childhood bed. My father kind of talk-singing, because he wasn't a good singer… but Claude's voice was beautiful.
The fox he said 'Better flee with my kill,
Or they'll soon be on my trail-o, trail-o, trail-o,
The fox he said 'Better flee with my kill,
Or they'll soon be on my trail-o…'

The safety of childhood, the safety of my new friends. I gently stroked Hazel's hair, as if I could protect her just by touching her, the way I felt when my father protected me by tucking the blankets tight around me.

"He ran till he came to his cozy den,
There were the little ones, eight, nine, ten,
They said 'Daddy, better go back again,
'Cause it must be a mighty fine town-o, town-o,
town-o '
They said 'Daddy, better go back again,
'Cause it must be a mighty fine town-o... ' "

The lullaby faded out, and no one made any more requests. I looked down at Hazel's face, the flicker of candlelight making her seem to shine from within. Her eyes were half open. She looked at me, then past me, up into the dark. I followed her gaze, up past my shoulder, into the dark of the obstacle course. A gargoyle-like figure sat up on a platform, watching over the group, but not part of it. Ace Mathews.

"Is he okay?" Hazel asked.

"Yeah, he's fine. I'll climb up and take him a blanket."

"You're a good friend, Will." I kissed her lightly on the lips, and she got up and went to the women's side to sleep.

33
Invasion

"Will. Wake up. *Now*."

I dragged myself to consciousness, for a moment not sure where I was, or even who I was. The urgent voice had called me Will...

"Ace?" I asked stupidly. "What the...?" My location in the space-time continuum was coming back to me. I'd climbed up to Ace with a couple blankets, and we'd talked quietly for a while...I must have fallen asleep up there, three stories up. Weak pre-dawn light showed at the upper windows, not far from where we were.

"Will, something's happening." Ace *never* panicked, but I heard panic in his voice now. And I heard something else, a soft rustling, almost like fire. I sat up, instantly awake. I looked to the narrow windows- slight movement at the edges of the glass, a darkness a bit deeper than the sky. The darkness was slowly increasing.

"Vines," I said in wonder, then I shouted it. "Vines! Wake up! We're being vined!" I looked at Ace, and said as I buckled the kukri at the small of my back, "Don't let them touch you. They'll cover everything then die. Gotta wait till they die. Get everyone on the climbing structure. Go!"

We were both shouting as we clamored lower on the structure. People were starting to wake up down below, Freerunners and soldiers grabbing shoes and gear and weapons before they even knew what the danger was.

"We're being vined!" I kept yelling. I reached the ground, and looked back at Ace, just about to join me. "Ace, you stay up here- help people up. I'll get you a blade." He nodded, and a tiny part of my mind thought, *wow, bossing Ace Mathews around, and he listens. Yeah, maybe I have changed.*

Someone, I don't know who, went to peek out one of

the fire exits. Before he got to the door, it was violently ripped from its hinges, and a mass of plant life burst into the opening. The guy was overwhelmed, pulled to the ground and instantly covered in grey-green vines. I could hear his muffled cries; and over it, the rustling sound, now louder, and a rapid clicking as if millions on insects were swarming the building.

"Get as high as you can!" I shouted to everyone and no one. I threw a machete up to Ace, then helped boost one of the kitchen ladies up. Ace grabbed her hand and hauled her up to a platform set on metal bars.

All around the structure, Freerunners, soldiers and staff were climbing, escaping the tide of alien vines that were swamping the floor and walls. I looked desperately for my friends.

By the stairs that led to Oliver's office, a small group of soldiers had set up a perimeter, machine guns pointing out. But there was no enemy that they could target; they backed up as the vines encroached, their perimeter growing smaller.

Too late, the soldiers started up the stairs. The vines reached their boots, and one of them started firing impotently at the floor…then they too were overtaken. I was roughly in the centre of the Runner's Haven, where I guessed it would take the vines longest to reach.

The edges of the training apparatus were starting to get vined, and slowly the room was becoming fuzzy, like an itchy green cloth was being draped over the world. I boosted people up to Ace as they reached me. Up went Sleigh, in his army pants but shirtless; he helped Ace pull Oliver senior up, the three of us struggling with his bulk; up Fee, up Hazel, thank god……

Hannah's foot was in the stirrup of my hands and she asked urgently, "Is Bear up there?"

"I don't know! I didn't see him!" I heaved her up, but instead of grabbing Ace's outstretched arms, she made a last second decision, and front flipped over me.

She landed behind me on her feet, machete drawn, calling "Bear! Where the hell are you?" I watched her heading toward the men's side, then I was hoisting the next person up.

Dim dawn light filtered in through the Haven's doors. All of them had been forced open now. I could see I only had a meter's grace all around me, the vines approaching like a plague.

"Your turn, Will!" Ace yelled. He was hanging upside down from a metal bar by his knees; I leapt and we grasped forearms like trapeze artists. The vines reached the spot I'd been standing a moment before. I lifted my legs up; leafy tendrils reached up, up toward me.

"Brace yourself!" Ace yelled.

"What?" I screamed back as Ace's grip tightened painfully. *Slam!* Something hit me bodily, and I thrashed, fighting back. Something was holding on to me, wrapped around me-

"It's me, Will," Claude's voice in my ear. With one arm and both legs clinging to me, he awkwardly sheathed his machete on his back. Severed vines clung to it, and around his neck. Above me, Ace grunted. How long could he hold on, supporting the two of us?

Suddenly the screaming subsided, but I heard occasional yells and yelps from behind me. And the clicking noise, with the background sound like someone scrunching tissue paper told me the vines were still growing, still alive.

I looked up. Maybe a dozen people clung to the training apparatus, hanging like ripe fruit ready to drop.

"Can you see Hannah and Bear?" I asked Claude through clenched teeth. For a small guy, he was getting awfully heavy. My shoulders felt like they were ripping from their sockets.

"She's free, but barely," he said calmly, looking over my shoulder. "Bear's vined, but he's got a hand free." He then called up, "You okay Ace?"

"Yeah," came the strained reply.

Claude called to the people above us, "Be ready! When the vines die, we must move quickly! The trees will begin to harvest immediately!"

Something tugged on my ankle, and I kicked violently. Claude clung a bit tighter.

"Wait for it...," he called out; "Wait..."

The only indication that the evil vines had died was the cessation of noise. Claude yelled, "Go!" and dropped from me. Ace let me go a moment later, and I was free falling the meter and a half to the floor. I landed, and Ace landed beside me in a crouch. Claude was already gone, to free people.

Like that, and the vines were dead, crispy underfoot, but still effectively immobilizing the people they'd captured. I raced to the door where the first man had gone down, ripping the plants with my free hand and slicing with the kukri. I uncovered his head, but there was no response from him. I was dragging him from the remaining branches when the first of the demon trees appeared in the doorway. Its tentacle shot at me, got around my free arm like a vice. I pulled back and chopped at it, severing its end; I went tumbling in the other direction, and the demon tree picked up the fallen man and brutally tossed him backwards out the open door.

It shuffled toward me.

I scrambled, tripping over the carpet of dead vines. Puff balls were being set off somewhere, and my throat and eyes were starting to burn.

Hazel called to me, and I focused on her voice. She and Ace were desperately trying to free people near the eating area. I rushed to help.

Machine gun fire erupted in bursts somewhere behind me, and ricochets buzzed like hornets around the room. We freed three, four, five people. The Freerunners we freed had their weapons, and set about helping cut others loose. Ace grabbed my arm, and turned me toward the open front doors.

The unmistakable low-slung lion-shape of a running tree was silhouetted there.

"What the hell is that?" Ace asked quietly.

"How are you with a rope?" I asked as way of answering.

"Will!" Hazel yelled, "I'm going to the lab!" And she was off, through the kitchens to Dr. Botsworth's lab on the other side.

Ace and I ran for the corner where the rock climbing ropes were neatly coiled. More demon trees and running trees were pouring in through the open doors, maybe eight, maybe ten in all; but more of us were freed now, forming little pockets of resistance to protect those immobilized by the vines.

I snatched up a long coil of nylon rope, and Ace took an end. We fashioned a giant loop, and rushed toward the nearest running tree, and past it, the loop hanging lose between us. The alien focused on Ace as he rushed by, and pounced. I abruptly changed direction to try to tighten the loop, and was pulled to my knees as the running tree pulled the lasso tight.

I scrambled to my feet, and trailing a dozen meters of rope, I parkoured the wall, and flipped up to a metal bar. The alien tugged at the rope, but it was focused on Ace, and I struggled to wrap the rope around the bar. It tugged again; I needed to wrap it a second time, but it was too strong. I strained backward, but the tiny bit of bar I was on didn't have room for me to adjust my footing.

"Ace! A little help!" I yelled.

I looked over my shoulder and down, trying to spot Ace.

Instead, I saw Hannah and Bear.

Bear was partially vined, flat against the wall by the men's sleeping quarters. He was thrashing, struggling with his left hand to reach the hatchet pinned to the wall in his right. In front of him, Hannah crouched like a wild thing, swinging her machete to keep a massive demon tree at bay.

Her dilemma: if she paused to free Bear, the tree would get them both. But she was brutally out matched. Could I get there...?

The rope in my hand jerked violently, ripping a furrow of skin from my palm. I jerked it back, got a length behind my butt to anchor it. I couldn't let go. I uselessly watched as the demon tree shuffled toward Hannah, slow and inevitable.

Hannah sliced at a tentacle, then made a sudden move, *toward* the beast. Bear screamed, the sound swallowed in the din of the battle, but I saw his mouth open wide, and he redoubled his efforts to get free. The tree's metallic canopy shielded my view, but I saw one, two lengths of tentacle drop, then the canopy closed, with Hannah inside.

From somewhere Geoff came running like a juggernaut, a red fire axe held before him. Dom was close behind, moving more cautiously. She had no weapon.

Geoff swung a might chop at the tree holding Hannah. The clang reverberated, and I felt it in my teeth. The tree ignored him, intent on the battle going on inside its canopy. Geoff swung again. Meanwhile Dom had Bear's hatchet, and was cutting him free.

Geoff swung the big axe upwards, and it caught under the metal leaves, like a cat's fur being rubbed the wrong way. He wrenched it loose, swung up again, and several leaves clattered to the floor.

By now, Bear was loose, and had regained his weapon. He imitated Geoff, and the two of them hacked madly at the beast, causing more and more leaves to drop. Its shield remained closed, totally enveloping Hannah, like an insect in a flytrap lily.

Suddenly, the rope I was holding went slack. I'd been pulling, and the running tree had been resisting; with the resistance gone, I tumbled backwards, barely gripping the rope as a free-fell. My shoulders screamed as the rope went tight again, and I was dangling a meter above the running tree. It was motionless, its tentacles limp and almost touching the floor.

Dr. Botsworth and Hazel were on the ground; the doctor held a now-empty jar.

Cautiously, I dropped and rolled. I looked up. The running tree's metallic leaves hung lifelessly; a thick black liquid dripped from them.

We rushed over to help free Hannah. Geoff and Bear were hacking away desperately. As I skidded to a stop, the big demon tree suddenly went rigid. A black mold appeared at the edges of its canopy, slowly expanding. It was the same black-green colour as the goo Dr. Botsworth had splashed on my alien. Dr. Botsworth had told us about this: the alien, realizing it was beaten, had released its self-destruct mold.

But Hannah was still inside. What would it do to a flesh and blood human?

"It's dead!" Dom screamed. "Get her out!"

Metal leaves clattered to the floor as Geoff used the fire axe as a pry bar. Bear rushed right into the fold of the tree, sawing at the tentacle vine around Hannah's neck, and the other wrapped tightly around her body. Her pretty face was an alarming shade of purple. She gasped as the vine cut free, and Bear lowered her gently to the floor.

A few meters away, the dead alien was quickly engulfed in its corrosive mold.

Bear cradled her head in his lap, his tears falling onto her upturned face. Dom yelled for Ollie. I stood there like an idiot.

Around us, people were dragging out the carcasses of the running trees we'd managed to kill, or standing around the walkers that had self-destructed. Others were cutting free survivors, or trying to locate friends.

"Can you breathe? You can breathe, right?" Bear asked frantically. Hannah's colour was returning.

"I can breathe, Bear," she said, then smiled sadly. "But my back, and...I'm all messed up inside."

Bear grabbed her hand in his. "You have to be okay," he pleaded, "You saved my life. You have to be okay."

She coughed, a little involuntary convulsion, and a tiny bit of dark blood showed on her lips. Bear gently wiped it away.

"Strength, Bear," Hannah said quietly, and I saw her slip his leather bracelet back onto his wrist. "You gave me strength." Hannah closed her eyes then, and Bear hung his head over her, as if he could still protect her.

I walked away, to help the others.

Bear would need me later, but not now.

34
The Plan

Oily smoke hung like a death shroud over the Runner's Haven.

A handful of giant spike pods sat burning in the parking lot where we'd lit them. One big one, almost two meters tall, kept twitching toward us, its instinct to collect bodies still active even though it was all but dead.

Military men and women bustled about, collecting alien remains, and helping to recover our own dead and injured. Jackson had arrived with a platoon and a tarp-covered wagon just after sunrise; early in the day, but still too late for Hannah. He'd sent a handful of his people to follow the aliens' harvester ship, but they'd returned without any luck.

Nine bodies lay in a neat military row, awaiting I don't know what. Four visiting soldiers, three Freerunners, and two support staff.

Dead, but not harvested. I couldn't find the silver lining in that.

Besides Hannah, there was the kitchen guy who'd lent me the Jack Reacher novel. I'd finished the book a week ago, but it was still in my bunk; I hadn't gotten around to giving it back. For some reason that bothered me.

"Will, Claude's calling us in," Hazel said at my elbow. She touched my arm. "Should we get Bear?"

I looked over to where Bear lay on top of our dead Beemer, his arm across his eyes.

"Yeah, I'll get him," I replied. "Jackson needs Freerunners, and Bear will want in."

"Let me start off by saying I'm sorry," Jackson began in his gruff voice. "The Haven has remained unmolested for five years." He looked out at us: twenty or so Freerunners, Dr. Botsworth and Gemma, Oliver and Ollie.

Ace and Mr. Scributan were with us too. "With the new species of aliens, we should have anticipated that they would track a Freerunner back here, and I feel responsible."

Jackson played with something in his hand while he spoke. Now he held it up: a green propane tank, like you'd use to cook on a camping stove. "But as tragic and ill-timed as last night's events are, I need you to pull yourselves together for the next three days." There was the Jackson I knew and loved.

"As many of you have heard through the gossip mill, we have been planning a major offensive against the invaders for a few months." More than a few of us shifted where we stood. A chance to strike back.

Jackson continued, "I have been arguing for the Freerunners to take on a new role in this offensive. A more ...active role." He looked at Claude, the Quebecoise's face more serious than I'd ever seen it. "Thanks to Claude's efforts over the past few weeks, General Hamilton has been persuaded to my way of thinking. So in three days' time, while the bulk of the army distracts the enemy, some of you will be paying a little visit to the mother ship."

Someone gasped, and beside me Bear rolled his shoulders.

So the rumours were true: Claude had infiltrated the domed stadium, where the aliens were fueling their ship on the rotting bodies of Earth.

"Now, before we start taking volunteers, I'd like Dr. Botsworth to explain a few things." He handed the little propane tank to Dr. Botsworth. The mousy scientist stood up straight, and cleared her throat.

"We know of several things that will effectively kill the aliens: fire, if it's hot enough. Cold, if it's cold enough." The doctor looked out at the small crowd. "And Will and Bear discovered that you can actually trample or hack them to death, but bringing a herd of cattle into battle seems rather awkward." She gave her smile, but even I didn't laugh this time. "Sorry. Right," she continued more seriously. "And of course, if they believe they are going to be captured, they release a corrosive mold that destroys them in minutes. Gemma, will you continue from there?"

Gemma, looking startled, went to the front with her mentor. "Ah, well, the mold has been a problem. It's prevented us from studying the aliens' physiology, how they tick. We never have more than small samples to study. So we haven't been able to figure out how to exterminate them. And even the mold dies immediately after its job is done, just like the vines."

"What about the running trees?" a Freerunner asked. "They don't self-destruct like the shufflers."

"But they *can*," Gemma said. Her confidence grew as she warmed to the topic. "But for some reason, perhaps because of their speed and versatility, or maybe because they are younger, and more aggressive than the previous generation…they rarely do." She looked at me, and smiled slightly. "And Will was able to kill one before it released its mold. We collected the mold seed pod, and were able to examine it."

Gemma reached over to Dr. Botsworth, and gingerly took the green propane bottle. She held it up. "And we were able to weaponize it."

Jackson still refused to take volunteers for the mission, or even really explain the mission, until the Freerunners had had a chance to speak to Claude and Oliver privately, with no military presence. Old Mr. Scributan shuffled off, but Ace hung around.

"Will. Claude." Ace gave us his steady gaze. "I want in."

Claude gave Ace a toned-down version of his grin, and shook his head. "Sorry, *mon chum*," and he put a hand on the bigger man's shoulder. "You are a fine athlete. A wonderful competitor. But this job is for *coureur des bois*."

He indicated the group of Freerunners around us, all finetuned machines, all with some experience at Running.

With an effort, Ace kept his anger in check. "C'mon man," he implored. "I beat you back at the race. And last night...if it wasn't for me, half of you would be dead right now." I'd never known Ace to boast, or let anything other than his actions speak for him. He really wanted to be part of this.

"Claude, he's got a point," I began. "He won't slow us down-"

"*Non*," Claude made a motion with his hand. "It is not about ability, Ace. You are a good man, and a good friend to Will, I think. But you have a different path. Mr. Scributan is leaving this afternoon; you should be with him."

Ace stood motionless for a moment, then finally nodded once. "Fine." He started to turn away, but he paused and stuck out his hand. Claude gave the full-wattage grin, and, ignoring the outstretched hand, wrapped Ace in a big hug. I barked a short laugh at Ace's expression, surprising myself. Then I said "Aw, Ace gets hugs!" And I wrapped my long arms around both of them.

Ace awkwardly endured it, and I heard him mutter "Freakin' Freerunners," under his breath.

When it was just Freerunners, Oliver took over.

"Okay, here's the score, people. We need a minimum of ten Freerunners to infiltrate the domed stadium."

Someone whistled, and someone else chuckled.

"You want that done before, or after lunch?" one called out.

"After, actually," Oliver said straight-faced. "Three days after, when there's no moon. The aliens seem a bit sleepy on the new moon.

"The basic plan is, the military will launch an up-front offensive from the north and east. Most of the aliens are clustered around the dome since the destruction of their little grow-op out at the mall, and Jackson thinks they can draw them out into a street fight.

"They'll need to make it look convincing, and a lot of good men and women are putting themselves at risk, so we can sneak in the back door." Oliver looked at Claude. "If we can release the mold on their ship, and contaminate their…food stockpile…at the same time, Toronto may be alien-free by Thanksgiving."

Claude picked up the thread. "Each volunteer will be carrying three to five of these canisters," he said, and passed the propane tank around. When it got to me, I hefted it. No big deal to carry: smaller than a football, bigger than a softball, maybe two pounds. But put five of them on your back, and try to parkour…

"Shit," I said, and handed it to Hazel. She looked thoughtful, passed it to Bear.

"Gonna slow us down, Oliver," Fee said. "I gotta be honest, five of those will get me killed." A few of the smaller Freerunners, like Adrian, nodded.

"Hopefully it won't be five a piece," Oliver said. "It really depends on how many volunteers we get."

"I'm in," Bear said.

"Now, wait till you've heard it all, folks." Oliver continued. "Claude has scouted the stadium several times, and-"

"I'm in too," Hazel and I said simultaneously.

"Okay, kids, fine, but-"

Hands went up all through the group, and a chorus of "I'm ins" drowned Oliver out.

Claude grinned and shook his head. When the noise had died down, he looked at Oliver and said, "Two apiece for most, three for me and some of the larger men." Geoff puffed out his chest at that. "Now we just have to re-learn how to parkour, with the extra weight."

35
Preparation

For the next two days, Runner's Haven thrummed with energy. Every single *coureur des bois* was home, and each one was training with a heavy backpack.

I carried three roundish rocks in mine, roughly the size and weight of the mold canisters. By wrapping them in a wool sweater, I distributed the weight as best I could, and reduced their movement on my back. I sweated through the obstacle course and out in the rail yard, focusing all my anger and hurt over the attack on the Haven, till it was concentrated to a pinprick of intense purpose.

The soldiers helped us tear down and burn the vines that covered the living quarters and kitchens of the Haven, but Claude insisted we leave them up in the training area.

"The exterior of the dome is more vine than concrete now," he explained. "We need to practice moving quickly and quietly in their environment. They have running trees that they've adapted to patrol the walls of the stadium. They are smaller, but faster than what we've seen on the streets."

On the second day after the attack, we buried Hannah and the others. I helped Bear dig her grave. The soil back beyond the creek was dry, and we needed a pickaxe to get down beyond a meter. Bear was silent as he dug. Nearby, soldiers laboured on eight other graves, professional and efficient.

We paused for water, and Bear broke his silence.

"She wanted a fish tattoo," he said out of nowhere. "Her last name was Pike. Hannah Pike."

I nodded. It fit. Hannah had been fierce, like a pike, and quicksilver fast.

"Do you think Ollie will still put a pike up on The Wall for her?" Bear asked, a bit of pleading in his voice.

"Of course he will, Bear," I answered. "Hannah was a Freerunner."

The funeral was sparse; we had nine people to burry, nine lives to sum up in one afternoon, so we relied on ceremony. There would be time to remember them properly in the weeks to come. Or there wouldn't be.

"Did she deliver her message?" Ollie asked after Hannah's name was spoken.

"She did," his father replied from the head of the grave.

"And did they harvest her remains?"

"They did *not*," came the ritual reply, and only the cicadas spoke after that.

We moved to the next fresh grave, and the next...

Oliver approached Bear that night. I couldn't hear what was being said, but I knew how the conversation would go: Oliver would tell Bear that he didn't need to practice with the weighted packs: Bear was a cyclist, he'd be message Running on the highways outside the battle. Bear would politely say *try to fucking stop me*, or something to that effect.

In the end, Oliver let Bear be part of the team infiltrating the stadium.

We weren't the only ones busy. Jackson's people were running a small assembly line in and out of Dr. Botsworth's lab. I went back there looking for Hazel, and instead found Gemma bossing soldiers about.

"Careful with that tank! It's full, and the nozzle isn't tight!" she was yelling. "You! We need more of the big tanks off the wagon! No, take this out with you! Don't go empty-handed!" The poor military men and women meekly followed her directions, lugging big meter-and-a-half long gas tanks in and out of the lab.

Gemma spotted me, and a smile lit her face up.

"Will! Come see!" She just loved talking about her work. "These big tanks are going with the army for their attack. It's a diluted form of the mold, but with a bit of luck, it might slow them down."

"How are they going to, uh, deploy it?" I asked, trying to sound intelligent.

"Well. The tanks are pressurized, like the little one's you'll be carrying. But where you'll be throwing yours down into the stadium from above, the soldiers will be shooting a spray from hoses. Garden hoses, actually." She smiled and shrugged at the simplicity of it.

"Cool," I said. "Is Haze around?"

"Out back, adapting tank nozzles." I turned to go.

"Wait!" Gemma said, and handed me some welding goggles. "Put these on!"

I went out the back, and quietly watched Hazel at work. She was down to her tank top and shorts, and a welder's mask, running a small welding torch on the big tanks. The August sun and the work had her sweating, and it dripped down her muscly arms. When she was done, she flipped off her mask and noticed me. She smiled her smile.

"Just how long have you been standing there?"

"Long enough. How's it going?"

"Good," she sighed. "My dad calls this kind of work *MacGyvering.*" I said I didn't get the reference, and she shrugged. "Me neither. Before our time, I guess. Essentially, I've got parts from barbeques, camp stoves, and ovens, and I've got to make them all fit on these acetylene tanks."

"My dad calls that 'making chicken soup out of chicken shit,'" I responded, and Hazel laughed. "You know, your talents are wasted in Freerunning, Hazel."

"You saying I'm not a talented Freerunner?" she accused.

"Course not!" I realized too late she was teasing me again. "But, seriously Hazel. You're like Ace. You can do so many other things, things to make people's lives better. You shouldn't be risking your life as *coureur des bois.*"

"There's gotta be some choice in the matter, Will.

231

Just because I can do something well, doesn't mean I have to. I want to be a Freerunner, not a blacksmith. Or rather, I want to be both. See?"

It was my turn to sigh. "Yeah, I see. It's just..."

"You're thinking about Hannah, aren't you?" she asked gently.

"Yeah, pretty hard not to," I said. "Right from when I first met her, she was so fierce, so brave. She had this little knife, and she was protecting a little boy-"

"At the ambush, right?" Hazel asked.

I nodded. "Yeah, and her whole family had just been taken, and I, like, didn't even know. And she made this instant decision to trust me. Like, she just had her head together, could make the right decisions, while the boy's parents were all uncertain."

"Will, this is all like your dad says," Hazel indicated the Haven, the whole world around us. "Since the aliens came- maybe since before, I don't know- it's all chicken shit. And we're just doing the best we can to make soup out of it."

I wrapped my arms around her. It sounds like I'm trying to be all macho, but she was so strong, and I was happy I was still bigger and stronger. "Maybe that's what you should get as your tattoo," I murmured into her hair; "A chicken."

She whacked me on the butt, and I held her tighter.

"Screw you, Will Dunmore," she said into my chest. "When this is done, Ollie's gonna draw me up a jaguar. Or maybe a hummingbird; I haven't decided."

We all met the morning before the attack up on the roof. Eighteen Freerunners who would be carrying cylinders to the stadium; the ones who would be biking and Running messages for the military; Oliver, Ollie, Jackson and the scientists.

232

It was a cool August morning. Gemma pushed up the sleeves on her hoodie and showed us how to work the nozzle to release the toxic mold.

"Pretty simple. Claude has the assignments, where you'll all be, but all of you will be above the alien ship. Then you just throw the canister down on the signal. The mold will disperse from the pressure in the canister, and if we can surround it, the living ship should die."

Lots of *ifs* and *shoulds*, I was thinking.

Claude had a map of the stadium, and we laid out our approaches. He did his best to warn everybody about the sights and smells, but really, how can you prepare for that? I shuddered. Claude passed out little containers of Vick's rub.

"Put a bit under your nose if you need to," he advised, "It might help with the smell. A bit."

We'd grown quiet with the enormity of our upcoming mission. Before we broke for breakfast and some last minute preparations, Oliver stood and spoke to the group. "Listen. You are like my own children, and-"

"Even me?" Ollie interrupted, and we all laughed, the tension broken.

"Except for you; the aliens landed before I could get the paternity test back." Oliver continued, a bit less seriously: "Now, listen. I don't want you taking unnecessary risks. The doc figures we've got enough mold to kill the ship two times over. No one goes down in a blaze of glory, hear?"

I put my hand on Bear's shoulder, and squeezed.

36
Infiltration

Darkest night. No moon, just the drunken dancing of the aurora borealis, while the sober stars watched disapprovingly from afar.

And we moved silently beneath.

We'd split into three groups of six, subdivided into partners, with an experienced leader for each group. Fee had a group heading east then south; Myles and Kat led a group south then east.

And Claude was taking us on a zigzag through the middle. Me and Hazel; Geoff and Adrian; and Claude teamed himself up with Bear.

We'd rendezvous with the other groups at three am- the witching hour, Fee called it- in the stadium itself.

Open canisters at three-thirty when Claude set off the flare.

Easy as pie.

Down into the sewer tunnels, the brackish light of plastic glow sticks not reaching our feet. We ran single file, under the outskirts of the city, at cruising speed. Claude knew the route, had travelled it several times, and assured us there was no debris.

It was weird to run without seeing the ground, and for a while I felt like I was floating. The three canisters in my pack were an added weight, but not a real hindrance.

The night air was warmer than in the tunnels when we emerged, and moister. We spread out on a broad street, running in jagged formation, always within sight of our partner. I could smell autumn in the wind, and I got that feeling of restlessness that makes you want to run around storing nuts or something. I had to check my stride, keep from speeding up.

The high rises of the financial district loomed in the distance, dark cut-outs against the colours of the sky. They seemed impossibly high, until you noticed the heavenly reach of the CN Tower that dwarfed them all. Very soon, the military would be initiating their campaign there, so we could sneak in from the west.

Claude led us on a complicated route, scouting rarely, always moving. I knew roughly the layout of the streets, and paid attention to street signs when I could make them out.

When we reached Adelaide Street running east-west, the choke vines clogged the path, and I resolutely buried my fear, deep down in my being.

But this was downtown, once a cool club district, and the close buildings and modern art sculptures offered *opportunities.* Claude didn't hesitate: up the side of a building, using the metal security gate like anyone else would use the stairs. He didn't look back at us, and I felt it as the gesture of trust it was. He knew us now, he'd trained us well. We followed him, not directly, but taking our own paths as we'd been taught.

The six of us knew each other, too: our paces and our styles. We stayed on the periphery of each other's awareness, sometimes coming close or even crossing paths on a roof top, or between a bus shelter and a retaining wall.

Adrian moved like a spider monkey, lithe and quick. Geoff muscled his way above the streets, mostly sticking to roof tops and solid footing, but he kept pace without difficulty. Bear was somewhere between the two: sure and confident without the fast twitch, sometimes moving from a pure strength handstand move to a full-out run with much more style than Geoff had.

And Bear had a bit of extra weight: besides the canisters in his pack, he wore Hannah's machete alongside his trusty hatchet.

Hazel and I stayed fairly close to one another, mirror images of each other. Or maybe we were like a cello and a viola, one weaving a counterpoint melody to the other.

But I'd never say that out loud.

And so we cruised the night city, above the tangle of deadly vines. Claude practically danced the rooftops and street lights. He freeran, expressing joy and freedom through his body, moving with a controlled abandon that was infectious. Following his example, we all found the zone, and we *lived* above those streets, in the dark, on what might be our last Run.

Two k without touching the ground: a new record for me. Claude paused on the third-floor balcony of an unfinished condo, and silently signalled for us to join him.

"Bear, scout for us," he said quietly, and handed the night vision goggles to him. I knew Claude was trying to keep Bear focused, in the game, and out of his own head. Bear scanned the dark city scape.

With the naked eye, I saw a major street running north-south, and it seemed fairly vine-free. Down by Lake Ontario, the Gardiner Expressway, an elevated highway, sat crumbling under its own weight. The stadium was near, behind more high rises and hotels. And rising above them all, the thin spire of the CN Tower.

"Three demon trees, big ones," Bear's low voice broke the silence. "Stationary along the far side of the street." He handed the binocs to Adrian, who took a peek.

"They've set up a perimeter," Adrian added. "A no-man's land. Probably more of them parked farther north and south that we can't see."

Claude nodded, pleased with his students' homework.

"Geoff, first option?"

Geoff shrugged. "Get down on the ground, blow right by 'em," the big man said. "They'll see us, but never catch us."

"Hazel, second option?" Claude asked.

"Freerun to the expressway," Hazel suggested, "If the surface is guarded, maybe we could traverse the structure under the highway." Claude nodded. He knew the best route already, but he was building our confidence, preparing us for the real trials.

"Will: decision?" he asked.

My favourite decision: no decision. "Split up, do both routes. That way we increase our chances of getting some of us through."

"Good," the Quebecoise said. "We'll put fewer on the ground, just Will and Hazel: you two are fastest in a sprint. If you're quick, you might escape notice;" he waggled his eyebrows. "I did it, once. They spotted me the other two times." He turned to the others. "We'll go the long way. Will and Haze, meet us at The Last Fumble Bar on Blue Jay Way."

"Okay," I said, "I'll buy the first round."

Being on the ground again felt weird, like I was exposed. Hazel and I crept nervously to the sidewalk. Far off to the left, we could make out the spread canopy of a massive demon tree, still as a statue. The other was to the right, but I couldn't pick it out among the derelict vehicles and real trees growing in neat lines along the street. We picked a relatively straight gap in the stalled traffic.

"Together, or one at a time?" Hazel whispered.

"Together," I said. "Think you can keep up?"

"Let's make it fair," she whispered, "I'll carry both the packs, and give you a head start."

We went on three, two fast shadows gliding low and silent across five lanes. We had no way of knowing if the demon trees detected us, and didn't wait around to find out. We skirted two more stationary aliens further on, and neither seemed on the alert.

The Last Fumble was a big sports bar with ripped awnings overhanging busted plate glass windows. We sat on the floor, only our eyes above the level of the windows, and waited. Hazel sniffed the air, and made a face. I smelled it too: rotting meat.

"Is that-?" she started to ask, and I nodded. "Crap! We're still three blocks from the stadium!"

Moments later, the sound of multiple explosions sent a new surge of adrenaline through my veins. They were distant: the battle to the east had begun.

Claude and the others came in ten minutes later on cat feet, not even making sound on the broken glass. Geoff's shirt was ripped, and blood dripped from long cuts on his arms and neck, black as syrup in the glow stick light.

Hazel pulled out a med kit and started cleaning him up. "Trouble?" she asked ironically.

Geoff played macho, said, "Not really," and we all laughed, quietly. Then Hazel got to his hands, and she gasped. I peeked over; they were torn up, the palms like shredded newspaper.

"You shoulda seen it, Will!" Adrian said in an excited whisper. "Running tree got a couple tentacles on Geoff, and he grabs the vine, thorns digging into his hands, and just starts to spin! Lifted the thing clean off the ground!"

Adrian grabbed Bear by the shoulder, and continued the tale. "Bear here steps in, as calm as if they'd rehearsed it, and slices the vine with the machete as the tree swings around! Bastard tree goes sailing off the expressway, lands like a sack of laundry!"

Bear shrugged and smiled. "One for Hannah," he said, with a glimmer of his old self.

Hazel said "Geoff, can you climb?"

Geoff looked at Claude, who remained expressionless. "Hell, yeah, Haze. Just tape me up." So she did, muttering something about more balls than brains. She was one to talk, but I tactfully didn't say so.

"How about the second tree?" I asked. "The partner?"

Claude shook his head. "It was way ahead, heading for the battle. We ducked down to let it pass. It was dumb luck that the other one stumbled upon us."

"Do we need to worry about it?"

"We need to worry about everything," Claude said.

We rested and hydrated at the Last Fumble, and Claude gave a few last minute tips.

"The creatures patrolling the wall are small, and fast. I call them aphids, 'cause they're bug-like, and there are a lot of them. You can't avoid them; I think their job is to, well, be gardeners as well as night watchmen. They help the vines grow evenly on the wall, and the vines are the protection."

He made sure we all had our leather gloves, and had us put them on. Geoff winced as he pulled them over his damaged hands.

"These'll protect you a bit from the thorns, and we're climbing in partners to deal with the aphids. But there are also these little purple flowers. Avoid them."

"Why? What do they do?" I asked.

"Don't know," he admitted, "Like I said, I avoid them. Whatever they do, it can't be good."

37
Little Purple Flowers

The domed stadium loomed like a giant moss-covered turtle, some ancient animal arising from a deep slumber into an unfamiliar world. The surrounding buildings, in contrast, were all angles and sharp edges, even with their vine coverings.

From the street, we couldn't see that the domed roof was open, but we knew it was; that's how the alien ship had entered five years ago, and that's what we were going to enter now. Almost three hundred feet up alien vines, and in.

Hazel and I made our approach cautiously, freerunning the city's concrete walls and abandoned vehicles to stay above the choke vines and traps. I could see that a direct approach on the ground, like the military would do with all their heavy equipment, would be useless.

The closer we got, the huger the stadium seemed, and the ranker the air got. Hazel gagged at one point, almost losing her grip on a street sign when her body convulsed, so we put a dab of sharp-smelling Vick's under our noses. It did help, a bit.

My compass led us to roughly our assigned spot. The others had dispersed, quiet as cats into a dark alley. We hadn't had any sign from the other two teams: the stadium covered about ten acres, and we all had our own approach vectors.

Off to the east, gunfire and occasional explosions were like a metronome in my head, steadily counting off the lives being risked so we could infiltrate this alien stronghold.

We saw more and more stationary demon trees, huge old beasts much larger than the ones I'd encountered at the corral and the Haven. Their canopies were spread wide, stretching two meters or more on each side. They showed no interest in the conflict going on downtown. I guessed they must be sentinels, some kind of elite guard around the home base. They didn't even twitch as we maneuvered the secret paths above them.

The wall stretched up, up, into the shooting colours of the sky. I noticed vaguely that the northern lights were dimming, veiled by storm clouds moving in from behind us. Thunder rumbled once, an echo of the gunfire in the other direction. I pulled the dim little glow stick out from my shirt. A few meters to my right, Hazel did the same.

We nodded to each other, and started to climb.

The first five meters seemed easy; maybe too easy. We climbed steadily, methodically. It was nothing like the rock face back home, where I'd lost my chance at the Race: the alien vines gave firm, easy grips, and solid footholds. The thorns poked right through the leather gloves if you grabbed them, but the low vines were old growth, so the thorns were big and sharp, but spaced far apart.

The biggest problem seemed to be muscle fatigue. A good rock climber stays tight to the wall, so the legs take the weight, not the arms. But those thorns had us hiking out, arms stretched, butts out, to keep our soft parts away from the thorns. The added weight of the mold canisters were starting to take a toll. My shoulders were getting tired, and we had eighteen storeys to go.

At seven meters up, we found the aphids. Or, they found us.

"Will!" Hazel called softly. She was up and to the right, and she'd stopped climbing. "Get over here!"

I put on some incautious speed, and headed to her. Something metallic glinted in the darkness, and then was gone. I hurried up.

Hazel's left hand was trapped to the wall, wrapped in vines as thin as twine. With her hybrid machete, she was swatting at an aphid. It was like a metal hedgehog, smaller than a racoon, with multiple vine-legs scurrying about. Its body was covered in small overlapping scales, the entire thing an armoured solar panel. It made a click-click sound as it scuttled around.

Another of the little critters was busy at her right leg, somehow coaxing the wall vines to send out fresh shoots that were quickly immobilizing Hazel, pinning her to the wall.

I started to cut her hand free with the kukri. "Don't worry about my hand!" she whispered. "It's stopping me from falling anyway. Just get rid of these bastards!"

The upper one was scuttling just out of reach of her blade. I climbed down a bit, and took a quick stomp at the one at her leg. I connected solidly, and the thing dropped like a stone. I reached over Hazel's back, waited till the second one dodged her blade, and I swung the kukri where I thought it would dodge to. I heard a clink as I connected, then Hazel took a solid chop at it. It limped away across the vines, with a big dent in its middle.

I quickly cut the vines, and we picked up the pace. There was not rest for us on this wall, only death if we paused.

More of the aphids came, and in greater numbers each time. Our own laboured breathing covered the clicking sound of their approach, and we had to hold our breath for a moment every few meters to listen. If you could hit them with a good swat of the blade on their first approach, you could knock them off. If you missed the first time, they learned, and waited for their friends.

Our world became the vines ten centimeters in front of our faces, the thorns pinching into our hands, whacking aphids, and climbing.

Up, up, up. We couldn't even see the top. Our awareness narrowed to climbing, and whacking aphids.

Climb, hold breath, swing! Whack! Breath, climb.

We'd beaten back a miniature army of mindless aphids, and I felt we had to be near the top. I looked down, but the storm clouds had moved in, and I might as well have been looking down a well. I focused on the faint green glow on the vines in front of me coming from my glow stick necklace, and on Hazel's presence off to the right. I climbed.

Slight movement, right in front of my nose.

Huh? A little twist of tissue paper, green in the light of the glow stick. The tissue paper was unwrapping... at the last second, I turned my face away and scrunched my eyes and mouth tight. Poof! The little purple flower released its powdery spores. Where they contacted my cheek, the skin tingled. I climbed quickly, blind, afraid to call to Hazel in case I breathed the poison in.

Wiping my face on my shoulder as best I could, I cautiously opened my eyes and breathed. I was almost even with Hazel, and she looked at me, concerned at why I'd sped ahead. The green glow at her neck seemed to throb and pulse with new energy. I stared at it. It was beautiful.

"Will?" Hazel asked.

The green light...how had I thought of it as sickly? In it, I saw an entire world of colour, every colour, in spectrums my eyes hadn't been able to perceive before. It was the essence of Hazel, around her neck like truth, like life... I had to touch that light-

"Will! What the hell!" I heard Hazel yell, but her voice was distant. I let go of the vines, and reached out to grasp the beautiful light...

Hazel grabbed my hand, and even as I fell and our shoulders jerked at my weight, I could only think about beautiful things.

"Will! Snap out of it!" Hazel screamed, but I was aware, more aware than ever in my life.

Pain in my face helped me focus, a bit. The next time I was alert enough to see Hazel's knee coming, and flinched before she kneed me in the cheek.

"Hey, stop-" I began, but I started to drift again. What was pain, after all, but an extension of the mind, an experience as valuable as any other? Like love, or hunger…my mind drifted inward this time, and the physical world withdrew. The hallucinogen from the little purple flower was blowing my mind wide open.

A new sensation. No, a familiar one…My brain struggled to identify it. Cold. Yes, cold and wet. Water. Face. Someone was dumping water on my face.

I opened my eyes. Hazel looked down at me. She looked as luminous as ever, even in darkest night.

"Hazel, I love you," I think I said, and she slapped me, not lightly.

"Oh, no you don't. You stay in this world, Will." And more water from her bottle splashed me.

With an effort, I pulled my mind back to reality. Somehow, Hazel had gotten me to the top of the stadium. We were on the upper level, the aisle above the topmost seats. And Adrian was there, too.

"Hey, guys," I said dreamily. "I just had the most wonderful dream."

This time, Adrian slapped me.

I shook my head to clear it. *Focus, Will*, I thought.

"Where's Geoff?" I asked.

"I had to tie him up with little vines," Adrian answered. "He's okay, but he keeps talking to little bunnies that aren't there. I think he got a fuller dose than you."

They got me to my feet, and Adrian led us to a niche where he'd stashed Geoff. The big Freerunner's eyes were closed, a euphoric smile on his face.

"How'd you get him up here?" Hazel asked. Geoff was probably twice Adrian's size.

"Told him the little bunnies were going up, and he had to follow. How'd you get Will up?"

In answer, Hazel flexed her muscular arms. "Woman power, pure and simple."

"Thanks," I said stupidly. The drug was wearing off, but I still felt unnaturally good. *Focus.* "I guess we leave him here," I said, looking around. The others agreed, and we salvaged his mold canisters. He'd carried five, and Adrian said it hadn't slowed him down at all. We cut his restraints so he could defend himself if he came to. It was still deepest night, and hopefully any patrolling aliens wouldn't notice him.

Lightning flashed as we were standing up, and in the brief strobe of light, we saw into the dome. It was a one second look, but it was imprinted on my mind. The stadium was huge, more than ten stories high.

The alien ship filled most of it, its top only a few meters below the bottom of the level we were on. I had the impression of a giant silver seed, almond shaped, sleek and smooth. Thunder rumbled ominously a few seconds later.

We crept down the stadium stairs, past twenty rows of nose-bleed seats to the railing, and waited for the next flash.

The lightning came again, a double flash, and as one we recoiled in horror. The top of the ship was shiny and beautiful; but the bottom half was nightmare come to life.

Tangled roots thick as a man's body protruded from the underside of the craft, as twisted and random as the thoughts of a maniac. Large alien aphids, giant versions of the ones that gardened the wall, crept about the mother ship, tending to its roots. The massive root system was like that of a cypress tree, diving into a bayou to find nutrients. But the swamp they fed on...

Staring into the darkness, waiting and dreading the next lightning strike, I asked, "What was the population of Toronto before the invasion?" Dr. Botsworth had taught us this, but I couldn't dig it up.

"Five million," Adrian said in awe.

"How many survived the attacks?"

"'Bout one million," Hazel answered this time.

I didn't say anything else. The next time the lightning hit, we knew that we were looking at a swamp, a giant bowl filled with the rotting soup of four million people.

38
American Beer

We were forced out of shock by a strange tugging at our
packs. It felt like they were being pulled down. I turned,
expecting to find an aphid or running tree behind me, but
there was nothing.

"Look up!" Hazel whispered, and in the next
lightning flash we saw a small alien craft, a body transporter,
directly overhead. It was flying in from the east, from the
battle. A miniature of the mother ship, I knew its top was
silver metallic. What we could see from underneath was the
horror show.

Its multitude of vines grasped the harvest, the bodies
of dozens of our soldiers, and even several horses.

The harvest ship released its cargo, and we heard the
bodies splat and splosh into the mire below us. Then the ship
turned around, back for the next harvest. Again, I felt the
peculiar tugging at my pack.

"They use some kind of repulsion with the earth's
magnetic energy to fly the ships," Hazel explained. "It's
pushing on the metal canisters. Gemma's parents are
studying it."

"We gotta get into position," Adrian said urgently.
"We got maybe ten minutes till the signal goes up." That got
us moving, and we spread out, looking for the seat row
numbers that would put us into position. More thunder and
lightning dotted the night, and I resolutely kept my eyes off
the hell below me.

Silver section, 109 C. We'd climbed into the silver
section, so I just needed to follow the seat numbers. I crept
along, Hazel ten meters behind me. There was a lull in the
lightning, and I had to use my glow stick to check the seats.
There were no vines here, and I relished the smooth,
manmade concrete floor and plastic seats like they were pure

gold. Like a silken road…I caught myself drifting away on the flower's happy drug this time, and pulled myself back to reality with an effort.

A slight noise, a rattle, and I froze. The darkness was absolute. The noise didn't come again; I started to creep…

Suddenly, the signal to release the mold went off. Claude had fired a flare up into the sky above the stadium, and in its red glow I saw three giant aphids within a five meter perimeter of me.

The flare hung up there, illuminating the entire stadium. The aphids froze, and I froze. They were much bigger than the wall aphids, big armoured spiders on gangly root-legs, the bodies two meters in the air.

Slowly, I pulled my pack off and started reaching in for a canister. The rattle noise sounded tentatively, and, without looking away from the creatures, I worked the valve on the canister. A hiss started to sound, and one of the giant aphids moved toward me, long legs straddling the stadium seats.

I pointed the pressurized mold at them, waving it frantically. The gaseous mold reflected the flare's red light, and the stupid aphids charged right into it. The mold attached to their metal bodies, and immediately the corrosion set in. They twitched and convulsed as if burned, and I ducked under their lashing legs.

Lying by the railing, I scrambled to get the other canisters out of the pack, two more of my own, and two of Geoff's. I opened them and chucked them over the side, as far into the stadium as I could. Without waiting to see the results, I turned and ran toward Hazel and Adrian. It started to rain, big fat drops in a sudden downpour.

Hazel was on the run. Two of the grotesque creatures were in pursuit, their long legs easily maneuvering the tiered seats. They chased her around the lowest aisle, the sheer drop-off to her left. Hazel was really moving, arms pumping like pistons. I poured on the speed too, heedless of the slippery wet surface.

Suddenly, Hazel dropped to the ground, hands over her head. The lead aphid overshot her, its thin root-feet unable to get traction on the wet concrete. Hazel stood up, and reversed direction. She was heading toward me, the second alien headed toward her at an angle from above. In a move that was pure Claude's teaching, she jumped at the railing, clearing it. The aphid followed. As it sailed over the edge after her, she caught the bottom most railing, and sprung back up and over to my side.

The aphid managed to catch the railing, too. Hazel hacked at the three clinging tentacles, and the beast dropped. I was still running toward her at a full sprint, and getting close. But the first aphid had gotten turned around, and we were charging toward each other like bighorn sheep. Hazel was right in between.

"Run to me!" I screamed, and she did, muscles pumping.

It was like ballet, though we'd never practiced the move. Two meters apart at top speed, and Hazel slid on her side under me, at the precise moment I leapt over. I was no Claude, but I managed one full somersault and a twist in the air, drawing the kukri as I sailed. I captured that relativity thing again: time slowed, and I was acutely aware of the horrid smell of decomposed bodies; the ridged texture of the metallic armour on the creature passing below me; and of the firm, supple feel of the leather-wrapped hilt of my weapon in my hand.

I landed on the aphid, astride it like a horse. It bucked and thrashed, and I used my thighs to stay put, as I steadied a two-handed grip on the kukri, and started hacking off limbs. Soon Hazel was chopping at it with her hybrid blade.

By the time Adrian caught up with us, we'd already heaved the alien carcass over the railing.

The three of us collapsed in the stadium seats, exhausted and content. A few indistinct human figures moved around the stadium opposite us, our fellow Freerunners finishing their jobs.

The huge, sleek mother ship was already being consumed by fingers of black mold. We watched for a minute as the giant gardener aphids scrambled about below us, trying to repair the damage, but the poisonous fungus consumed them even faster than the ship.

"Hey, look," Adrian said, pointing across to the far side of the stadium. The flare's light was refracted by the downpour, but I could see a figure, waving his or her arms overhead. "Is that Bear?"

I stood up to get a better look, and leaned over the railing. Whoever it was, they'd stopped waving and were running up the steep steps between the seats.

"I think it's-" I began, but a loud gurgle from below cut me off. I looked down as a massive tentacle-root burst up from the bloody mire below, sending thick, ropy slime in all directions. All around the stadium, the dying ship's feeding roots were erupting, blindly questing for a purchase on the upper decks. The one nearest us sent out smaller vines, still as thick as my leg, and suddenly I was grabbed around the waist and lifted into the air.

The ship itself was moving, rocking in its nest, using its extremities to lift itself up out of its vulgar pool, trying to perform an emergency lift-off. I heard my friends' yells as I was thrashed around, and desperately I tried to reach the kukri strapped to the small of my back.

Hanging upside down, ten stories above the mire, I had a strange vision. From the far side of the stadium, a stocky figure was jumping from the railing *onto* the alien craft.

As I watched Bear running sure-footed across the vast metallic surface of the giant ship, I wondered if I were still hallucinating. But the details were so specific: the hatchet gleaming in the flare's red glow; the handle of Hannah's machete poking up over his shoulder; his shaggy black hair plastered to his head by the rain. This was real.

The ship rocked and heaved, but Bear adjusted, and even picked up speed.

And then he leapt. I vaguely thought of the phrase *blaze of glory*; then the impact of his body hitting the tentacle that held me shook me hard. Just below where I hung, clinging like a koala to a tree, Bear started hacking with his hatchet. The tentacle thrashed more, and I lost all sense of direction. The world was a smear to my eyes.

Then Bear yelled "Hang on!" and I tried to; but I couldn't reach anything to hang on to.

I was freefalling, the tentacle around my waist suddenly slack. I briefly caught sight of Bear, still clinging to the thick stump of tentacle. He somehow managed to grab me by my pack, and muscled me over to where I could grab the tentacle below him.

Adrian and Hazel were at the railing, screaming and reaching out. As the alien limb thrashed violently toward them, Bear and I pushed off, and our friends grabbed on and pulled us to safety.

We all scrambled up the steps, out of the ship's reach. For a moment it looked like it might achieve lift-off, then the roots on our side gave out, and the whole thing listed, and crashed wetly back down into the stadium.

I gripped Bear's forearm in silent thanks. If the ship had collapsed with me in its grip, I would have drowned in body soup.

From the far end of the stadium, beneath the Jumbotron, Claude shot a second flare, a green one to let the military know the job was done. The rain gave it a halo, a lighter green circle that reminded me of spring.

A vast migration of the little aphids scuttled into the stadium, responding to some alien signal to repair the ship. They ignored us as we went off in search of Geoff, and we ignored them back. If Dr. Botsworth was correct, the mold would continue to expand for a few days, infecting any alien plant life it came in contact with.

Adrian spotted Geoff first. He was sitting along the railing, his feet dangling above the macabre soup. He was watching the green flare, with something like rapture on his face.

"C'mon, big guy," Adrian said, helping him to his feet. "Claude said to meet at the luxury boxes. You can watch the pretty lights from there."

Thirteen Freerunners made their way to the luxury seating area. Thirteen out of eighteen.

We were the last to arrive. I counted heads, checked off the faces of Freerunners I saw. I made a separate tally of those that weren't there. There would be five new tattoos on The Wall soon. Helen's charging rino. The B-52 bomber for that short Freerunner who went by the name Gunner. Big Al's ridiculous yellow happy face, with the bullet hole in the forehead. And two other missing Freerunners, who I couldn't even name.

Among the survivors, there were a few injuries as well. A dislocated shoulder, some broken bones. Some minor whiplash on my part. And of course, Geoff was still a lot happier than usual. "I love you, man," he kept saying to Adrian.

Claude greeted us with a big hug when we straggled in, and then handed us each a can of Bud Light, salvaged from the luxury box's bar. We settled into the plush leather armchairs of the box with the others, and pulled the tab on the beers. The overhang above protected us from the rain storm.

Down below, demon trees and running trees were scrambling into the stadium, desperate to save their ship. They met only death there.

"To the *coureur des bois*," Claude said formally, raising his can. We echoed him, and drank. Hazel grabbed my hand and held tight.

Adrian made a face as he swigged from his can. "Whew! What the hell is this, Claude?"

"That, *mon chum*, is five-year old American beer," Claude said.

"It's disgusting!" Adrian said, and took another big drink.

"I love it, man," Geoff said, examining his can. "No, I mean I *really* love it."

Epilogue

Early autumn sunlight streamed through the upper windows into the Haven's training area. Fifteen students, most of them military privates, stood or sat on the training mats, listening with rapt attention to their new parkour instructor.

"Don't think of them so much as obstacles," Geoff was patiently explaining to the group, "Think of them more as *opportunities.*"

I had to smile at that. I smiled at the whole scene. The destruction wreaked by the alien invasion of the Haven was mostly cleaned up, except for a small climbing wall of alien vines that we'd decided to leave up for training purposes.

And the training would continue. There was still no word from John C, the military camp down in Hamilton. Captain Kordts would be heading up a campaign to find out if there were any survivors, as soon as his young soldiers had completed some elementary freerunning sessions.

On my way to the kitchens, I paused when I saw Bear emerge from the sickbay. He was walking and trying to look at his calf at the same time.

"Better get that thing covered up, or it's gonna get infected," I said mildly. "Let's see it."

Bear proudly showed me his body art: a fierce bear, stylized in native Canadian reds and blues.

"Nice squirrel, man!" I said with enthusiasm. "Takes a real man to wear a rodent tattoo out in the open like that!"

Bear punched me in the shoulder, hard. "It's a bear, dickweed," he said, and then we both laughed. "So, is Hazel going to come home with us?" he asked more quietly.

"Better ask Hazel," I said, shrugging. I'd invited her to winter up in Hockley with us. From there it was only another fifty k to Barrie, where her Grandma lived, and her parents would probably be there over the cold months.

"Better ask Hazel what?" Hazel said, coming up behind us.

"What your intentions are with my young friend here," Bear answered. "You gonna come up and meet his parents or what?"

Hazel made a show of thinking about it, with her fingertip on her lips. "Well, I guess I'd better," she conceded. "It's going to be a long winter, and I don't want to lose him to some farmer's daughter, or a sheep or something."

"Hey, you're the one who's going to have to sleep in the barn," I countered. "My parents are very old fashioned."

My friends followed me to the kitchen, and we sat at an empty table drinking tea, and husking corn for that night's dinner. Talk turned to where everyone in our group was headed.

"I hear Dom's calling it quits," Bear said. "Ollie's trying to get her interested in training as a medic, but I don't think so. When the aliens attacked the Haven, I think it freaked her out."

"Gemma's staying for the winter," Hazel put in. "She and the doc are building up the stockpile of mold to ship to Montreal and Hamilton." Hazel chucked another cob of corn onto the pile. "But they're worried the other mother ships carried a different breed of demon tree, and maybe the mold won't work. Claude's cousin made it in from Quebec last spring, said their demon trees have different shaped leaves or something."

"What about Claude?" Bear asked me. "Montreal, or Hamilton?"

I didn't know. I hadn't seen Claude much since that night at the domed stadium, two weeks earlier. Seemed everyone wanted a piece of the infamous Claude, the

Freerunner who'd orchestrated the destruction of the Toronto mother ship. Captain Kordts had been pushing him to come south; Jackson had been arguing for Montreal, a bigger city where they could establish a new school for *coureur des bois.* And of course, Oliver wanted him to stay put, right here at the Haven.

"Know what?" I said, standing up abruptly, "I think I'll go find out exactly what his plans are."

I finally found my mentor and friend upstairs in Oliver's office. He was seated with Oliver, Jackson and several military bigwigs around Oliver's desk. Claude's cheeks looked hollow, and there was no sign of the laugh lines at the corners of his eyes.

"Sorry to interrupt, gentlemen," I broke in, "But I need to borrow Claude for a minute." Relief flooded Claude's face, but the older of the two army brass was outraged.

"Excuse me, boy, but we are discussing the future of Canada right now," he exploded. "You may certainly not *borrow* anyone."

Jackson put a calming hand on the General's arm. "Ease up, Hank," Jackson said in his most condescending tone. "Canada ceased to exist five years ago," he continued, and nodded to me respectfully. "Besides, you really don't have much say in the matter. Claude and Will here aren't under your command. They're not army; they're *coureur des bois.*"

I led Claude out to the training area, where Geoff was pulling out the Frisbees.

"Thank you Will," Claude was saying. "Those men want to analyse and quantify every single move we made infiltrating the stadium. I try to tell them, it is like parkour; the next time will be different, there is no formula," he shook his head. "I do not understand the military mind.

"So, Will, what did you want to talk to me about?"

256

"I want you to come to Hockley for the winter," I said without hesitation. "You're burnt out, Claude, and these army guys are gonna use you up. Come winter with us. My folks would love to have you."

Claude looked at me, but didn't answer right away.

"Hazel and I are probably going to be Freerunning again in the spring," I said into his silence. "Bear too, if I know him at all. You can start up again then; or not. Your choice. But for now, take a rest, Claude. After five years of Freerunning, you've earned one."

"*Mon chum*, I think that is the best idea I've ever heard," Claude said, smiling, and he put his hand on my shoulder.

We paused to watch Geoff's students in action, but Geoff had other plans.

"Okay boys and girls!" big Geoff boomed. "For your edification, two of our most esteemed *coureur des bois* are going to perform a demonstration!" Geoff started handing out plastic discs to the trainees. "Will and Claude are going to traverse the obstacle course. The Frisbees represent alien contact.

"The rules are: the first trainee who can hit one of these two experts is exempt from tomorrow's Toxic Death Run!"

"What's a Toxic Death Run?" one young soldier asked.

"None of your damn business," Geoff replied. "Now, the number of times a Frisbee is thrown but misses represents the number of shots you must drink at tonight's party. We're on the honour system around here, but trust me, I'm keeping track.

"And the final rule!" Geoff dragged it out, "The *coureur des bois* that is hit first must clean the latrines for the next week!

"Who is the better Freerunner? Will it be the veteran, Claude Carron; or the young gun, William

257

Dunmore? Gentlemen, on your mark!"

Geoff had us, that's for sure. Claude looked at me, and for the first time in weeks, I saw the spark in his eyes.

Geoff yelled "Set!" and the trainees readied their disks.

Claude grinned a little Claude grin at me, and his body tensed for action. I grinned back, and, without taking my eyes off of Claude, I said, "Hey Geoff? You know what?"

"Yeah, I know; I know," Geoff answered. "I'm an asshole.

"Go!"

About the Author

Curtis is a husband and father, a writer, an aging athlete and a wanna-be farmer. He teaches high school English in a small farming community north of Toronto.

You can reach Curtis at *curtis.symons@outlook.com*, or check out his web page: *http://curtissymons.wix.com/freerunnersnovel*

About the Artist
Alissa Kaay Morrison created *Will at the Barricade* as a digital painting, but she works in traditional paint and other media as well. Alissa attends OCAD University in Toronto.

Music
Irish Rovers. "Wasn't That A Party." *Wasn't That a Party.* Epic Records, 1980.

Lowest of the Low. "Subversives." *Shakespeare, My Butt.* AM Records, 1991.

The Proclaimers. "I'm Gonna Be (500 Miles)." *Sunshine on Leith.* Chrysalis Records, 1988.

"The Fox and the Goose." Traditional.

45449424R00150

Made in the USA
Charleston, SC
22 August 2015